BAKER STREET
TRANSLATION

ALSO BY MICHAEL ROBERTSON

The Brothers of Baker Street

The Baker Street Letters

The BAKER STREET TRANSLATION

MICHAEL ROBERTSON

MINOTAUR BOOKS
A Thomas Dunne Book
New York

A THOMAS DUNNE BOOK FOR MINOTAUR BOOKS.
An imprint of St. Martin's Publishing Group.

THE BAKER STREET TRANSLATION. Copyright © 2013 by Michael Robertson. All rights reserved. Printed in the United States of America. For information, address St. Martin's Press, 175 Fifth Avenue, New York, N.Y. 10010.

www.thomasdunnebooks.com
www.minotaurbooks.com

The Library of Congress has cataloged the hardcover edition as follows:

Robertson, Michael, 1951–
    The Baker Street translation / Michael Robertson.—1st ed.
        p. cm.
    1. Brothers—Fiction. 2. Lawyers—England—London—Fiction. 3. Letter writing—Fiction. I. Title.
    PS3618.O31726B38 2013
    813'.6—dc23

                                                                2013002520

ISBN 978-250-04391-7 (trade paperback)

Minotaur books may be purchased for educational, business, or promotional use. For information on bulk purchases, please contact Macmillan Corporate and Premium Sales Department at 1-800-221-7945, extension 5442, or write specialmarkets@macmillan.com.

First Minotaur Books Paperback Edition: March 2014

P1

ACKNOWLEDGMENTS

My thanks to my editor, Marcia Markland; to my agent, Kirby Kim; to Laura Bonner for representing international rights, and to assistant editor Kat Brzozowski; production editor Elizabeth Curione; designer Phil Mazzone; publicist Justin Velella; jacket designer James Iacobelli; and copyeditor Carol Edwards at Thomas Dunne Books/St. Martin's Press.

And a special thanks to Rebecca Oliver, my first agent, who believed in these books early on.

BAKER STREET
TRANSLATION

LONDON, JANUARY 1998

When Arthur Sandwhistle woke up on the morning of what he knew would be the greatest day of his life, he couldn't get the bloody rhymes out of his mind.

One, two, unbuckle my shoe.

That one went through his head, unbidden, as he was pulling on his Doc Martens.

He threw an overstuffed rucksack over his shoulder and grabbed a hard black pudding off the kitchen table on his way out the door.

"You're twenty-four," shouted his uncle, standing at the stove. "Get off the dole. Get a real job!"

Arthur didn't answer. He knew he no longer needed to.

Three, four, shut the door. And he slammed it.

Now he was out on the street.

Five, six, she's turning tricks.

Okay, he'd just made that one up on his own. The team had changed that rhyme, as it had many of the others. But it had become "throw down sticks," instead of "pick up sticks," and it certainly wasn't "turn tricks."

But tricks were what she'd been turning, and a trick is what he'd been, though she hadn't let him know until the very end.

When he did find out, it had been almost enough to make him bail on the whole deal. But not quite.

"I don't know who paid me," she'd said, with one hand clutching her purse and the other on the door. "I got a phone call and a few quid put under my door, but I never saw his face, and I never got his real name, just like you never got mine."

"You mean your name isn't even—"

"Of course it isn't. Grow up. I was to sweeten the deal. I was paid to be the sugar on your cornflakes. And breakfast is done. Get over it, sweetie."

And then she was gone.

But she was right. He'd get over her quick enough. And he bet that if she knew just what the cornflakes were—just how much he was getting paid for his own part in it—she'd have thought twice about skipping out.

She had no idea how important he really was. Without him, the whole thing would be a bust.

Programming and installing the microchips had been easy. No one was better at that. Certainly no one who had to live and work in his uncle's cellar.

The problematic part had been the degrees of separation—all this insistence on the right hand not knowing what the left hand was doing, the anonymous, encrypted communications—just so much cloak-and-dagger twaddle. A gigantic pain in the bum.

Personally, he didn't care one way or the other about the royals. And he himself was no anarchist, so far as he knew. He wasn't even sure what one was.

But no matter. His own part of it was finished and delivered. When he got his money, the birds would flock. And the tail in Rio would have an all-over tan.

Now he would just pick up his payment at King's Cross station. Then it was forty minutes to Heathrow for the flight to Brazil.

Perhaps he'd even learn to surf. They did surf in Rio, didn't they? For a moment he had a vision of himself, tanned and buff, riding the crest of a twenty-footer, like some Hawaiian god— or Brazilian, whatever—to the giggling applause and adoring stares from the smoothly waxed—now that part was Brazilian, he was sure—beauties waiting on shore.

His adrenaline was pumping now.

Seven, eight, lay 'em, mate.

Seven, eight, don't be late.

He laughed. The damn singsongs were swimming in his head. It was a bloody good thing he had already sent the code, or the whole thing would be completely bollixed up, the way he was making them up now. Hey, how about "Little Jack Horner craps in the corner"? Why didn't they use that one?

He reached the corner of Euston Road and Upper Woburn Place, and the light was against him; he had to stop to let the traffic go by.

Across the street, a bobby stepped out of the small Indian grocer. That was no concern. If necessary, Arthur could outrun and lose him in a block. But there was no need; the bobby did not even look in his direction.

The light changed; Arthur stepped back from the curb as a delivery van sped through, and then he trotted on across. He dodged and weaved around other pedestrians, keeping an eye out all the while, until he approached Euston and Midland.

Now he looked toward the intersection ahead. There was a Tesco convenience store on the corner, and he didn't like what he saw standing at the entrance.

Not bobbies. It was worse than that. Probably MI5.

Three men, two tall, one short, all in their early or mid-thirties, and each wearing the sort of Marks & Spencer friendly gray suit that business gits like to wear on casual Friday.

Only it wasn't Friday.

And now they'd seen him. They were all three pretending to be arguing about something in the sports section of the *Daily Mirror*, but Arthur knew that was a sham. He had been warned about their type. He knew what to look for. He knew to check their shoes.

And though it was hard to tell from this distance, he was pretty sure they were wearing rubber-soled Oxfords.

Not good, the rubber-soled part.

Arthur quickly looked away from the three gray suits and continued walking. He was not far now from King's Cross at Pancras, and the pedestrian crowd was getting thicker; he would make his move there and lose the gray suits.

Then, from the corner of his eye, he saw the man with the tabloid lower it suddenly and look straight in his direction.

Bloody hell. They'd read his body language, just like he was reading theirs.

No point in disguising things now.

Arthur stepped behind an old man with an umbrella. He skipped around a woman with two children and a stroller.

And then he took off running for all he was worth.

He was only blocks from the entrance to Kings Cross station. He could make it; once in the station, he could disappear in the crowd. They wouldn't know whether he was heading for the tube or the trains, and there were too many exits for them to cover. King's Cross, and he'd be home free.

Arnold looked back over his shoulder. Bloody hell, they were gaining. The shorter pursuer was faster than the others. Bloody overcompensater. He was catching up.

But now Arthur was at the intersection of Euston Road and Pancras. King's Cross was within sight.

The light was red and there was heavy morning traffic—and that was perfect. Arnold knew his pursuers would slow down and try to be safe; he would not. All he had to do was time it right and pick his spot.

He saw the entrance to King's Cross station across the street, heard the roar of trains pulling into the station, and he bolted suddenly, quick like a rabbit, into the street—for King's Cross and freedom.

King's Cross, King's Cross, you can't touch me now.

It was his last thought. The impact from the lorry he didn't see left no room or time for anything more.

The sickening sound of the impact carried the length of the block.

The shorter gray-suited man, the first in pursuit, ran up to the intersection and saw that Arthur Sandwhistle had been separated from his Doc Martens, and most of his blood, by about fifty yards.

The second gray-suited man arrived on the scene. He allowed himself the luxury of leaning forward, hands on his knees to catch his breath, and then he said, "There'll be hell to pay when the director hears of this."

"I can't see we could have done anything differently," said the first man.

The third gray-suited man trotted up and looked the scene

over. "You know the rules," he said. "Do not pursue into dangerous traffic unless there is risk of imminent harm to civilians."

"Well, I'd say delivery of an explosive device poses a risk of harm, wouldn't you?" said the first man.

"Unless he already delivered it. And now we'll never get to question him. Was he a pawn, or a planner?"

"He ran too fast for a planner," said the first man.

"Well, whatever he was," said the second man, as an emergency crew put Arthur's body onto a carrier, "he's no good to us now."

"Or to anyone else," said the first man. "I'm feeling winded. Let's get a pint."

2

In his penthouse on top of the *Daily Sun* headquarters in Tobacco Wharf, Lord Robert Buxton was about to commence a milestone celebration.

He had already checked the headlines for the next day's papers, as he always did in the evening. Nothing extraordinary happening, nothing worth shouting about in any of the papers that he owned. His editors had done their best to exaggerate and insinuate where they could. Some royal events were coming up this week, which he gave more play than usual, with the slant that there hadn't been many of those recently. Aside from that, it was an unremarkable news day, at least for the kind of headlines he liked to run.

But he had something else on his mind tonight anyway.

It was late evening in London, a chilly winter rain had passed through, and there was no fog as he looked out over the Thames. The clarity and brilliance of the reflected lights just made the disappointment he was feeling now all the more keen.

In the Buxton family tradition, one's twenties were for randy romping and honing one's skills—mostly the financial ones—for one's thirties, which were for expanding the family fortune. One's forties—the corner Buxton was about to turn—were for truly getting down to business and expanding the Buxton family itself.

But there was a problem.

The rich and famous and powerful partygoers had already assembled downstairs, drinking and gossiping by the river, ready to be escorted up to the penthouse to flatter Buxton.

But Laura Rankin was not among them.

It was hard to believe; things had been going so well just a few months earlier. But there it was—he had proposed, and she had said no.

Well, not quite no. She had asked for more time to think about it, but Buxton was no fool, and he could guess what that meant. Probably.

He was astonished. And now he found himself reevaluating his criteria:

Of all the women he knew, who had the grace and presence to make the best impression in public? Laura Rankin.

Of all the women he had ever known or met or seen, who had a body structure that would most likely yield three children and still maintain the perfect curvature of her figure? Laura Rankin, although it was a close call between her and several other possible candidates, because sustainable figures are not nearly so rare as excellent public presence.

And of all the women he had been with, who was the best shag? Well, that was a German pantyhose model from the ad pages of a *Der Spiegel* wannabe magazine that Buxton had bought last year, but no matter—he did not plan on giving up that occasional entertainment in any case. It was fine for sex and marriage to overlap, but no need to get carried away and make one a subset of the other.

There were other criteria, of course, but these were the big ones, and when he added them all up, they still came to the same result: Laura Rankin.

Therefore, "No" would simply not do, and neither would "I need to think about it, if you don't mind," at least not for very much longer.

But in the past several weeks, Laura had found reason on several occasions to be at Baker Street Chambers until well after dinnertime. And rumor had it, as reported by Buxton's own security team, that she had been seen driving back across the bridge from Butler's Wharf.

Laura seemed to be slipping back toward Reggie Heath, her earlier love. It made no sense that she should do so; Buxton racked his brain trying to think of what had changed.

It was not Buxton himself, surely. His own power and prestige were simply increasing. And his physical appearance was only getting better with age; he knew this, because half the partygoers downstairs had said so at one time or another, and without any prompting whatsoever. And in his gut he knew it was true.

Then it occurred to him—given that he had not changed, and Laura had not changed, then it must be his rival—Reggie Heath had changed.

Not physically. In that respect, in fact, the two rivals had some similarities—Heath was perhaps two or three years younger than Buxton; equally tall at just over six feet. Heath was thin; Buxton was proud of his own girth, of which there just enough to show the world that he was established and unapologetic about it.

But something had changed.

The surface events were obvious: Less than a year ago, Reggie Heath had been nothing more than a self-important

London barrister who waffled rather than commit to a woman who was plainly above his league. Laura had tired of waiting and was about to dump him. Lord Buxton had stood at the ready; indeed, as he thought about it now, he took some satisfaction in having done everything he could to help push things along.

But then something unexpected had happened—Heath, who in Buxton's opinion still carried a chip on his shoulder from his East End upbringing, established his new law chambers at Dorset House, a building that comprised the entire 200 block of Baker Street. Most of Dorset House was occupied by a bank, Dorset National, and all of it was miles away geographically and eons away socially from the traditional confines of the Inns of Court. A barrister would have to be a complete git to locate there; it was more foolish a move than even Buxton had hoped for. Surely Reggie Heath's career and fortunes would flounder— and indeed they did, at first—and Laura would finally cut the ties.

But no. She didn't. Reggie floundered, but she didn't cut him loose. Not quite.

And then there were the letters to Sherlock Holmes. Within weeks of locating his chambers at Dorset House on Baker Street, Reggie Heath had begun receiving the letters that previously had been dealt with by the Dorset National clerical staff. Then, in reaction to one of those letters, Heath and his younger brother Nigel had jetted off to the States, dragging Laura into an adventure that she surely regarded as embarrassing, to say the least.

Or so Buxton had assumed. He had made much of those events in his tabloid publications, and for a while, that seemed to have had the desired effect on Reggie's career.

But not on Laura.

He had misjudged the situation, Buxton realized now. Whatever Reggie's attitude toward them, Laura apparently did not regard those letters as an embarrassment. She seemed to regard them as a good thing, almost as if—though it was hard to say why—they represented some sort of opportunity.

For exactly what, Buxton could not quite say—but he was certain that Laura's renewed attraction to Reggie had something to do with the letters to Sherlock Holmes. Receiving them had somehow given him a panache that he had not heretofore possessed.

Buxton considered it carefully. He could see no other cause. It was the letters.

Something had to be done.

Buxton looked out on the Thames reflections again, feeling better now. He had decided what to do. And he knew he had the resources to do it.

But that was for tomorrow. For tonight—having now decided on a course of action—he could enjoy his party.

Buxton directed his chief of staff to open the doors and admit his birthday guests—and first among them, the blonde from the ad pages of *Der Spiegel*.

O n the fourth floor of Harrods department store, in the toy section for preschoolers, twenty-two-year-old Emily Ellershaw was using all the skills she had learned in her new-hire training—and still she was having a rough go of it. She couldn't quite understand this customer's complaint, and she was having a hard time mollifying him.

"I'm very sorry for the mistake, Mr. Aspic," she said as she placed a medium-size boxed toy on the counter between them, right next to another one, already opened, that to her eye was exactly the same. "Do you mind very much—explain the problem to me again?"

The customer was in his mid-fifties, with wispy brown hair, pale skin even by English standards, and a vague scent of vanilla that seemed to waft whenever he moved his heavily calloused hands—which he was doing now as he took the toy out of the box that was already open.

"I bought it yesterday afternoon," he said in a tone of forced patience. "For my niece, you understand."

"Yes, certainly," said Emily with a hopeful and encouraging smile.

"When I got it home and opened it, I discovered that it is the wrong version. The toy itself is correct, but the instruction sheet that came with it is not the most recent version. I must have the most recent version. I mean, my niece must have. I . . . I don't want her playing with something that is out-of-date, you know."

"Of course, I understand completely," said Emily, although she didn't quite. "I hope this other one will do, then. It is the only other one we have in stock. We received only these two."

The man nodded, as though that was a given. Rather eagerly he began to open the second box. He reached in and pulled out a folded instruction sheet that accompanied the toy. He unfolded it and began to study the tiny print on the thin paper.

As he did, Emily looked at the toy from the first box, unpacked on the counter between them.

It was a plastic duck. From the title on the box, Emily guessed it was actually supposed to look like a goose; but in both appearance and size, it was much more like a duck. It was white, with a yellow bill that the child was supposed to press.

Emily tested it. She pressed down carefully on the yellow bill.

"One, two, buckle my shoe," said the duck in a tinny voice intended to sound matronly and British.

The man looked up with a glare. Emily immediately withdrew her hand from the duck.

"Sorry," she said. "Just wanted to be sure it works. It appears to."

"As I said, the toy is fine. You do not need to test it. It's the instructions. They are not the right version. Both packages are wrong."

"I'm very sorry," said Emily, reaching for the instruction sheet. "Would you like me to have a look at them?"

"No," said Aspic. He quickly put the duck and the instruc-tions back into the box. "You're certain these are the most re-cent two you've received?"

"Yes," said Emily. "We have no others. They've just come in, and we haven't sold any, except for the one you bought. I'm very sorry it's not right for you. But we'll be happy to do a full refund. Was this a credit card purchase?"

"No, it was cash," said the man quite impatiently. He quickly packed up the toy that he had brought in with him. "And no refund is necessary. I'll just keep the one I've got, thank you very much."

He turned on his heel, with the package under his arm, and strode quickly away toward the escalators.

Emily got ready to tape the second boxed toy back up again.

Just on a whim, she pressed the duck's bill once more.

"Humpty Dumpty took a great fall," said the duck.

Works fine, thought Emily. She closed the box and taped it shut.

4

"Do you perhaps have something that is very easily customizable after the fact?"

Reggie Heath, Q.C., was speaking to a jeweler in Hatton Garden, and he felt very much out of his depth.

He had gotten there early—before they even opened, in fact—to beat the morning crowds, and to nail down the details that had kept him up all night.

"Well, gold is malleable, of course," said the woman, "but not with just your average kitchen utensils. If you really want the lady to have what she wants, perhaps you should ask her to pop in and have a look around?"

"Is that how it's done?" said Reggie. He stared through the glass at the many rings—too many—and he realized that he really hadn't a clue.

"Actually, I'm not sure anything off the shelf will do," he said, stepping back just a bit, as if the display were hot to the touch. "Perhaps I need to go to a bespoke jeweler—"

"Nonsense," said the woman quickly. "We have every sort of engagement ring imaginable. Here, take our catalog." She leaned forward, scrutinizing Reggie across the glass counter.

"Ah," she said after a moment. "You haven't asked the lady yet, have you?"

"Well . . ."

"Don't let that stop you. Our rings can be returned within a week, for just that very reason."

"You mean, in case she says no."

"Of course. Happens all the time. You would get a full refund."

"Yes. Well. Considerate of you to point out the possibility of a negative outcome. Good God, is that the hour? I believe I'm due in court. Thank you very much."

Reggie escaped the jeweler's, though he was not, in fact, due in court, and he fled in a cab back to Baker Street.

It was January, not high season—but even so, there was a gaggle of camera-toting tourists in front of Dorset House as Reggie arrived. This particular group looked French, the second most common Sherlock Holmes tour group after the Japanese—milling about in the 200 block of Baker Street, with uncertain and slightly annoyed looks on their faces, searching for 221B.

Reggie tried to avoid eye contact as he got out of the cab, but it didn't work. An apparent leader of the group maneuvered between him and the heavy glass doors of Dorset House.

"Is this Two twenty-one B Baker Street?" the alpha tourist demanded.

"No."

"We are looking for—"

"Yes, I know. Try the little museum up the street. It has an actual sign."

The tourist turned his head, and Reggie negotiated quickly around him and into the Dorset House lobby without having to issue any further travel advice.

It was enough that he had the letters to deal with. The Sherlock Holmes Museum was happy to receive tourists, especially if they bought something, and Reggie was completely fine with that.

From the lobby, Reggie took the lift up one floor to Baker Street Chambers. Also known as Heath's Chambers. Reggie Heath's formerly muddling, but now doing all right, thank you, law chambers.

Lois—a rotund fiftyish woman who looked as though she'd been incarnated directly from an advert for baking flour—greeted Reggie at the secretary's station.

"Where were they from this time?" she said quite cheerfully.

"France."

"Oh. It still surprises me they would bother. I thought they preferred their own detective icons."

"I wish all tourists would prefer French detective icons—I'd have an easier time getting into my office in the morning."

Lois laughed.

"And the same goes for the letter writers," added Reggie.

"Oh, you can't mean that," said Lois.

"I certainly do mean it."

Lois stopped what she was doing and looked up.

"Why, if it were not for the letters, where would this chambers be?"

"Humming along nicely and without distractions," said Reggie.

"Really? Would you have had the Black Cab case, and all the wonderful publicity that came with it?"

Reggie thought about it. "No," he said after a moment. "But I'm not sure coverage in the *Daily Sun* constitutes wonderful publicity."

"But now you have more clients."

Reggie nodded.

"And were it not for the letters, would you have ever had need to hire me?"

"You have a point," said Reggie, "If it were not for the letters, my previous secretary would not have murdered my previous clerk, and I would not have needed to hire you. But I did not hire you as a law pupil, Lois, so there's no point in your practicing cross-examination on me."

"Of course," said Lois, "But I think you should show more respect for the letters. I, for one, and I know I'm not the only one, think they're wonderful."

"Duly noted," said Reggie. He opened the door to his interior chambers office.

Before he could go in, Lois said, "I put the new ones for this week on your desk."

Reggie paused, and sighed. He had instructed her, more than once, to just routinely send all the letters to Nigel in the States.

"I will leave them on the mailing cart," said Reggie. "They are to go to Nigel in tomorrow morning's post."

"Yes," said Lois, slumping back into her chair. "Of course."

Reggie tried not to get annoyed. In most other respects, Lois was working out quite well. And he had more important things to think about.

"Did you clear my calendar for next Tuesday?"

"Oh yes," said Lois. She recovered her chirpiness. "No appointments at all on Tuesday, and just two new briefs for the entire week. They're both rolled up and tied with their little red strings on the shelf, and both are quite simple pleadings, pure formalities, no more than a page or two each, which you can stand up and deliver next week in your own inimitable style, with no advance preparation whatsoever."

"You are catching on, Lois."

"Thank you," she said.

Now, finally, Reggie made it into his office and closed the door behind him.

Reggie's interior chambers office was a sanctuary. He had made sure it was so: a massive mahogany desk, rows of law books lining the wall, a tall swiveling leather chair behind the desk for Reggie, and two subordinate, but nevertheless expensive chairs in front of it, for solicitors and their clients.

But this morning, there in the middle of all the gleaming hardwood and leather and brass were the incoming Sherlock Holmes letters that Lois had plopped on his desk. The bloody things were beginning to accumulate.

It made Reggie uneasy.

Most of the letters that arrived every week were simply from dedicated fans of the Sherlock Holmes canon. People who knew perfectly well that the man was fictional. They just wanted to express their knowledge of Doyle's work, like *Star Trek* fans dressing up at a convention.

But there were always a few that were—well, different.

Some of the letter writers—typically the very young, or the very old—believed Sherlock Holmes to be real.

In theory—and as stipulated in the lease—Reggie was obliged to open the letters personally and respond to them— always in a standard way—assuring the letter writers that Sherlock Holmes appreciated their interest but was now retired and keeping bees in Sussex and was unable to respond personally to their inquiry.

But in practice, Reggie always had Lois bundle the things

off across the pond to Nigel, Reggie's younger brother. Reggie did not want these letters accumulating on his own desk. Lois was supposed to put them on the cart at the other end of the corridor, to get picked up for Express Mail to Nigel in Los Angeles.

Nigel didn't seem to mind wading through them, and to Reggie they were at best a bother, and at worst a dangerous liability.

But at the moment, they were on Reggie's desk, staring him in the face.

He sat down, hesitated, and then in the same way one pushes on a tooth to see if it is still sure, he took one off the top.

The first was from a ten-year-old schoolgirl in Iowa, asking if Mr. Sherlock Holmes could please tell her how to know whether the boy in the next row liked her. Should she boldly just go up and ask?

No one at this address can answer that one, thought Reggie. Try Dear Abby.

The first one hadn't been too bad. Reggie relaxed a bit and looked at another. This one was from a centenarian in Texas who was making out her will.

Get an American lawyer, thought Reggie; they're plentiful.

The next was from Taiwan. This letter writer was grateful for an earlier, very helpful response from Sherlock Holmes's personal secretary, and he requested further assistance regarding some additional attached documents.

This was annoying. The earlier response from "Mr. Holmes's personal secretary" could only have come from Nigel. And if Nigel had, in fact, sent anything helpful, then he was departing once again from the standard reply.

The letter writer had obligingly included a copy of that first response. Reggie picked it up and looked at it:

Dear Mr. Liu—

Thank you for your inquiry regarding the enigmatic nursery rhyme. Unfortunately, Mr. Sherlock Holmes is at the moment unavailable, and children's verses are not within his particular area of expertise anyway—but perhaps my poor attempt at a response will help.

First, be aware that there is no such thing as a "dub-dub." It is not, in fact, a word. When used in English following "rub," all those words together constitute an idiom that means, roughly, "scrub away with abandon." That is only an approximation, of course; such is the way with English idioms, and especially the ones that rhyme.

Other English phrases for which you should show caution in translation include "Bugger off, mate!" and "Bob's your uncle." These are not meant to be taken literally.

You may find it comforting to know that this particular nursery rhyme has many variations in its English form. When it first popped up, it referred to "Three maids in a tub," and shortly after the enthusiastic scrubbing, all the young ladies went off to the fair. The Victorians found this tale a bit too titillating, and so they tried many variations to take the fun out of it. Perhaps that's why your version of it uses "toffs" instead.

But it is just a nursery rhyme, after all, and I'm sure that your translation of it, whatever it turns out to be, will be fine.

Yours truly,

Mr. Sherlock Holmes's personal secretary.

Reggie looked at the signature at the end and sighed. Yes, it was Nigel's. Reggie's brother just couldn't seem to leave well enough alone

And no good deed goes unpunished. Now this letter writer

politely wanted to verify the exact meaning of more phrases in other nursery rhymes.

There are lexicons for such things, thought Reggie. Look it up. Stop thinking of Sherlock Holmes as a sort of general help center.

Reggie had had enough. He made a mental note to remove the letters from his desk and put them on the cart on his way out to lunch. For now, he pushed the entire stack onto the corner of his desk nearest the door.

And anyway, he had plans to make. Lois was rapping on the closed chambers door, but Reggie called out for her to go away. At least for the next five minutes.

It was time for his next step. Laura would be back in London in just a few days, and Reggie did not intend to bollix this up.

As he picked up the phone, he briefly considered whether this was really the best way to go about it. Perhaps a moonlit dinner above the Thames would be more romantic.

But no. She would be terribly impressed; she would love it. There really was no doubt about it at all.

"I would like to speak to the person in charge of catering," said Reggie.

"Sir, we do not do catering for the general public," said the woman on the phone. "Would you like to make a reservation to dine in?"

"No, I'd like to set up a small catered affair," said Reggie. "For two. Next week."

"Sir, we do catering only for the royals. And we are quite busy this week."

"Yes, but I have it on good authority that there was a particular type of chocolate raspberry tart that you served at one of those affairs a year or two ago, and I know a lady who would very much like to—"

THE BAKER STREET TRANSLATION

"Sir, we are a purveyor of catering services to Her Majesty the Queen."

"Yes, but that doesn't mean exclusively, does it? I know barristers who buy socks from purveyors to the queen. Half the point of being such a purveyor is that you can demand exorbitant prices when you sell similar things to commoners, correct?"

"Well, yes."

"So what would that exorbitant price be?"

There was a short pause, then—

"How many people?"

"Two."

"How many courses?"

"All of them. And the dessert cannot be just similar; it must be exact."

There was another pause at the other end of the line as the woman crunched some numbers.

The she stated a price to Reggie.

Reggie gasped.

It took a moment, but he gathered himself.

"All right," he said. "Let's do it."

Reggie hung up the phone and exhaled.

It would be worth it.

Lois was at the door once more, and now Reggie could let her in.

"Yes?" said Reggie.

"There's a solicitor here to see you. He doesn't have an appointment, but he says it is urgent, and since your calendar is clear, I thought—"

"All right," said Reggie. "Show him in."

Lois stepped away for a moment, and then she returned with a man of about forty-five, unremarkable in appearance, wearing a standard middle-range solicitor's dark brown suit.

"Thank you for seeing me, Mr. Heath," said the solicitor. "I apologize for not making an appointment, but I was told you are the only person for this job, so I came to you at once."

"What are the specifics?"

"It is a civil case. My client wishes to have a purchase contract nullified so that he can recover his original possession or be compensated for the actual value of his loss. All attempts for settlement have been rejected, the court briefings have been filed, and because the article in question is worth well over one hundred thousand pounds, he wants a Q.C. to do the oral arguments."

"Contract nullification is never easy."

"Yes, but this was a mistake of fact. My client thought he was selling one thing, and the purchaser claims that he was buying something else."

"And what was the thing that caused all this confusion?"

"My client sold a plaster bust—not an original, mind you, but a simple reproduction—for ten pounds. Moments later, he saw the purchaser take the bust down to the street, smash it on the pavement, and retrieve from it a very rare and valuable black pearl."

"Well," said Reggie, "This would be difficult to—" And then he stopped. He looked hard at the solicitor.

"A black pearl, you say?"

"Yes."

"A plaster bust?"

"Yes."

Reggie sighed. There were the positive results from publicity. And then there were the negative ones. "Whose bloody prank is it this time?" he said, glaring across at the stone-faced solicitor, if indeed that's what he was. The man was probably from the Sher-lockian Society, which had begun taking great pleasure in needling Reggie—plain jealousy, in Reggie's view—but the Sherlock Holmes letters had received so much publicity that even Reggie's legal colleagues were not above setting up such a joke.

"Why, I've no idea what—"

"Please," said Reggie. "Even I have heard of the 'Adventure of the Six Napoleons.'" And with that, Reggie pushed the button for his secretary. "Lois, is my ten o'clock here yet?"

"No, sir. You don't have one today."

Bloody hell, thought Reggie. He really needed to get Lois up to speed on the office code words.

"Well, come and escort this gentleman out of my chambers anyway."

Reggie turned to the still-poker-faced prankster. "Good day, sir. And please tell your friends from whichever Sherlockian society you belong to, to stop wasting my time."

"I've no idea what you mean," said the solicitor, getting up from his chair. "Cheers."

Then, exiting Reggie's chambers office, the man finally betrayed just the slightest smirk, and Reggie caught it. It was just too annoying to let pass.

"I even know that the Napoléons weren't pastries!" shouted Reggie as Lois escorted the man to the lift.

This had to stop. As the lift doors closed on the Sherlockian solicitor, Reggie took all the letters from his desk out to the cart in the corridor, and plopped them there unceremoniously. Then he returned to his office and resolved to have a chat with the leasing committee about the whole thing.

Yes, there was that bloody provision in the lease that made Reggie responsible for them.

But leases were made to be broken and to give lawyers employment in breaking them; that was the very nature of them. Reggie was good at it himself, especially at arguing the case;

and for finding the most subtle nuance and the most obscure precedent that could expand it into an actual loophole, there was no one better than his brother Nigel.

As Reggie was beginning to consider this, the phone rang.

It was Lois again. She said that Mr. Rafferty, from the leasing committee, wanted to have a word.

"Perfect timing," said Reggie. "Tell him I'll be right up."

Reggie stopped at Lois's desk on his way to the lift.

"Oh, and Lois—"

"Yes?"

"Just for future reference—the type of gentleman who was just here? That was not an urgent matter."

"I'm very sorry, sir. He said he had a legal problem that couldn't wait, and he even told me what the point of law was."

"Yes," said Reggie. "I understand, and it's not your fault that one sneaked by you, when they're going to be so devious about it. But for future—when you get walk-in solicitors who didn't even go to the trouble of making an appointment—I want you to give them a little test."

Lois gave Reggie a puzzled look. "You mean like a written exam?"

"No," said Reggie. "Just do this: Ask if they are familiar with the entire canon."

"The canon?"

"Yes. And then watch their eyes. If their eyes get all sparkly when you say 'entire canon,' or if their pupils dilate—that's a warning sign. That will mean they are a Sherlockian. Not a humble Trekkie university nerd, nor a wannabe Jedi knight quasi-religious sycophant, but a genuine, dyed-in-the-Shetland-wool, grown-up, I've-already-got-a-life, adult Sherlockian. An original. Don't let them in. Don't let anyone who claims to know the entire canon near my office. I mean, except Nigel, of course, if he should return."

"Yes," said Lois doubtfully. "I'll try to remember."

"Thank you," said Reggie.

Then he took the lift to the top level of Dorset House and walked across the hardwood floor to Rafferty's office.

The floor was polished and gleaming but entirely bare of furnishings—just as it had been months earlier when Reggie had first come up to talk to Rafferty. It was a little surprising; Reggie thought they would have found some additional use for the space by now.

But no, it was still just Rafferty's little office alone on the floor, tucked away in a corner, and conveying an impression not so much of prestige as of slight embarrassment.

The door was open; Rafferty, a smallish man in an immaculate gray suit and wire-rim spectacles, was seated behind his desk, looking out on the floor, and waiting—almost anxiously, it seemed to Reggie—for Reggie to get there.

"Sit down," said Rafferty as soon as Reggie reached the entrance. "Close the door behind you, please."

There was clearly no one else on the floor, but Reggie shut the door, as requested.

"I suppose that technically," began Rafferty, "legally, I am not really allowed to tell you this. But I will anyway."

In Reggie's opinion, Rafferty had always had a bit of a Napoleonic complex—but that was not his demeanor today. He seemed quite sincerely concerned—and not at all confident—about whatever it was he was about to convey.

Reggie sat down. Rafferty took a deep breath and then spoke in a hushed voice. "An offer has been made for Dorset House."

Reggie absorbed that statement for a moment, and said nothing.

"I thought you might want to know," continued Rafferty, "given that your chambers have been doing so well, and that your tenancy might be at risk. There is a provision in the offer that Dorset House will not be obliged to move its banking offices or its direct employees. But there is no such protection in the offer for building tenants not directly employed by the bank. There are only two such tenants, and one of them, of course, is you."

"I have a lease!" said Reggie.

Rafferty nodded somberly, then gave a little shrug. "You know how it is—leases are made to be broken."

"Has Dorset accepted this bloody offer?"

"No," said Rafferty. "They have declined it—at least for the moment. I don't believe Dorset National Building Society wants to be at risk of ever having to lease back its own premises, or to move its headquarters—any more than you, I presume, would want to move your law chambers, now that your practice has gotten off the ground."

"No," said Reggie. "I would not. And Dorset was bloody well right to decline."

"Yes, well, so far so good," said Rafferty. "But there's more." He paused and looked about now, as if someone could have actually sneaked into the office with them.

"Yes?"

Rafferty spoke in a whisper. "The buyer has said that if they are unable to agree upon terms for purchasing Dorset House, he will consider a hostile takeover of Dorset National Building Society itself!"

"He can buy the whole bloody company?" said Reggie, not whispering at all.

"Apparently. Or at least a majority interest."

"Who could do that? Who is this person?"

"I don't know. I don't have access to that information."

"Why in hell would anyone want the building so much that they'd buy the entire company for it?"

Rafferty just sat back in his chair and glumly shook his head. Then he said, "How are the letters? Able to keep the responses going out, aren't you?"

"Yes," said Reggie, fidgeting just slightly. He didn't mention the batch he had just put on the cart for Nigel; strictly speaking, he knew he was supposed to be doing them all himself.

"That's good," said Rafferty. He seemed distracted. "Do try to keep on top of them," he said now, almost apologetically. And then he added, "For as long we have them."

5

On a South Seas island, Laura sat with her shoes off, letting the sun pleasantly warm her bare shoulders and bare toes, and not thinking at all. She had, in fact, already made up her mind about the who, although she had not yet informed either of the men who most needed to know.

The only question was the what. Marriage was fine in and of itself. The question was, What then? She could not wait forever to decide.

Babies, or no?

Laura glanced down involuntarily at her bare toes, and then away again.

Reggie loved those toes. He had said so many times.

Nigel had not quite ever seen them. He almost had once, before Laura had met Reggie, and before Nigel had met Mara. But not quite.

Buxton seemed to have noticed them once, but apparently he had been neither impressed nor concerned, either way.

Only one woman in ten thousand had toes like that. One in one thousand, Laura had heard someone say, if the woman is a redhead. Probably an old wives' tale. There were all kinds of old wives' tales about what red hair and a couple of webbed toes might mean: a sign of intelligence; a sign of sensuality (Reggie said so); a sign, three hundred years ago, that a woman might very probably be a witch.

What other genetic quirks might she have lurking?

And what about Reggie's lurking genetic quirks? She was sure she had identified several. And never mind the genetic ones, what about all the social and behavioral ones? He had tons of those. What about his using his fingernails for all sorts of tasks that toenail clippers and screwdrivers and surgical scalpels had been designed for? Was that tendency hereditary? God, she hoped not.

And never mind all hers and his genetic and behavioral quirks, what about the state of the whole bloody quirky world?

Life being random, and so frequently unfair, there are so many things out of one's control.

She knew clearly what she wanted, yet somehow it was not an easy decision.

Just a couple of years ago, she could have blamed her own indecision on Reggie's noncommittal attitude, and just let it go at that, and so she had done.

But no longer. Blast him. She knew he was about to put the ball squarely in her court.

6

In the predawn hours at Regent's Park, a taxi pulled over on Outer Circle Drive near Clarence Gate, just south of the little takeaway patio at the boat-rental station. Two geese, gliding silently as the vehicle approached, took flight when the passenger door opened.

Robert Buxton stepped out. He was a bulky man, not inclined to being inconspicuous in either temperament or physique, and his white macintosh stood out in relief against the color of the cab.

He sensed that, and he quickly waved the driver on.

He had taken a cab, rather than his limo, specifically for anonymity. Total secrecy wasn't necessary; he wasn't concerned about the stray dawn jogger. But there was no sense in being obvious about things, either, and so he had made a point of arriving before the morning commuters—and of getting out of the cab before he reached his actual destination.

And then Buxton began walking south. He had to pause his rolling stride for a moment at the intersection of Park Road and Baker Street; the red signal light by itself was not an impediment, but an accelerating lorry was, and he had to stand for a few seconds, impatiently, until it had passed.

Then he continued across the intersection. His destination wasn't far. A hundred yards or so south from Park Road, just past the middle of the 200 block of Baker Street.

He entered the marble and glass lobby at Dorset House. He had indeed beaten the business commuters; there was no one but the thin, white-haired security guard, who was seated at his station in the middle of the lobby.

The old fellow's head was nodding down at a tabloid newspaper he had opened; he appeared to be asleep. But the sound of Buxton's footsteps on the marble floor roused him. He glanced up from the tabloid—the *Daily Sun,* Buxton was pleased to notice—as Buxton approached.

Buxton decided it was best to say something.

"Heath's chambers?" said Buxton, facing the security guard's station but with an eye on the lifts.

"You mean Baker Street Chambers?" said the guard.

"Yes," said Buxton.

"First floor up," said the guard. "But no one is in yet."

"That's fine," said Buxton. "I'll just go up and leave a note."

The elderly guard just nodded and did not challenge Buxton. Few people did.

And Dorset National Building Society did not know whom they were dealing with, if they thought he would simply accept a turndown and walk away.

Buxton got in the lift, rode up to the next floor, and then stepped boldly into the before-hours dark of the law chambers.

As he stepped out, he heard a sound from somewhere on the floor. He paused and waited—and the heating unit crackled and started up. That was, no doubt, the sound he had heard.

But no need to take chances. He was Lord Robert Buxton; he did not need to skulk unless he chose to. He announced his presence.

"Hello there," he called out. "This is Heath's law chambers, is it?"

No one answered. No more sounds, except the hum of the heating unit.

Excellent.

He took a moment to look around. He had not been here before.

It was a simple layout—one central corridor, which led directly from the lifts where Buxton was standing to the corridor at the opposite wall, and two additional corridors on either side, at far left and far right.

All the lights were off. But even in the dark, Buxton could easily tell how little the interior on this floor—Reggie's floor—must have cost. It was so apparent in the flimsy cubicle structures and furnishings of the support offices: Compared to Lord Robert Buxton, Reggie Heath, Q.C., was simply a pauper. He couldn't even put on a good show.

Buxton couldn't help but smirk. How humiliating to be Reggie Heath.

He strode down the center corridor until he reached the secretary's desk at the far end.

To his left, the intersecting corridor led to two offices.

The first was quite small, with a window that faced toward the secretary's desk. The law clerk's office, probably. Along the wall just beyond that office was an arrangement of partitioned barrister's shelves, with incoming briefs and such. And then, beyond the shelves, was a corner office. That one had to be Reggie Heath's.

The door was closed, but Buxton checked it anyway. Locked,

of course. No matter. Given the casual attitude Reggie was known to display toward the letters, Buxton did not think he kept them there.

Buxton tried the door on the clerk's office. Not locked. The door pushed open. But this office was almost empty—a typewriter, a wooden file cabinet, an empty metal In basket, a nameplate that Buxton could not quite read in the dark. Nothing of use here.

Buxton came back out and turned his attention to the secretary's station.

There was nothing to explore on the secretary's desk itself. But there were some shelves in back of it and around the corner to the side. Buxton walked around the desk to take a look.

And then, in his haste and in the dark, he almost fell over it—a small metal delivery cart, waist-high, tucked behind the desk, out of the way of the cleaning crew.

This made a noise—not loud, but startling on the quiet floor—as Buxton put out his hand to steady himself.

"Bloody hell," he muttered under his breath.

He took a moment to look about—no lights had come on anywhere in the floor. All was silent. There was no one to hear the noise he had made. But something had fallen to the floor.

He didn't want to have to tidy up, but probably it was best not to make it obvious that someone had been rifling through the secretary's station.

He got down on his hands and knees to pick up what he had spilled. He saw a large express mailing envelope, and at least a half dozen pieces of correspondence that had spilled out of it.

He picked them all up and placed them back on the cart— and then he stopped. An address had caught his eye.

Had he found them?

He lifted one sheet up to catch the residual light that came through the windows on the Baker Street side. He could just make it out:

To: Mr. Sherlock Holmes, 221B Baker Street

Eureka. Yes. The letters to Sherlock Holmes.

He bent down again to make sure he had them all, including a couple of stragglers that had landed under the desk.

He stood and checked his watch—there was still time before anyone should begin to arrive. He put the letters on the secretary's desk in front of him, turned on the small desk lamp, and began to shuffle through them.

He was entirely prepared to buy Dorset House—or possibly even a majority interest in the bank that owned it if need be—to take away the letters and whatever it was about them that had made Reggie more attractive to Laura. But he had no intention of buying a pig in a poke—he wanted to know what he was paying for.

He began to scan through the letters. He quickly read one after another, trying to understand what could possibly make any of them matter.

But there was nothing to them. Just nothing. All he could think of was how amazing it was that there were so many losers in the world.

And then he came to a letter that made him pause.

He read it through once, and then he repositioned the lamp so that he could read it through again, more carefully.

It read as follows:

Dear Mr. Holmes—
    You are receiving this letter because I know that I shall soon pass away.

Do not grieve. I go to a better place, or at least to one no worse. And as I am writing this letter and recording this document at age 102, I cannot complain about the timing of things. Indeed, my entire life story is one of the most excellent timing.

Which brings me to the purpose of my letter: I have no heirs. I have outlived them all (even my lovely beagle Paulo, whom I cannot bear to replace). There is no charity that I know well enough to trust, and no political or social cause that I fully believe in. And so I have done the only sensible, logical thing I can do:

I have willed my entire fortune to you. I know it's not much; it dwindles away daily, as you might imagine. But what little I still have will be yours.

Hilary Clemens

Buxton looked at the return address, which had no street number, but just "Shady Oaks, Texas," and he started to laugh. It was the name of a rest home, probably. A woman on her deathbed in a rest home was writing to Sherlock Holmes to give him her remaining valuables; no doubt a few coins stashed in a shoe box under her bed, or perhaps a few dollars tucked between the pages of old novels.

So this was the sort of thing Reggie Heath had to deal with. What a git.

But then Buxton had an inspiration.

He looked about the secretary's station until he found some stationery. It had Heath's law chambers letterhead. Perfect. Then he took the letters and the stationery and went to the small open office.

He sat at that desk and rolled a sheet into the old typewriter. Yes, he thought, this was indeed a brilliant idea. The damage to Heath's reputation would be incalculable.

Then he hammered out a letter:

Dear Ms. Clemens:

Thank you for your kind letter, and your interest in bequeathing your entire fortune to me, Sherlock Holmes.

Your generous gift can enable me to bring many nefarious villains to justice.

However, I fear it would prove difficult, given the convoluted and irrational intricacies of American law, for your bequest to me to be honored by the court. At best, it would be tied up for years, allowing many scoundrels to continue doing bad deeds unfettered.

And although I would like very much to meet you in person and explore other possibilities, I will be off to the moors very shortly to deal with an occurrence so evil and borderline supernatural that I hardly dare take pen to paper to describe it to you. Or a typewriter, either.

However, I have appointed my good friend Reggie Heath to act on my behalf. If you will kindly make your bequest to him, I know that he will see that it is disposed of properly.

                                                    Yours truly,

Buxton prepared to sign the letter, and then he stopped. He had no real idea what a Sherlock Holmes signature should look like. Neither did this old woman, surely. Nor, in fact, did anyone, given that such a thing did not actually exist.

But it did need to look like Reggie Heath's attempt at such a signature.

Buxton looked quickly about at the secretary's station again, until he found a document that Heath had signed. There was no *S* in his signature unfortunately, but there was a distinctive *H*. The rest could just be a blur.

Buxton forged the signature and held the letter up to a lamp. Oh yes. This would do.

He found a mailing envelope with the Baker Street address on it, sealed the letter inside, and dropped it in an outgoing mail basket so that it would get the appropriate postmark. For good measure, he marked it for overnight delivery.

And then he heard a sound from down the corridor—the single chime of the lift arriving . This was surprising; it was still well before opening hours; he should have had more time.

But clearly he was no longer alone. One or more individuals were on the floor with him. And at any moment, whoever had just gotten out of the lift would probably come his way.

Buxton held his breath and listened—no, no one was coming down the central corridor. Whoever it was must have gone around the side. That meant he had a couple of moments before he was discovered.

Buxton considered his options. Certainly he could make up an excuse for being there and carry it off with a bluff; that would not be difficult, unless it was Heath himself who had just arrived.

But it would not do to get caught holding the bunch of Sherlock Holmes letters. And he could not get them back to their original location without being seen by whoever had just come up on the lift.

Buxton looked about at the law shelves and documents and wondered what to do.

And then he knew.

He worked quickly; he knew he had only seconds left. And, in fact, it took less than a minute.

Of course, someone would discover them soon enough during business hours. But it wouldn't matter; he would be long gone by then. And even if they were found within a day or two, no one would think it had anything to do with him.

There. It was done.

And then he turned and walked quickly straight down the central corridor, prepared to bluster past whoever had come onto the floor, should that person turn up in his path.

But no one did. He reached the opposite side of the office and turned a sharp left, heading for the stairs. He congratulated himself on another job well done.

And then he felt a flash of burning white pain at the base of his skull.

7

A FEW DAYS LATER

At midmorning in Los Angeles, Nigel Heath shuffled in flip-flops down the red masonry steps from Mara's apartment, carrying his second cup of Earl Grey tea with him on his way to the mailbox.

His natural British sensibilities told him that there was something indolent and irresponsible about wearing flip-flops on a weekday. Certainly Reggie would never do it.

And, in fact, flip-flops or no, Nigel felt that he was indeed verging on indolence—even by his own standards. It simply would not do to have Mara going off to work in the early morning while he sat sipping tea. He needed to get back to work. And given where he was and what he knew how to do, that meant practicing law in the States, and that meant passing the California Bar.

And so he had taken the exam six weeks earlier. He hadn't thought it would be necessary to study much for it; surely it would be nothing compared to what he had waded through at King's College.

But it had been much more difficult than he anticipated, and he wasn't sure now that he wanted to see the results. The casualness of his footwear was entirely a bluff—in fact, he was approaching the mailbox with some trepidation.

With any luck, the results wouldn't be there yet. With any luck, what he'd see instead would be a large yellow express package of Sherlock Holmes letters from Reggie. It had been a while since he received any, and at the moment he wouldn't mind the distraction. The previous batch had, in fact, been quite fun, even though—well, actually, specifically because—he had departed from the standard responses a bit.

Now Nigel opened the mailbox and looked inside. Lots of coupons and junk mail. No letter from the California Bar examiners, and that was a relief at first, and then it wasn't.

And still no new letters to Sherlock Holmes.

Damn, thought Nigel. No distractions. Now there was nothing to do but go back to worrying about the bar.

8

There were days when it was good to be a barrister, and today was one of them.

Reggie's last remaining hearing for the day had concluded early, he was already back at chambers on Baker Street, and it wasn't even yet five in the afternoon.

In theory, court was in regular session until half past four. But the pubs beckoned, and judges and lawyers always began checking their watches at quarter past. Only clients, wary of the hourly fees if their barristers had to come back another day, wanted to stick it out and extend the session.

It wasn't all quite fair to the clients, in Reggie's view. But today he was glad for it. The early adjournment had made it possible for him to go to the jeweler again before returning to Baker Street Chambers.

And now he was done with court for the day, and he was done at chambers, as well. He turned off the desk lamp.

He had not heard anything further about the alleged buyout offer for Dorset House, and he was determined not to give it any more thought. Probably Rafferty had been misinformed. Or he had misunderstood, or been exaggerating.

In any case, Reggie had other priorities. He had Laura's ring—the best choice he had been able to make after hours of study—in a little jeweler's box in his coat pocket. He intended to leave now, get a pint at the Olde Bank pub to relax his mind, and mentally rehearse how he would approach the subject.

He was planning it for her first day back from the shoot in Thailand. He didn't intend to wait to make his move. And he would do it in a way that she did not expect.

But now Lois stuck her head through the open office doorway.

"There's a client to see you," she said. "I think. I mean sort of."

"Who does he have as solicitor?"

"I don't think he has one."

"Well, he can't retain a barrister directly. You know that."

"Yes, but . . . he's come a very long way to see you, I think. Perhaps just a word?"

Reggie looked at his watch and began to drum his fingers on the desk.

"I told him you would see him," said Lois apologetically. "I know I shouldn't have. I couldn't help it. And I did the test for walk-ins that you told me about earlier."

"The test?"

"I asked if he is familiar with the entire canon."

"Oh," said Reggie. He had forgotten about the Sherlockian incident from before; he made a mental note to be more careful in the future about giving Lois instructions when he himself was either annoyed or hungry.

"He seemed quite genuinely confused by the question," said Lois. "He replied that he is not familiar with any aspect of English weaponry at all. His exact words. And his eyes were not sparkly, or twinkling, or any such thing that would indicate a prank."

Reggie sighed and stopped drumming.

"Very well. Bring him in, then."

"Yes," said Lois, and then she quickly disappeared from the doorway.

Minutes went by, with Reggie waiting at his desk. He was about to get up and see what the delay was—and then he saw the end of a smooth wooden cane plant itself, unsteadily, just inside the doorway.

Gripping the top of the wooden cane was a gnarled, heavily wrinkled left hand, calloused and scarred from what had to be a lifetime of manual labor. The hand was just barely visible, almost lost, in the gray sleeve of an ancient cloth coat.

The wearer of the gray coat tapped the cane unsteadily forward about half a foot; the gnarled hand was trembling, and Reggie got up from his desk and went to the doorway to assist.

Lois was already on the other side, hovering to help.

The man was Asian—probably Chinese was Reggie's guess— and from the look of him, Reggie suspected he might reasonably lay legal claim to being the oldest man in the world.

Reggie hastily positioned a chair—it felt disrespectful to try to assist more than that until clearly necessary—and watched in suspense as the man lowered himself very slowly but calmly into it.

When the man had accomplished that, he said, "Thank you, Mr. Holmes."

Bloody hell, thought Reggie, and he cast a glare in Lois's direction, but she had already fled.

It was too late to do anything about it now. Reggie sat behind his desk.

"I am most grateful that you are willing to see me," said the man. "When I was a boy, I read about you first in my own language, and then in yours. There is not any shadow of a doubt that you are the greatest detective who has ever lived." He lifted his head slightly to survey Reggie for a moment. "And you are very well preserved."

"Thank you."

"In the small village where I grew up, I used the accounts of your famous exploits to teach English to myself as a child. And now, many years later, it has opened up a great new opportunity for me. I was a humble farmer in my youth. My children want me now to open up my home as a vacation farm for tourists, but I cannot bear to do so, now that my wife is gone. My country is modern, and I shall be modern. Now I shall be a . . . a professional man, like my grandchildren."

He said this with evident pride.

"I see," said Reggie. "Congratulations." Then, guessing that he was supposed to ask, he said, "And this new career path is . . . what, exactly?"

"I have recently become a translator. I am able to translate my native traditional Mandarin into both French and the British variation of English."

"Ah. Yes."

"And that is why I have come to see you, Mr. Holmes."

"Yes. Well. The first thing you need to understand is that I am not Sherlock Holmes. My name is Reggie Heath, and I am merely a barrister. These are my law chambers."

The man looked first puzzled, then very much embarrassed.

"I am sorry for my mistake. I believed this to be Two twenty-one B Baker Street. I must have come in the wrong door. Is it the next building?" He half-stood, and Reggie reached across the desk, ready to support him, just in case.

"No, no, you came in the correct door. I mean, this is where

Two twenty-one B would be, or would have been, if it had existed. At least the Royal Mail and a few other people seem to think so."

The man sat back down.

"Then I am glad that I have not made a mistake. I saw the statue of you at the entrance to the underground station. It is you, although not a perfect likeness. I hope you did not pay too much for it. In any case, I shall keep your identity a secret if you wish me to do so."

This was the first Reggie had heard of any slight resemblance between himself and the bronze of Sherlock Holmes at Baker Street station. He did not regard it as a compliment, but then, the old man's eyesight probably wasn't all that good.

"No," said Reggie, "It's true there is a statue of Sherlock Holmes. But he is simply a very well known character of fiction."

"Yes, your exploits are well documented in the guise of novels, and your fame is written everywhere. It was in the books that I studied in my class for students of English as a second language. *The Hound of the Baskervilles*."

"Yes, but again, fiction. Written by a man named Arthur Conan Doyle."

"Sir Arthur Conan Doyle," said the man, correcting Reggie.

"Yes," said Reggie. Now they were getting somewhere.

"I know that he is Dr. Watson's literary agent, and he arranged for the publication of the accounts that Dr. Watson created of your exploits. Your English experts have said so."

"No, Conan Doyle is not my—is not Sherlock Holmes's—is not Dr. Watson's—literary agent."

"That is sad news. But I know he must be quite old. He has died? Is there a new agent?"

"Conan Doyle died in— Well, it doesn't matter, as he was never— Look, there never was a Sherlock Holmes. I'm sorry, but there it is. He was entirely made up. No such person exists or has ever existed."

The man stared at Reggie, and then he looked at the floor for a moment, and then back at Reggie again.

"In my country, it is necessary that a person first exist, and also that he accomplish great things or espouse great philosophies, and only then would we consider placing a sculpture on a large boulevard to honor him."

Reggie thought that was a very good point.

"Sometimes we do things oddly here," he admitted.

The man nodded, and having scored that point, he raised another. "And how would a person who does not exist manage to employ a personal secretary?" asked the man.

"I'm not sure I follow," said Reggie.

The man gave Reggie a puzzled look. "Follow . . . where?"

"I mean," said Reggie, "I do not understand your reference to a personal secretary."

The man took that in, considered it, and nodded. Then he removed a letter from his coat pocket, and suddenly Reggie knew what he must be referring to.

Reggie waited as the man began to unfold it painstakingly. Reggie's visions of a pint of Guinness were evaporating.

Now the man had the letter open.

"I wrote to you," he began, and then he paused, gave Reggie a knowing look, and corrected himself. "I mean I wrote to Sherlock Holmes, not to you, several weeks ago because I know that you—that is, he—having traveled so widely all over the world, and being conversant in many languages, and surely an expert in the quaintness of your native tongue, could help me confirm my translation of one mysterious English phrase. Here is the letter that I received from you in response."

He placed the letter in front of Reggie. Reggie recognized it, and sighed. It was the letter that Nigel had sent, explaining the term *dub-dub* in a nursery rhyme.

"I found your response to be very helpful," said the man, "even though you are only Mr. Holmes's secretary."

"No," said Reggie, "I am not Sherlock Holmes's personal secretary."

"Ah," said the man. "Yes. As I thought." He leaned forward and spoke in a conspiratorial whisper. "You are, in fact, the man himself. I knew that if I came this great distance to London, I would have the honor of meeting you in person."

Reggie wanted to object again, but it didn't seem to be much use.

And the man had traveled halfway around the world. Next thing, Reggie feared, he would be saying that he had mortgaged his house to do it.

As if on cue, the man said, "It took all of my savings for the flight. But what are savings for, if not for such an emergency?"

Reggie took a breath.

"Mr. Liu, perhaps you'd best tell me," said Reggie, "exactly what you hoped Sherlock Holmes could do for you."

The man nodded and smiled slightly, as if this outcome had never been in doubt. He began to pull more documents out from a deep pocket in his coat.

"That letter helped with my first translation as a professional. But it was only my first. I then received a much larger translation, with many more rhymes. My employer was no doubt impressed at my success in translating the very difficult English word *dub-dub*.

"No doubt," said Reggie.

"And so I did the complete set of translation, and I sent it to

my employer here in London. Here, you see: Mrs. Elizabeth
Winslow, Standard Translation Services."

"Yes."

"But she returned them to me. She said that my translations
were incorrect and told me to try again. But I am certain that
my translations are correct. They were not nearly so difficult as
the first one. And so I informed her that if she did not accept
my work and render payment as agreed, I would be forced to
send the rhymes to Sherlock Holmes—as I had done with the
first one—and you would confirm that I had them right."

"Let me guess," said Reggie. "That did not resolve the matter?"

"No," said Mr. Liu. "It did not. Her most recent response
said that she suspects me of being—I remember the words she
wrote exactly—'quite possibly bonkers.'"

Reggie nodded. "Mentioning that you were consulting Sherlock Holmes might not have been the best argument for your
case."

"I don't understand why that would be so. But I am sure
that if you will respond regarding the most recent letter that I
sent to you, she will believe you that my translations are correct. I know that you are a very busy man, with much more
important matters than mine, and that is why you have not
responded to me already."

Reggie drummed his fingers uncomfortably on his desk.
The truth, he knew, was that he had simply been a tad negli-
gent and had not been sending the letter packages promptly on
to Nigel. And although he resented the letters, that was not an
excuse for his own tardiness.

"I apologize for that," said Reggie. "I'll ask Lois to find your
most recent letter, and we'll have a look. It might take her a few
moments to hunt it up."

"That is not necessary," said the man. "The final translation was such a large piece of work that I took the trouble to make a copy before I sent it, and I have brought the copy with me."

The man stood, leaned forward just a bit unsteadily, and unfolded a double-wide sheet of paper on Reggie's desk.

The sheet had been laser-printed on the kind of thin, cheap paper used in instruction booklets for small items—toys, electronics, and such—sold internationally. One of the folded sections was in English, another in Chinese, and another in French.

Reggie glanced at the titles: "Rub-a-dub-dub"; "One, Two, Buckle My Shoe"; "Humpty Dumpty"; and several others. Typical of such sheets, most of the typeface was so small that you could hardly read more than the titles, and Reggie didn't try. But each language section contained—so far as Reggie could tell—a set of Mother Goose nursery rhymes.

"So you not only did the translations," said Reggie, "but you produced the final copy?"

"Yes," said the man proudly. "On my laser printer. And I did not make errors. I am a good translator. I need help only with the occasional idiot."

"I think you mean idiom."

"Yes. And so when she still refused to pay, I had no choice but to come myself."

"Surely this trip has cost you as much as the payment that was due?"

"I must have honor in my career, Mr. Holmes. I must respect myself, and my clients must respect me."

Reggie nodded slightly and then said, "Personally, I would have saved the cost of the trip and put the money toward respecting myself with a few pints at my local pub."

"That is what you say," said the man. "I do not think it is

what you would do. And you are young. When you are older, you will value honor more than beer."

"Anything is possible," said Reggie. "Have you spoken to this woman since you arrived in London?"

The man shook his head. "No. I went to her address and found that it was not her home, and not her place of business, but nothing more than a little store that sells stamps and other necessities."

"I see. So her address is a postal box. That's not unusual."

"Surely the world's greatest detective can find her for me?"

Reggie laughed. He handed the printed sheet of translations back to the old man.

"You don't need the world's greatest detective, Mr. Liu. And you don't need a barrister, either. You just need a garden-variety solicitor. It's not terribly unusual for some unscrupulous contractors to attempt to cheat their subcontractors out of payment, thinking the subcontractors will simply give up, especially when the distance is so great. But now that you are here, I expect a good solicitor will be able to obtain your payment, and perhaps even reimbursement for your trip. If you will come back tomorrow afternoon, I will find one for you."

The man shook his head. "I must go home tomorrow."

"Well," said Reggie, "this will likely take a few days. Before he can even get started, your solicitor will have to obtain the woman's actual address from the Royal Mail."

The man shook his head very slightly in disappointment. He began to roll up the document he had brought.

"If you were Sherlock Holmes," he said, "you would tell me from the weight of the stationery and the manner in which it is cut where it was purchased and the economic and social standing of the person who purchased it, and from the smudges on the edges, you would tell me where the person lives in this city, and from all those things together and other things I cannot think of, you would know where I can find this person. And I brought one of her envelopes to show you as a reference."

"I'm sorry, I don't think that would help. As I said, I am not Sherlock Holmes."

"And now I believe you. Do not take offense; it is not an insult."

The man tucked the document back into his coat and rose very slowly from his chair.

"And now I must go," he said. "I believe I am suffering the effects of running in a race just slightly behind a jet plane. Thank you for your gracious time with me."

The man stood, looking wobbly for just a moment; Reggie stood as well and came around to the front of the desk just as the man reestablished his balance. Lois came to the doorway to assist.

The man turned suddenly back to Reggie and said, "I was told I should take in a show before I return home. Do you have a recommendation?"

Reggie was stumped. It was not a question he had expected. And for an instant he wondered if he was being pranked again.

"The standard tourist recommendation," said Reggie, "based on the fact that it has been running forever, is *The Mousetrap*. All the characters are fictional, of course."

"Of course," said the man, "I will consider it. The bellman at the hotel had some other suggestions."

The man turned away and wobbled on through the doorway. Reggie frantically gestured to Lois to go with him.

"Get him into a cab," said Reggie, "and pay for it if he'll let you."

Several minutes went by, during which Reggie turned off his lamp again, picked up his mac, and prepared to leave but did not. He remained seated at the edge of his chair, as if some task remained to be completed.

And now Lois returned. She stood in the doorway of Reggie's chambers, put her hands on her hips, and glared.

"Yes?" said Reggie.

"Well he came quite a long way now, didn't he?"

"Yes. An astoundingly long way, given the money involved."

"And what does he get in return?"

"I'm not sure what you mean."

"What he gets is you showing him the door is what I mean. Or me doing it for you."

Reggie wanted to object to that indictment, but he couldn't. He had been chastising himself over the same thing for the past ten minutes. As annoyed as he was that Nigel had departed from the standard reply in his response to Mr. Liu, it occurred to Reggie that he himself had compounded the problem by not sending the subsequent letters on to Nigel in time. He had just been ignoring all of the letters, letting them accumulate on the corner of his desk. Had he not done so, perhaps the man would not have come all this way.

"I'll call his hotel," said Reggie. "Perhaps I can do something for him in the morning. This is work much more suited for a solicitor, if I can find him one in time. But if not—well, sometimes a barrister on your side can make a trial seem imminent, and the potential defendant more cooperative."

"I should think," said Lois before exiting triumphantly. "Especially if you wear the silly wig."

9

What woke Robert Buxton was the stench.

It filled his nostrils. It permeated the air. There were familiar elements in it, but it was more intense than any scent he had ever encountered.

He opened his eyes. But doing that seemed to hurt, and he closed them again; it was too dark to see anything anyway.

His head was still throbbing. Not just in the back but in the front, as well—sinuses, forehead, neck, everywhere.

Damn that smell.

He knew he was lying on a flat, hard, damp surface; he was in the dark; and something stunk. Beyond that, he had no clue.

Except that somewhere, water was running.

Somebody call a plumber, he thought, still trying to clear his head.

He opened his eyes once more and tried to raise his head to look around. He put his hands on the cold surface beneath him, then shifted his weight and pushed with his arms, trying to raise himself up.

But the surface he was lying on—whatever it was—was slick, and his hands slipped. He heard something splash.

And then a wave of nausea swept over him; chills ran from the base of his neck all the way down his spine. He lost consciousness, and his head dropped down again onto the hard, damp floor.

10

Reggie arrived at Baker Street Chambers at midmorning
the next day, with Laura's ring secured in the inside pocket of
his mac.

He had told Lois to set up no appointments for him on the
day that Laura returned from her shoot. Today was that day.

In fact, there should be nothing more on his desk than a
follow-up to his call from last night to Mr. Liu's hotel. The old
gentleman had been out; probably to take in a show, as he had
said. But Reggie had left a message, and with luck he might
easily wrap the whole thing up in a day. A brief word with the
translator's overly picky employer would take care of it.

Reggie stopped at his secretary's desk before going into his
chambers office.

"Good morning, sir," said Lois, cheerily. It had not been
possible to keep her in the dark about his plans today; she knew
something was up.

"Good morning, Lois. My calendar is still clear?"

"Yes, sir. Pretty much for the entire week." She giggled
slightly, then stifled it.

"And the other preparations?"

"Everything is set up. The caterer will return at the top of the hour."

"Brilliant."

Reggie went into his chambers and closed the door behind him. He looked about at the advance preparations—the small round dining table, the white linen, the silver service. Yes, it would do.

He sat down behind his desk and reviewed the plan one more time: Transfer the ring from his mac into his suit pocket. Done. Office rearranged. Done. The best caterer in all of London delivering an early lunch at the top of the hour. Done.

Everything was ready.

Now he had a quarter of an hour before Laura would arrive. Nothing on his calendar. Nothing to do.

He picked up the phone and rang Lois.

"Did I get a message back from Mr. Liu?"

"No, sir. Do you want me to try his hotel?"

"No, no. Not now. We'll try him again later."

"Yes, sir."

Reggie hung up the phone. He still had several minutes before Laura was due to arrive. He took the ring box out of his pocket and opened it on his desk to take another look.

And then—sooner than expected—there was a distinctive knock on the chambers door: Laura's knock.

Reggie scrambled to get the ring back in the box and into his pocket.

"Come in," he said. He was still behind his desk; there wasn't time to come around to meet her.

The door opened. Laura stepped just inside and hovered, Bacall-like, in the entryway, tall and slender.

Reggie caught a slight scent of coconut and oranges; either she had adopted a new perfume or she had come directly from the airport and hadn't yet washed off all the sunscreen. She had picked up only a little sun, just enough to darken the freckles that had already been visible and highlight a tan line in the front. That was good. Reggie liked tan lines; they were the major thoroughfares that led to the freckled side streets, which led, pale and enticing, to interesting places to visit.

Laura paused, looking first at Reggie and then at the fancy dining arrangements he had imported into the chambers.

She raised an eyebrow and the corners of her mouth tweaked up.

"When you said brunch at chambers," said Laura, "I quite thought you meant tandoori takeaway."

"It turned out that my calendar is open this afternoon. So we have time for more than one course. Perhaps even three of four."

"I'm surprised," said Laura, clearly pleased. "Everyone says clients are quite charging through your doors.

"Yes," said Reggie. "Ever since the Black Cab case, I have become known as the barrister who did not, in fact, kill his client. Who knew that by itself would constitute a positive recommendation?"

Laura smiled and sat down. "Or that appearing in the *Daily Sun* could actually be a good thing?"

"Yes, that, too," said Reggie. "How was the location shoot? Was it, as they say, a wrap?"

What Reggie wanted to hear was that the far-off location shoots for this particular film were, in fact, now done, and that Lord Robert Buxton hadn't been dropping in on her on the slightest pretext, as he had managed to do on the first round.

"The weather got a bit sticky," said Laura. "And little orange-and-black beetles kept getting through the mesh on my tent and popping up in the oddest places. But everyone else tells me the shoot itself was boffo. I've been so looking forward to using that word. And yes, I do believe this wrapped it up."

"Word of a sequel?"

Laura laughed. "There's some sort of a publicity do tonight that I'm supposed to attend. Along with Robert as the principal financer. Perhaps he'll hint at something."

"Ah," said Reggie very carefully, with no inflection whatsoever. But bloody hell, he thought. Would the man never go away?

Laura continued. "I need to talk with him anyway, and he's been difficult to reach the last couple of days."

Now that sounded better. But Reggie resolved to make sure the name Buxton did not come up in the conversation again at all.

"Why do you keep putting your hand in your coat pocket?" Laura asked.

"No reason," said Reggie. He smiled slyly, or at least hoped it was sly. He let go of the ring box—just for the moment—and put both hands back on the table.

"I expect the main course will be arriving any moment," he said. "And for dessert, I understand they do something very special with chocolate and raspberries."

Reggie saw her eyes light up. Perfect. According to plan.

And now his desk phone rang. That would be the caterer, arriving with the first course.

Reggie felt very much in command. He punched the speakerphone button to let Laura hear the caterer announce the menu directly.

But it wasn't the caterer.

"I'm glad I caught you, Heath," said a male voice over the phone.

It was Inspector Wembley.

"I was just about to have lunch," said Reggie.

"Bring it with you," said Wembley. "I need a word. You can eat it on the way. Or after you get here, if your stomach is cast iron."

"What I meant," said Reggie, "is that I have an appointment for lunch."

"Heath, courts are not back in session until two, and the thing I've got here takes priority over any business lunch you have scheduled."

"It's not a business appointment," said Reggie. "It's social."

"You don't have a bloody thing of social importance in your life, Heath."

"Hello, Inspector," said Laura now, quite cordially, through the speakerphone. "How are you today? You sound tense."

There was a pause. Then: "I'm quite well, Miss Rankin. Thanks for asking. And sorry to interrupt. But Heath, I'm in an alley in Soho, looking down at a freshly dead body—and the only thing the recently deceased has on him that would explain his presence here in London is your business card. That and a playbill for *The Mousetrap*."

Reggie made no immediate response. He remembered the recommendation he had made to the old man the night before, and his diaphragm tightened in apprehension of what else Wembley might have to say.

"It is a very popular play," said Laura into the phone, covering Reggie's silence.

"Agreed," said Wembley. "But I wouldn't come here all the way from Taiwan for it."

"Bloody hell," said Reggie.

He looked across at Laura.

"I have to go," he said.

"Perhaps I'll go with—" began Laura.

"Heath only," commanded Wembley through the phone. "No disrespect, Miss Rankin, but this is not for civilians and you have no stake in it."

She smiled slightly, nodded, and sat back down.

"As you wish, Inspector," said Laura. "I'll just stay and have both Reggie's lunch and my own."

"Cheers," said Wembley.

Reggie was still clutching the ring box in his pocket, and for a brief moment he thought about bringing it out right then and there.

But surely he could time it better than to propose on his way to a murder scene.

Reggie let go of the ring and stood.

A look of disappointment flashed across Laura's face. Reggie assumed it was because of Wembley's refusal to let her ride along to the crime scene. After all, she had no idea what he'd been up to with the lunch.

"Very sorry," said Reggie. "I hope you don't mind. I'll be back as soon as possible."

"I hope you don't mind," said Laura as Reggie picked up his mac. "I'm going to eat your dessert while you're gone."

11

The moment after Reggie exited the chambers, Laura took out her list.

She had written it down during the flight from her South Seas location shoot. It had been a long flight, but it was a short list.

Item one: "Say yes to Reggie."

Well. She could hardly cross that one off now.

She had been quite expecting the proposal to happen as soon as she returned; even before she flew out for the shoot weeks ago, she had been sure it was coming. Her best guess had been that it would be at dinner on the weekend.

But then had come the lunch invitation, and Reggie's unwillingness to specify in advance just exactly what the lunch would be. "I'll surprise you," he had said. And then she thought she knew.

And when she saw all the expensive white linen and silver set up in Reggie's chambers—well, then, she really did very much know.

And now the whole thing was on hold—for hours at least, probably for another day. She would have to wait.

She sighed and looked at the next item on the list.

Item two: "Tell Robert."

Now, in fact, she had been trying to tell Robert for several days now.

Friends had advised her that he was a hard man to say no to. She didn't think they meant he would simply make himself unavailable.

She had rung him before she got on the plane. But no answer.

She had rung him again when the plane touched down at Heathrow. Still nothing.

She had rung both his private mobile line—the number that he said he shared with no one but her, the prime minister, one cabinet member in each of the major political parties, and the king of Bahrain—and the private office number, which he shared with only his immediate staff and the directors of each of his major holdings—and still no answer.

So item two was still on her list, as well. But she could take care of it now, and she was about to pick up the phone.

But then Lois knocked and stuck her head in. "The caterer is here," said Lois. "And it smells delicious."

"Does it?" said Laura. "Then you'll share it with me, of course."

Lois hesitated. "I should be at my desk. . . ."

"Then that's where we'll have it," said Laura.

"Lovely," said Lois.

Moments later they started in on sole soufflé Francine at Lois's open office station.

Lois first had to push aside what looked like about half a dozen tabloids and newspapers.

"What's all this?" she asked.

"Oh, it's just a hobby of mine," said Lois. "I never do it when there's work, of course, but it's very quiet today."

"I noticed that," said Laura.

"Yes, Reggie cleared his calendar so that . . . well, I'm not supposed to say what for, but anyway, when it's quiet and I have time, as it is today, I like to read the newspapers, like Sherlock Holmes would do."

"And what way is that?"

"You read the paper," said Lois. "And you solve a crime. Or recover a missing diamond. Or save a lady's reputation from scandal. You don't even have to get out and about anywhere. You just do it from your chair."

"Sounds fun," said Laura. "Had any luck at it?"

"Well . . . no, not yet, at least not so far. But I keep trying. For instance—"

"Yes, go right ahead."

Lois picked up the *Daily Telegraph* and read from it.

"Today we have 'IRA Peace Talks Continue'; 'Pedestrian Fatally Injured at King's Cross Station'; 'Lady Ashton-Tate Birthday Bash to Support Red Squirrels.'"

"Surely that last one's not a crime, is it? I have friends who'll be in jail if it is."

"Oh no, but it's not just crimes you should pay attention to. It's everything. Except the things that don't matter."

"And which are those?"

"For the life of me, I don't know, and that's what makes it such a challenge."

"I see. So do you see any solutions to crimes in any of those?"

"No," said Lois. "I can't think of a thing to say about any of them."

"Nor can I," said Laura. "What a couple of dunces we must be. We aren't Sherlock Holmes at all. Although, between you and me, I'm not sure the fellow really ever did have any fun. So you know what I think we should do instead?"

"No."

"Eat dessert. You can have Reggie's portion."

"Lovely," said Lois.

Moments later, the chocolate raspberry tart having been demolished, Laura left Lois with her newspapers and returned to Reggie's chambers. She shut the door behind her.

She picked up Reggie's desk phone and tried Buxton's private number once more.

It rang half a dozen times, and then—to her surprise—someone finally picked up.

"Who is this?" said the male voice—not Buxton's—with no preliminaries at all.

Laura was just a little put off.

"Well, who are you, then?" she said. "I was expecting Lord Robert Buxton."

"You might as well tell us who you are first," said the man on the phone. "We'll have your number in a moment."

"You'll have it wrong, then, because I'm not calling from my own phone."

"Well, this is a private line. So someone's in trouble, either way."

"Perhaps it will be you," said Laura. "I suggest you let me speak with Robert."

Now there were a couple of other voices in the background.

"One moment," said the man on the phone.

For a moment there was silence, with Laura on hold, and then the man came back.

"Are you Laura Rankin?" he asked.

"Yes."

"Please come to Lord Buxton's headquarters," said the man, somewhat friendlier now. "We would like to speak with you. I'll tell the security station to let you in."

"They always do anyway," said Laura.

"Not anymore," said the man.

This sounded ominous, and Laura was about to ask for clarification, but the man had already hung up.

Laura rang Lois on the interior line.

"If Reggie returns while you are still here and complains about missing the dessert, tell him it's his own fault," said Laura. "Also, tell him I've gone over to Buxton's—well, let's not put it that way exactly. Tell him where I've gone, but not to worry."

"Why should he worry?" asked Lois.

"Well, I don't want him to think that— Oh, never mind, just tell him."

"I will, but you should know there's someone on his way to Reggie's chambers right now. I'm sorry I couldn't stop him. I was just about to ring you—"

Now there was a heavy, angry knock on the door, and then, with no courtesy pause whatsoever, the door opened.

Laura looked up.

She saw a man wearing cowboy boots. Nicely done cowboy boots, to be sure, in two tones of expensive leather and with fine tooling up the sides—but pointy-toed cowboy boots, all the same. Also a dark brown blazer with a yoke that ran the length of the shoulders, and contrasting tan slacks.

And one of those hats.

An American. Probably from Texas, thought Laura, or possibly Arizona, but quite unapologetic about it either way.

The man was in his fifties, with jet black hair and a strong build, and a surprised look on his face. Clearly, he had not been expecting to see someone like Laura.

He paused in the doorway; his eyes scanned quickly back and forth about the room, and when he had confirmed that there was only Laura, he gathered his bravado again and spoke.

He said, "I want to talk to the idiot here that's pretending to be Sherlock Holmes."

Now that she heard the accent, Laura made her assessment more precise: a Texan. And an angry one at that.

"I'll handle it," Laura said into the phone to Lois, "And then I have to be on my way. Don't forget about the leftovers."

Laura hung up the phone.

Really, this should be easy. She never had any trouble with this type.

"Why, there's no one here like that at all," she said as she closed up the last takeaway container. She said it with what in her mind was a pleasant American southern drawl. She couldn't help it; she was always trying to get her accents right, and the man's initial attitude warranted some sort of a comeback.

The Texan looked back at her suspiciously. "Are you messing with me?" he said.

"I've no idea what you mean," she replied, now with no trace of any accent at all. Almost. "But in any case, there is no person here who pretends to be Sherlock Holmes. There never is. And even if there were, I'm afraid I just couldn't be of any help to you at all."

She slurred those last three words together, and with just a bit of a twang, which made them sound, when run together, like a nautical term. She smiled just slightly when she did it.

Mistake. She saw the man take a moment, his eyes appraising her more fully now, and then she saw the look that crosses a man's face when he's shifting the agenda from business to sex.

"Oh, I don't know about that, ma'am," he said with a quick grin.

In a flash, he'd gone from annoyed to randy.

Which meant that, as angry as he was, his stake in the matter—whatever the matter was—had its limits.

The Texan sat down at the linen-covered table. "Maybe we can talk about it over dinner? I'd suggest an Italian place that folks have been telling me about, but it looks like you're already set up."

A lawyer, Laura concluded.

"And don't worry about this," said the Texan, removing his Stetson. "It comes right off."

"Now you're messing with me," said Laura. "And I'm in no position to be messed with."

"Sorry to hear that," said the man. "I'll tell you why I'm here, then."

"You aren't here to see me," said Laura. "And I don't have the time in any event. You may leave your card, if you like."

"As you wish," he said. He stood and gave her a card from his wallet. Laura glanced at it.

Carl Stillman, J.D. Houston, TX.

Yes, a lawyer.

For a moment, the man was all business again. "You can give that to whoever needs to see it; I'll expect to hear from someone at this chambers, and I won't leave London until I do."

And then he paused at the door. "Or," he added, "you can use it yourself, at your convenience. In my book, there's no such thing as geographically undesirable."

"Bye now," said Laura.

Laura closed the door after Stillman left. Then she picked up the phone and got Lois on the interior line.

"I don't know what he wanted, but be sure he leaves," she said. "And don't let him back in until Reggie returns."

"Of course," said Lois.

Laura hung up the phone. She looked about at the linen and trappings for the nice brunch she and Reggie had not quite enjoyed together. After all his preparation.

She sighed. Then she stepped into the corridor and shut the door to the chambers office.

She exited Dorset House on Baker Street and took a cab for Robert Buxton's headquarters at Tobacco Wharf.

12

Reggie had taken a cab from Baker Street; to find parking in any of the business streets in Piccadilly or Soho at almost any hour was always impossible.

The taxi drove down Regent Street to Piccadilly Circus, where four transportation arteries and the busiest tube stations in the city conspired to dump all manner of people, with all manner of purposes and destinations, into one bright square of neon lights. At any hour, Piccadilly was always filled with black cabs and roaring double-deckers, and a mass of humanity trying to dodge them all and get to Lillywhites, or the Criterion Theatre, or to the Boots pharmacy or the Burger King, or down the side streets that led to something more off-track in Soho. There was street construction under way, as there always was; Reggie had concluded long ago that the only purpose of it was to make the whole place more difficult to pass through, in the same way that department stores position display cases to block any direct route out of the store that might let you escape without a purchase. It was Piccadilly Circus. You were obliged to stop and buy something.

In front of the winged statue of Eros, the driver turned left

onto Shaftesbury. Then the cab slowed as they passed the Tro-
cadero, with its throngs and video-game arcades.

Now there were several narrow lanes, all of which ran for no
more than a block or two, off the main commercial street and
into the more specialized blocks of Soho. The businesses here
were more cautiously and specifically lit, like courtesans, brightly
enough to attract their clientele, but not so much as to annoy the
mainstream establishments on the connecting streets.

On one of these lanes, the cab stopped at the entrance of an
even narrower alleyway. Here there were deep shadows and no
lights at the moment; nothing in this alley had a midmorning
clientele.

Reggie got out and showed his identification to a young
and skeptical officer standing in front of the fluorescent yellow
crime-scene tape. It took several minutes of persuading, but finally the bobby called out over his shoulder to Detective Inspector Wembley—a fiftyish man, with the shoulders of a former
boxer and a coat that was fitting too tightly with the passing
years—who was huddled with another Scotland Yard professional over something in the interior of the alley.

Wembley looked up and waved Reggie in.

Reggie stepped over the tape and into the alley. The alley
dead-ended at an eight-foot brick wall. Several feet in front of
that wall was a Dumpster; at the perimeter of the small space
obscured by the Dumpster were Wembley and a medical examiner.

On the near side of the Dumpster, an exterior set of stairs
led to a purple door, closed at the moment, with a sign above it
that identified the entrance to the Body Shop, a strip club.

As Reggie approached, Wembley stood and looked toward
him expectantly, or accusingly—Reggie wasn't quite sure which.

Wembley shifted his position slightly to give Reggie just enough space to see what they had found.

Reggie looked down.

It was Mr. Liu, the old gentleman who had visited Reggie's office the day before.

The wisps of the old man's white hair were plastered against his head with blood. The collar and lapel of his gray coat were saturated with blood, as well; the hem of the coat was damp and soiled from a rain puddle and Dumpster muck. Altogether, the man's frame seemed to be even smaller now than when he had been in Reggie's office, and much too inconsequential in death.

Reggie wanted to turn away. "How was he found?" he asked. He took a moment to mentally focus before continuing. He looked back up the alley toward the street. The foot traffic was fifty yards away, and the body was partly obscured by the sides of the Dumpster. Then he added, "I would guess he could have been here for hours without being noticed."

"He was," said Wembley. "We didn't get a call until the cleaning crew showed up this morning for the strip club upstairs."

"No one leaving the club saw him here when it closed?"

"Apparently not. But the light is poor, and he could have been missed on this side of the Dumpster. From a few yards out, all you see is an old coat on the ground. And the club employees leave by the front entrance when they close."

The forensics examiner, a woman in her early forties, stood up now.

"I think you've got a four-hour window," she said. "I'll get you details after I get him back to the lab, but my first guess is between eleven last night and three this morning. Step back, please?"

Reggie and Wembley moved back.

"My theory," said Wembley, "is that he came here last night looking for some special Soho entertainment and got robbed. I rang you because he had this on him. Have anything to say about it?"

Wembley showed Reggie his Baker Street Chambers business card, already captured in a clear plastic bag.

"He came to my office yesterday," said Reggie. And then, just out of tactical habit, he changed the subject instead of providing the details he knew Wembley wanted. "Did anyone see him inside the club?"

"Don't know yet, but we're going to check it out." Wembley turned and gestured for the young officer to come over.

"Meachem," said Wembley, "This is your lucky day. When the club opens, you get to interview the young ladies. I'd do it myself, but I'm just too damn busy."

"Thank you, guv," said Meachem. "I'll do my best."

"I know you will," said Wembley.

The officer went back to his position.

"Of course," said Wembley to Reggie, "it's possible our victim never made it that far."

"I agree, given the steep stairs," said Reggie. "Although he might have done, if you gave him all evening to do it. From what I know of him, he was a very determined man. But I think he was a little old for this to have been his destination. Are you sure the body hasn't been moved?"

"Forensics is checking on that. But I don't accept your premise. You can't get too old for a good strip club," said Wembley. "And the dancers are friendlier when they think you're harmless. Or so I hear."

Reggie nodded. "They're most friendly when you have cash in your pocket. Or so I hear. Does he have a roll of five-pound notes in his pocket?"

"No. Just seventy-two pence in change."

"Then either he was misinformed about how strip clubs work or the body was moved. Or perhaps he was in Piccadilly for some other reason."

"Or he was robbed before he could get inside, as I said. His wallet is gone."

"The man came all the way from Taiwan on a point of honor," said Reggie. "It would surprise me if he'd been trying to spend his one evening here at a strip club."

"Wouldn't surprise me a bit," said Wembley. "But I'm guessing you know something you haven't told me."

"He was doing some contract work, remotely, for someone here in London. Translating some mundane nursery rhyme twaddle. But he was having trouble getting paid."

"And he consulted a barrister for that?"

Reggie shrugged. He wasn't about to tell Wembley that someone had come to him thinking he was Sherlock Holmes.

"Not everyone understands our clever division of labor between barristers and solicitors," said Reggie. "He just needed a lawyer."

"So what's your theory?"

"I don't have one yet. He did ask about going to see a show. And I don't mean the kind upstairs. There are theaters nearby; I suppose he might have taken the tube to see a stage play in Piccadilly, then got lost walking back afterward, and ended up here in Soho."

"Maybe," said Wembley. "The divine and the decadent do tend to be right next to each other in this part of the city. But I think *Mousetrap* is playing too far away for your theory, if that's the one he saw. Any other ideas?"

"Just one: He confronted his nonpaying client and got killed for his trouble."

"And they chose an alley in Soho for their business meeting?"

"I can't explain the location. But it's not uncommon for remote workers to get stiffed. Happens a lot. The big companies just stonewall the smaller contractors and tell them to bugger off. Cases that come to me are much higher up the corporate food chain, of course. But it's an annoying sort of behavior, at any level."

"I think you're making more of it than it is, Heath. But do you have a name for this nonpaying client?"

"When I get back to my office, I can send you both the name and the postal box address his employer was using."

"Send it on, then."

Wembley started to turn away.

Reggie hesitated, still staring down at Mr. Liu's body.

"Was there something else?" asked Wembley.

"No," said Reggie.

"Step back, then. You'll hear from me if we have more questions."

Reggie turned away and started back toward his cab.

At the entrance to the alley, just past the crime tape, Reggie stopped. The wind had blown a small slip of white paper into a rain puddle by the wall.

Nothing unusual about that. But the item looked relatively fresh. Reggie picked it up.

A receipt from a souvenir store. Cash purchase. And the change back was seventy-two pence—the same amount Mr. Liu had in his pocket.

Probably it meant nothing whatsoever.

Still, Reggie looked back at the crime scene. Wembley and the forensics expert were busy, focused on the body. The novice bobby looked available, but taking the receipt back to the inexperienced recruit didn't seem like the most efficient thing to do at the moment, and the taxi was waiting. Reggie stuffed the receipt into his pocket and got in the cab.

As he rode back to Baker Street, Reggie reminded himself that Mr. Liu was already dead. There was no reason the exact circumstance of his murder should matter.

But it did matter. The more he thought about it, the more he connected the image of the stubborn man in his office with the frail body in the alley, the more he thought of Mr. Liu coming all this way for a sum that was less than the cost of the trip, the more the circumstance of his death mattered. It just did.

And although he wanted to do so, Reggie knew he would not be able to leave it alone.

13

Laura's cab arrived at Tobacco Wharf, where Robert Buxton, like another publishing magnate before him, had located his multiacre publishing compound.

There had been time on the short drive to rehearse once again what she wanted to tell him—what she would have told him already, if only she had been able to reach him in the last three days.

And time to wonder why he had made himself unavailable for her to do so.

It must surely be a very good reason—at least from his point of view.

Something involving royalty, probably, or highly placed politicians. Even Lord Robert Buxton knew better than to put her on hold for mundane corporate matters.

Not that it would matter. She had already made up her mind.

The cab drove down a dark red corridor of ten-foot-high brick walls to a gated entrance.

Laura had been here many times before. The supervisor at the guard station recognized her, made a quick phone call, and waved her on through.

In the lobby of the main building, journalists and office workers for the tabloids Buxton owned were coming and going; a few stood chatting by the public lifts. It was all normal.

She used the pass card Buxton had given her months ago to access the private lift. She got in alone and entered her security code to get to the top floor.

The lift opened on a broad reception area, with indoor shrubs and deep comfortable chairs and a skylight. At the center of it, immediately across from the lift, was a gleaming brass reception bar—staffed at various times, depending on the purpose of the occasion, by either a bartender or a stunningly beautiful receptionist. Sometimes, on more intimate occasions, Buxton himself did the honors.

The stunningly beautiful receptionist was, of course, purely for public-relations purposes. Buxton had found a way to mention that to Laura the first time she had visited this floor. Laura had found a way to convey that she hadn't even noticed.

But today it was none of those people. Today Buxton's chief of staff, his second in command, stood in front of the reception area.

He was a tall man, quite thin, with graying hair and horn-rimmed spectacles. As Laura got out of the lift, he stepped forward at once and introduced himself—Alex Simpson—unnecessarily.

"Yes," said Laura. "I'm sure we've met."

"Of course," said Alex.

Laura followed him through an interior door and into Buxton's private conference room.

One long side of the room was lined with bookcases and framed first issues of each of Buxton's publications. The other side was a broad window that looked out over the Thames.

Three men in black suits, with chests like anvils, and

electronic devices in their ears, Lord Buxton's private security team—Laura was sure of it; she had seen at least one of them before—stood talking in front of that window.

They all turned and stared in her direction. Then one of them pressed a button that automatically closed the heavy window drapes; the other two came and joined Laura and Alex Simpson at a polished oval conference table in the center of the room.

"Henry is in charge of Lord Buxton's internal security," said Alex, indicating the man seated at his left. "Ian is first operational officer. Their entire team will be working with us."

Laura looked from one to the other and then back at Alex. "Working with us?"

Alex looked over at Henry, and Henry nodded to confirm.

Then Alex looked at Laura and very carefully said, "Lord Buxton has been kidnapped."

For a moment, Laura was completely speechless. She had imagined a number of scenarios to explain why Robert had not contacted her. This was not among them.

"How . . . I mean, why haven't I heard . . ."

"You haven't heard of this because no one outside this room knows," said Alex. "We need your word that it will stay that way."

"Of course," said Laura, without giving it any thought at all. "Naturally."

Surely all kidnappings were done that way.

"But the police?" she offered.

"Are not under any circumstance to learn of this," said Alex. "We have been told this by the kidnappers. As you might expect. In any case—well, Lord Buxton has always anticipated the possibility—"

Henry interrupted him, speaking now for the first time. He leaned forward and lit a cigar, then leaned back in his chair as if he were making a point of some pride, "The fact is, we are more prepared for this and better able to handle it then the police have ever been."

Laura looked from Henry to Alex, who seemed to shrug in the affirmative.

"I don't doubt you in the slightest," said Laura. "But then—why am I here?"

Henry gave Alex a look that indicated he had been wondering exactly the same thing about her.

Alex did not hesitate with the answer. "Because Lord Buxton's emergency instructions specifically state that in such an eventuality, you are the one person in the world he would trust to deliver his ransom."

"Oh."

The entire room was silent for a moment. Laura tried to grasp the full meaning of what had just been conveyed—both in terms of Robert's attitude toward her and in terms of what might come next.

Alex apparently interpreted her silence as a demand for more details.

"We don't know how much they want yet," he said. "But Lord Buxton set aside a precautionary fund for this purpose long ago. And of course he is insured. The kidnappers have requested a meeting, at which they will communicate the particulars. And as it happens, because your relationship with Lord Buxton has been well publicized—after all, you are getting married, are you not?—not only are you the representative he would want us to use but you are also on the very short list of the representatives the kidnappers are willing to meet with."

"Who else is on that list?" asked Laura.

"Well . . . no one, actually. Just you."

"A meeting with the kidnappers," said Laura, pondering it. There seemed little reason to point out a flaw in the marriage assumption at this moment.

"Yes," said Alex. "Alone, per their instructions."

"Armed and potentially violent men, are they?" asked Laura.

Henry shrugged.

"Well," said Laura. She looked about her at the four men in the room. Alex and the barrel-chested security detail with guns under their coats, she assumed, looked back at her expectantly.

"I'll do it," she said after a long moment. "I mean, of course I'll do it. But isn't there supposed to be a proof of life, or some such thing?"

The men looked at one another. Alex nodded to Henry, and then Henry placed a briefcase on the table.

He opened it, reached inside, grasped something—and then he dropped it on the table in front of Laura.

Laura shrieked.

"My God! They've scalped him!"

"Hairpiece," said Alex. "Custom-made. We verified it's his."

"Oh, that can't be," said Laura quickly. "I surely would have noticed such a thing."

"He's worn it for years," said Alex. "It is his best-kept secret."

"I should say so," said Laura. She ran her fingers through the locks of the hairpiece and gave that secret some thought.

"Well," she said, "I suppose it might explain his reluctance for—well, one or two particular activities."

She put the hairpiece down.

"All right. I will do whatever I can. What needs to be done. But there's someone I'd like to notify before we get started on this."

"I'm sorry," said Alex. "But as I said, no one can know."

"He's very smart," said Laura. "Perhaps he might even be able to—"

"It's quite impossible, Miss Rankin. And I can't see how a barrister would be of use in any case."

Laura paused at that and looked hard at Alex.

"What made you think I was referring to someone who just happens to be a barrister?"

Alex hesitated, then said, "You were, were you not?"

"That's not the point. The point is, how did you know whom I was referring to?"

The man squirmed.

"Please understand. I am Lord Robert Buxton's chief of staff. It's my job."

Laura took a deep breath and looked hard at each of the three men, and then very directly at Alex.

"When we get Robert out of this," she said very deliberately, "perhaps there will be a discussion regarding just what your job is."

The chief of staff cleared his throat.

"Understood," he said. "But does that mean you will help us?"

"I will," she said. "But I must make a call. I at least have to let him know that I will be unavailable for a bit. If I don't, he will wonder—and if you want something kept secret, you are well advised not to set Reggie Heath to wondering."

The security chief turned toward Alex and said, "I really don't think we should—"

"It's not up to either of you," said Laura, "and there is no 'we' in this regard. I will make this call."

"Or course," said Alex quickly. "But please just leave a message. We can't risk his asking you questions."

As Laura started to dial, Alex put a cautioning hand on her forearm.

"I know you're an actress," he said. "Sell it."

Laura gave that advice the dismissive look it deserved.

She punched in Reggie's number at Baker Street Chambers, bypassing the public number that Lois handled and going directly to his private line.

As she expected, he had not yet returned. The answering machine came on.

"Thank you for the lovely lunch, almost," said Laura. "Sorry I left no dessert, but I did warn you. I have to leave now for . . . an emergency. With my cat. I must take Tabasco to the vet, poor thing. You would not believe what she has coughed up. I will ring you soon. Don't wait up."

She hung up the phone. The security detail in the room with her all nodded.

There, thought Laura. That should do it. At least for now.

14

Robert Buxton was awake again. He had a suspicion that he must have been fading in and out of consciousness for some time. This time, he resolved to maintain it.

He took a breath—and then he remembered why he shouldn't. There was that stench again.

He knew his eyes were open; the air was so damp that he could feel it hitting his eyeballs with the stink. But he could see nothing but pitch-black.

He blinked his eyes, trying to focus. There had to be something, some light somewhere. He raised his head, tried to turn it. The nausea returned when he did that, but this time he did not succumb, not yet—and yes, somewhere to that one side, there was something. There was a light.

It was coming toward him. Now it was so close that it was blinding. He shielded his eyes.

And then he heard a voice.

"Where is it?"

God, what an annoying voice. Was it talking to him? It might be.

"We know you had it. Where is it?

Buxton raised his head, tried to look past the blazing bright lantern and see the face of his interrogator, but he could not. The nausea returned, from his head to his gut, and his head dropped back down.

15

It was late afternoon when Reggie arrived back at Baker Street Chambers from the crime scene in Soho.

Lois was at her desk but didn't look terribly busy, at least not with law chambers work. Which was to be expected today, Reggie knew, given that he had told her to keep the calendar clear.

She had newspapers spread out over her desk.

"Sorry," she said as Reggie approached. "It's been very slow. An American lawyer dropped in and said he would call again later. And Miss Rankin departed an hour ago. But other than that, well . . . I was just looking through the headlines, trying to do that Sherlock Holmes thing with the newspapers. Solving things. Would you like to hear? The headlines, I mean?"

Reggie shook his head. "Not necessary. But I do have a task for you. Please get the contact information from my meeting with Mr. Liu yesterday and send it on to Detective Inspector Wembley. Also, in my notes there's the name of a woman Mr. Liu was working for; send that to Wembley, as well."

Lois turned from the newspaper and looked up questioningly.

"I'm afraid that . . . Mr. Liu was killed last night," said Reggie.

"Oh." Lois stared back down at the papers. "Oh my."

Reggie told her briefly what had happened. Then he took the receipt from the alley out of his pocket.

"I want you to go to this shop in Piccadilly and ask what this purchase was. It might be something that Mr. Liu bought shortly before he died. He had nothing on him. Whatever he had, if he had anything, was taken during the robbery, if it was a robbery. I'd just like to know what the purchase was."

"Yes," said Lois, taking the receipt from Reggie. "I'll get right to it."

Reggie opened the door to his interior chambers office.

He hadn't expected Laura to still be there, of course. Yet it caused a bit of a twinge to see the remnants of the catered lunch lying about.

Timing is everything, and he had sworn to himself that he would not bollix it up again.

Then he saw the message light flashing on his phone. Reggie immediately punched the button and listened to the message. It was from Laura. A sick cat. All right, then.

Then he punched the replay button and listened to it again.

He could not recall ever hearing this exact tone of voice from Laura before. It was hard to know what to make of it.

She was an actress, of course, and even more than most women, she knew how to convey what she wanted to convey just by her tone of voice.

But for the life of him, Reggie could not figure this one out.

He wasn't at all sure, but it sounded as though—just possibly—something might be wrong.

He hoped to God it had nothing to do with the proposal

that he had not quite been able to make before rushing off to Soho.

Was "I have a sick cat" the new code phrase for "I won't marry you"?

He hoped not.

But if it was not that, what was it?

He rang Laura's home phone. No answer.

He rang her mobile. No answer there, either; it played her usual personalized greeting and invited the caller to leave a message. He did. He asked her to please ring him back.

For several minutes more, Reggie sat at his desk and re-sisted the impulse to just get in his car and drive out to Laura's home in Chelsea.

And then, with no other urgent task available to distract him, Reggie gave in to those instincts. He left chambers, and instead of driving directly home to Butler's Wharf, he drove to Chelsea.

He pulled up underneath a tree directly across the street from Laura's home. The porch light was on. None of the other lights in the house was. She was either not home or she was home and had gone to bed.

But if she was home and had gone to bed, she would have picked up when Reggie rang her. That assumed, of course, that she had gone to bed alone. Reggie considered the alternative for just a moment.

Was she with Buxton? If she was simply going to a publicity conference or some such thing with him, why leave a message about a sick cat?

Perhaps Reggie had just been fooling himself. Perhaps there had never been any hope at all.

He resisted the impulse to go up and bang on the door. If

she answered, he would be standing there like a fool. If she did not answer, it meant she would be at Buxton's.

And his earlier sense that something was wrong, that Laura might be in some kind of trouble, was surely mistaken. He had simply been projecting—something was seriously wrong from his own perspective if Laura was going back to Buxton. But that did not translate into something going wrong for Laura.

And it was one thing to be concerned; it was another to become a stalker.

Reggie started the XJS and drove on.

16

When Reggie arrived at chambers the next morning, he immediately checked for a phone message from Laura.

There wasn't one.

But there was a message waiting for him from Wembley.

Reggie returned the call.

"I had an officer talk to your translator's employer," said Wembley.

"What did he find?"

"A woman running a small business. But nothing of particular interest."

"What do you mean by 'nothing'?"

"Don't cross-examine me, Heath. I mean we talked with the woman, we found no reason to suspect her of anything, and there's nothing there worth our time."

"Who did you send?"

"I forget his name. Someone from Traffic Division."

"Bloody hell, Wembley, is that the best—"

"As a matter of fact, yes. We're just a tad understaffed at the moment."

"How so?"

"I'm sure you know Scotland Yard is responsible for protecting the royals. Not my usual assignment anymore, but I used
to do it back in the day."

"And so they're recruiting you from Homicide?"

"For the next few days. There's not just one but two royal
events coming up. First and foremost, we've got the Prince of
Wales. He hasn't been out and about all that much, since the
death of the princess last year, but now he's set to host a bunch
of foreign dignitaries at a dinner party at the palace, so that's a
big deal. At the same time, there's a birthday party and celebrity half marathon, or jogathon, or whatever it's called, to honor
Lady Asthon-Tate for her conservation efforts. That's at Hyde
Park. One of the queen's cousins is attending that one; apparently, it takes a royal to help protect the endangered red squirrel, and it takes Scotland Yard to protect a royal, so we not only
have to cover the prince but we also have to spare a team to
cover the Hyde Park event and look after the cousin."

"Which cousin? The Duke of Kent?"

"No, the other one."

"The Duke of Gloucester?"

"No, the other one."

"The Viscount of Linley?"

"No, that's a nephew."

Reggie racked his brain. He'd never really tried to keep close
tabs on the royals.

"Anyway, it's a duke," said Wembley. "And on top of that,
apparently there are blokes at MI5 who spend all their waking
hours on the Internet, and they think they've detected some
chatter about shedding some royal blood, damaging international relations, and accomplishing whatever the bloody hell it
is that anarchists hope to accomplish. In any case, most of my
team is either on the royal protection detail itself or indirectly

assisting MI5 in some lowly and subservient way. If there were five of me, I couldn't keep up with everything that needs to be done. As my dear mum used to say, might as well jam a broomstick up my arse and ask me to sweep the floors while I'm at it."

"So MI5 jumps in and brings half of Scotland Yard along for the ride," said Reggie, "even if there are more than twenty other royals between you and the throne?"

"Of course they do. Doesn't matter how high up the target is."

"Seems like a lot of bother," said Reggie. "They wouldn't do this for a commoner."

"Well, MI5 would," said Wembley. "Or so they say. For them, it's the terror threat that counts. They'd jump in even if it was your birthday party that was threatened." Then Wembley thought about it. "Well, maybe not yours. I'm sure they have some standards. But for Laura's they would."

"Fine," said Reggie. "You're shorthanded because you're protecting a self-promoting royal toff and you can't afford to send a full-fledged inspector to investigate a full-fledged murder. I take it you won't mind then if I talk to this woman on my own?"

"Under the circumstances, I won't try to stop you," said Wembley. He told Reggie the woman's address. "You just make it clear to her that you're in no official capacity."

17

Reggie drove to the address Wembley had provided. It was not far, just a few miles north of Regent's Park.

Reggie drove through Camden Town, past flea markets that sold cheap knockoff jackets and hats, and music stores that sold used vinyl LPs to the town's resurgent bohemians. He continued across Camden Lock, and the muddy stretch of the Fleet River that ran beneath it, flowing with just barely enough water to support a struggling tour boat on one side and about a ton of floating trash on the other.

Now he was in Kentish Town. He stopped at a block of recently constructed estate flats—not extravagantly built by any means, but recent enough to at least not be run-down.

The sort of place for a young, ambitious, midlevel entrepreneur trying to work her way up and maybe someday own a mansion overlooking Hampstead Heath. And perhaps cut a few corners along the way, thought Reggie. Cheat an overseas contractor who she thought was too far away to do anything about it. Save a few extra pounds. Murder him in an alley in Soho when he comes to collect. Well, by itself, that hardly seemed sufficient motive. But sometimes things get out of control. And in any case, Reggie already knew he wouldn't like her. He didn't like cheats.

He walked up the exterior stairs to the second-floor flat and rang the bell.

A thin, fiftyish woman opened the door.

"Yes," she said. "I am Mrs. Winslow."

She had dark hair drawn tightly back, with no apparent attempt to hide that it was going gray. Narrow metal spectacles sat rather sternly, just a little lower than they should, on the bridge of her nose.

She didn't give the wannabe-upscale appearance Reggie had expected. If he had guessed, he would have said she was a public school headmistress.

Thank God he wasn't eight years old any more. And he was very much taller than she was.

Reggie introduced himself and gave her his card. "I'm here about Mr. Liu," he said.

She raised an eyebrow, scrutinizing Reggie, staring at his barrister's business card and then back at him again.

"The man the police said was killed?"

Her voice was carefully modulated, but she couldn't help but put an inflexion on the last word of that question. It betrayed tension. But there could be all sorts of reasons for that.

"Yes," said Reggie.

"Has there been an arrest? Are you handling the prosecution?"

She seemed quite eager about the prospect.

"No, and no. But Mr. Liu had contacted me earlier regarding the work he did for you, and I feel obliged to follow up."

"Really?" she said. She paused, apparently taken aback. "He actually engaged a barrister?"

"In a manner of speaking." There was no point in mentioning that Mr. Liu had come looking for Sherlock Holmes.

But the woman looked again at Reggie's card. "Baker Street Chambers," she said pointedly.

"Yes."

"One hears things about that chambers," she said.

Reggie made no response.

"Mr. Liu told me that he was going to take the matter to Sherlock Holmes," said the woman. "I chalked that up to just one more of his misunderstandings."

She looked at Reggie on that, clearly expecting some sort of confirmation from him. But he said nothing, hoping his silence would keep her talking. Maybe that tension behind her voice would cause something to spill.

And she did continue. But Reggie didn't like what spilled.

"If Mr. Liu really wanted to make an issue of it, he should have just had his solicitor send a letter," she said with a hint of exasperation. "Instead, he wrote a letter to Sherlock Holmes. And then, when I told him I would not take the word of someone claiming to be Sherlock Holmes that Mr. Liu's translations were fine when I knew they were not, he engages you—a barrister. Do I have it right?"

"Close enough," said Reggie. The letter had put him on the defensive; now she was grilling him, instead of the other way around.

But now the woman paused, sighed, and said, "Given the terrible thing the police told me about, I wish he had just gone with the solicitor approach and stayed home."

"So do I," said Reggie.

"Or," she continued sadly, "that I had been able to accept the work that he sent. But I simply couldn't. Do you want to see the errors he made?"

"I don't think that will be necessary," said Reggie. Perhaps Wembley was right. This woman was seeming less and less murderous. She was not likely to have gone herself to confront anyone in a Soho alley, and her business wasn't large enough for her to hire someone for it.

"Do you happen to know whether Mr. Liu was working for anyone else in London?" asked Reggie.

"No, I don't.'

"How did you come to hire him?"

"He answered an ad that I placed in a Chinese language newspaper. He had completed appropriate course work and he did fine on the proficiency exam I sent him. But his actual work product was another matter."

"In what way?"

"When I hire new translators, I look very carefully at the first translations they return to our customers, as a quality check. I don't think most of my competitors take the time to do that, but I personally regard accuracy as critical in my business."

"Of course," said Reggie.

"And unfortunately, Mr. Liu's work had many errors. The first one—'Rub-a-dub-dub'—was accurate enough, but for that one he seems to have had the assistance of someone in your office. And a couple of the other rhymes were acceptable, as well. But several rhymes had clear errors. And although I pointed them out to him and asked him to try again, he still came back with the same errors. He insisted he had it right, but I knew he didn't. I was very sorry to reject him, but it couldn't be helped. He was causing me to miss my deadline; I could hardly send the translation on to the customer's distribution list with blatant mistakes in it. Could I?"

"No," said Reggie, "I suppose not."

" 'Suppose'?" said the woman, as though she were about to rap Reggie's knuckles with a ruler.

"No, of course you couldn't send it on with errors."

But he didn't say it with enough conviction, and he immediately wished he had, because now he could see in Mrs. Winslow's eyes that she was going to defend her position further.

"I'll show you," she said.

She led Reggie to the back of the house, to a smallish room that she used as an office.

"I've got one of the older versions, from a few years ago, right here."

She turned to a set of shelves that had been converted from a bedroom closet. She dug deep into one of them, located a cardboard box, and from it she pulled out a large yellow-and-white plastic duck.

She plunked it on the desk in front of Reggie. "You can press the bill if you want to see how it works." she said.

"What?"

"Press the duck's bill. I mean the goose's. I swear it looks like a duck to me, but Elgar Imports markets it as Mother Goose."

Reggie pressed the plastic bill as the woman began to unfold a sheet of thin laser-printed paper.

"One, two, buckle my shoe," said the toy duck in an annoyingly tinny female voice.

"If you press it twice quickly, it will recite the entire rhyme," said Mrs. Wixted.

"Must we?"

"No, the first line is all I need to show you. The correct line is 'buckle my shoe,' as the duck said. But Mr. Liu got it wrong when he printed the instructions. Here, I'll show you."

She placed the paper in front of Reggie. It was exactly like the one the translator had brought to Reggie.

"Previous versions of this toy were just in English, but now my client is adding French and Chinese. Mr. Liu's job was to add in the English changes from the client, then translate the English into those additional languages, and then print out the final sheets with all three languages and send them back to me. I then take them to the client's assembly warehouse, in this case Elgar Imports, where I add them into the packaging for the toy. I provide a full-service shop, as much as possible."

"Understood," said Reggie.

"Now, here's one of the errors," she said. She pointed to a specific location on the translated sheet. "This is the final printed version that Mr. Liu sent back. And he not only got it wrong in Chinese and in French—and I know, because I read both—he actually introduced the same error into the English, as well."

"I'm not sure I follow—"

"Do you read Chinese?"

"Well . . . no."

"French?"

"Enough to order dinner."

"Well, then just look at the English section, then—read what it says right there."

Reggie read it aloud: "One, two, unbuckle my shoe."

"You see? He got it wrong. In fact, it's the exact opposite. The line should be 'buckle my shoe,' of course, not 'unbuckle' it."

"And accuracy is critical," mused Reggie, allowing just a little skepticism in his voice.

She looked up defensively. "Yes, it is. I know it's just a toy, but this is a printed copy of the rhymes that the duck—I mean goose—speaks, so that children can follow along and perhaps learn to read a bit. He made several errors like that one, getting a word clearly wrong, sometimes the exact opposite of what it was supposed to be. I know that these aren't instructions for assembling a rocket or arming torpedoes, or some such, but accuracy is critical, all the same."

"You're quite right," said Reggie after a moment's consideration.

"Mr. Heath," said the woman, "I'm not an unreasonable person. I mean, I try not to be. I could hardly run my business and make a living at it if I routinely paid for shoddy workmanship. However, I recognized that Mr. Liu did put sincere effort into his work, and I was willing to send him a minimal payment for that, even though I could not make use of what he returned and will need to have it redone. In fact, I was preparing a check and a letter to him, to that effect—until the police showed up on the step."

She turned away for just a moment and then turned back to Reggie, with a check in her hand that she had to have written out earlier.

"Perhaps there is someone you can deliver this to—on his behalf?"

Reggie looked at the woman, who was remorsefully offering the check, and in his judgment, she wasn't faking it.

"I'll see what I can do."

"I . . . I . . . am so sorry about what happened, " she continued. "When our new hires mistranslate, I sometimes fire them—but I never kill them."

Reggie believed her. As much as his initial instinct had told him there was some connection between this woman and the death of Mr. Liu, he was certain now that she could not have been involved. It had to be something else. Perhaps Wembley's theory of a simple robbery was correct.

Reggie took his leave and returned to Baker Street Chambers. Along the way, he rang Laura on his mobile, but there was no answer.

At chambers, he checked his own answering machine again, and with Lois, but there was still nothing from Laura since the phone message from her the day before. And by the time he drove home that evening, Reggie was beginning to worry again.

Just how much time does one need to spend with a sick cat?

18

One million pounds? Is that all?"

It was very late at night; only a few hours before dawn, more than a day and half since Laura's interrupted lunch with Reggie.

Since arriving at Buxton's compound the night before, Laura had spent all of her time sequestered there, with all the luxuries imaginable and servants at her beck and call, but with no further communication with the outside world. The security team had consented to the one initial phone message to Reggie, but after that, it had to be complete secrecy, they said, as they negotiated with the kidnappers. Laura was growing impatient with their rules.

But now they were all in Lord Buxton's private conference room again. This time Laura was seated at the head of the long table.

A special privilege, she supposed. Like the kind afforded Polynesian virgins before they were sacrificed to the volcano god.

Seated to her immediate left was Henry, the head of security. Standing on her right was Alex, the chief of staff. Each was flanked by an additional dark-suited security person. The brains were next to Laura, apparently, and the muscle stood on the periphery.

Alex dropped a heavy brown leather satchel on the table in front of Laura.

"That's all they asked for," he said.

"It seems so little," said Laura. "I mean, relatively speaking."

But even as she said that, Laura was resisting the impulse to open the bag and see what that much cash looked like.

"Go ahead," said Alex. "Open it."

She did. The heavy bag unzipped with a low-pitched purr. She looked inside.

There were more banded packages of one-hundred-pound notes than she could count.

"It is quite a lot of money. But I would guess Robert spends that much each year just on his private jet," said Laura.

"More," said Alex. "And you have a point. A kidnapper who does his due diligence would know he could be asking ten times this amount."

"So what does that mean?"

"I think it means we're dealing with amateurs," said Alex. "The choice of such a public and easily accessible drop spot suggest that, as well."

"Easily accessible for you, maybe," said Laura. "You're not the one who'll be rowing the little boat."

"I am sorry about that," said Alex. "It's one of the few things they insisted on. But as kidnappings go, making the drop in the boating pond at Regent's Park is as safe as anything I can imagine."

"Doesn't she know how to row?" muttered one of the muscle-men at the far end.

The security chief next to him gave him an elbow.

"He'll be fired later for that remark, won't he?" said Laura.

"If you want," said Alex.

"All right, then," said Laura. "Let's review: I'm to row out with all this money in a bag. They are to put Robert—unharmed, of course—into my little boat, and I row back with him. Or perhaps I'll give him the oars and he'll do the rowing. But is that basically how this works?"

"Yes."

"All right. But how do I make sure we've got Robert before I turn over the money?"

"Well, they're going to want the money first, of course," said Alex. "That's the way these things are done. And you are not to argue with them. The fact is, they haven't chosen the best location for this, from their perspective. One more reason I know they're amateurs. The park is surrounded by the outer circle road, so they won't be able to escape unseen on foot, and we'll be watching all the gates where they can get out with a vehicle. We will see anyone who tries to leave the park, and at the very early hour they've chosen for the drop, there won't be any crowds around at all to confuse the issue. Once we know Lord Buxton is safe, we can call in Scotland Yard. It's really perfect. So you just deliver the money and let us worry about the rest."

"How do they know that we haven't just surrounded the entire park with police?"

"We have to presume they have lookouts. Just as we do. But we'll tail them when they leave the park, and after we have Lord Buxton secure, we'll notify Scotland Yard and get the wankers nicked. All you have to do is row out and then row back."

"I think you mean make the trade and then row like hell," said Laura. "But all right. Let's get on with it."

Two hours later, at not quite 4:30 in the morning, before even the earliest dawn joggers, a shining black fortified Range

Rover pulled up at the Regent's Park gate just south of the duck pond.

The passenger window rolled down. Laura wanted a better look.

"Don't put your head out the window," advised Alex, who was behind the wheel.

"I wouldn't worry," said Laura. "I doubt that I could be any more ostentatious than this vehicle you chose to use."

She surveyed the scene, but she did, in fact, keep her head inside as much as possible.

It was still dark out, but there was enough light from the streetlamps to make out the little sandwich shop and boathouse—she had been there a few times before, actually, but it was closed just now, of course. On the near side of the little park lake, the ducks and white geese were faintly visible along the shore, with their heads tucked beneath their wings.

"Will I be in an actual rowboat," said Laura, "Or do I have to use one of the silly foot-pedal ones?"

"We don't know," said Henry, the security chief, seated in back. "You're supposed to take whichever boat has already been cut loose for you."

"Now, it appears to me that I will be exposed to all and everything as I row slowly across to the little island with the bushes where bad people are probably hiding. Is that how it seems to you?"

Henry and Alex looked at each other. Then they nodded.

"And where will you big strong men with guns strapped to your sides be?"

"Right here, at the ready," said Henry.

"At the ready, two hundred meters away, behind all this armored plate?"

"Yes."

"And do I take a weapon with me?"

"Are you licensed for the use of a firearm?" asked Henry.

"No."

"Then no."

"If they caught sight of it, the whole deal would be off," said Alex. "Or worse could happen. Especially because, as I said, we're dealing with amateurs."

"I see," said Laura.

Alex looked apologetic. He opened up his briefcase and took out a small spray cylinder.

"You could take this," he offered.

Laura looked at the little can of pepper spray.

"That would indeed be useful," she said. "If any of the kidnappers should turn out to be small terriers."

"Sorry."

"Let's just get on with it, then, shall we?"

"Yes," said Alex, checking his watch. "It's time."

Laura got out of the car alone.

She walked a few yards along Outer Circle Drive, heading toward the boathouse—and then she looked back toward the vehicle, just on instinct, to see if her well-armed allies had any further advice.

But they had already rolled the window up.

Laura sighed. Just out of habit, she looked both ways before crossing the street, then walked on past Clarence Gate, into Regent's Park, and onto a paved path than ran the length of the lake shoreline.

In the dark, she bumped into a mallard that had settled in just a little too close to the walkway; it squawked and flapped on out of sight.

Good thing we're not depending on the element of surprise, thought Laura.

Between the dark and the mist, she could see no more than about five yards in front of her. But she knew where the boat-house was, and she continued on in that direction.

She hoped she would not bump into any geese. They were not nearly so easily intimidated as a duck.

In a few minutes, she was at the boathouse. Closed, of course. But the gate that led to the boat tie-up was open.

Laura could see that one boat had been cut loose from the chain that linked them all together; it was attached only by a rope with a simple loop.

There was no wind at all; the water looked black and completely still.

Laura stepped down from the dock into the wooden row-boat. It wobbled just a little as she got in, but there was no issue of her falling—she and Reggie had, in fact, rowed here before; she knew how to handle a boat on a pond.

She looked out toward the little island. It was only about a hundred yards out, but in the dark it was barely visible. It was lucky she had been to the park before.

She grabbed hold of the oars. The handles were damp; slime dripped from the ends of the oars when she raised them out of the water, and in the overall silence of the pond, the first oar stroke made a very loud racket of clanging metal and splashing water as she set out.

She resolved to try to row more quietly—she wasn't sure why—and she proceeded in the general direction of the island.

In perhaps five minutes, she had covered nearly half the distance. The bow of the boat was toward the island, and she was facing the stern, of course, in order to row, and so after each stroke, she had to crane her neck and look over her shoulder to see if anyone had yet appeared.

She was halfway there, and still she could make out no one in the darkness along the shore. And quite probably the kidnappers were not going to announce themselves with any sort of light.

And then, on the very next pull of the oars, her boat struck something hard.

"Ease up." It was a man's voice.

Laura stowed her oars and turned to look. Her boat had struck up against another.

In the boat—a ten-foot dinghy, like Laura's—was just one man.

Laura didn't know if it would ever matter, but she tried to pay attention to the details.

The man was of average height, though he was sitting, so it was not easy to tell. He had a gardener's hat pulled down low over his forehead, and he had a cloth scarf or handkerchief of some kind wrapped around the lower part of his face.

In the predawn darkness, this was all undoubtedly sufficient for the man's purpose; Laura could see nothing about his face that she would be able to recognize again.

"Show it to me," he said.

The man's voice was muffled by the scarf. It was a deep voice, but not naturally deep, it seemed to Laura; rather, it was deliberately deep, like that of a radio announcer who was trying too hard. But more than anything else, the voice was just plain whiny. Laura was sure she would recognize that voice if she ever heard it again.

The leather bag full of one million pounds was beneath Laura's feet at the stern of the boat. She bent down and raised the bag up so that the man could see it.

"Put it there," he said, pointing to the stern of his own boat.

Laura immediately and deliberately dropped it back again into her own boat, keeping it out of his reach.

"Show me Lord Robert Buxton first." Laura said this in the same quiet tone of voice the kidnapper had used; she made it as much of a command as she could.

The man stared at her, and for a short moment they both just sat there in their respective boats, glaring their respective glares, in silence except for the faint sound of the pond water lapping ever so slightly against the boats.

Then the man turned and flicked a large flashlight one time in the direction of the island.

It was a small island—less than a hundred yards across. But the bushes and trees were densely packed along the shore, and in the dark Laura could see only the general outlines of the foliage.

After a moment, someone flashed a light back in response.

"Well?" said Laura to the man in the boat.

He flashed his own torch once again. And then the shoreline light came on again, briefly. But this time, instead of pointing out, it was held chest-high and pointed upward, illuminating a mans' face, from the chin up, in the way that children would do to frighten each other.

There was tape over the man's mouth, and Laura guessed that his hands were bound and someone else was holding the flashlight on him.

Now the lamp was switched off.

This all took place at some distance, in an instant, and in the dark. From the outlines of his torso, and the general shape of the captive's head—minus the nice, expensive hair—it might very well be Buxton.

Or it might not.

"I need another look," said Laura.

"No," said the man in the boat. "That's all you get. Take it or leave it."

Laura hesitated.

The man in the boat pointed at the leather bag at Laura's feet and gestured for her to transfer it to his boat.

"Throw it in," he said.

Laura considered it.

She didn't give a damn about the money. Even if it had been hers—well, a million quid could not be hers, but if it had been something like it, relatively speaking—she still would not have given it a second thought at all.

It just seemed to her a poor negotiating tactic.

But Buxton's chief of staff and the security chief had both said to give the kidnappers the money. And what reason would they have for not releasing Buxton once she had done so?

And surely they would not simply kill him. Not in a location in the heart of London, where they had to anticipate that the security team was scattered all around, watching, as in fact it was, and with daylight approaching.

They could not hope to escape. They could only take the money and hope that no one really tried very hard after that to apprehend them.

"Now, please," said the man.

Laura nodded. She bent down and grabbed the bag with both hands. She hoisted it up onto her lap.

She looked at the man in the boat, who looked expectantly back at her.

Then she grabbed the bag from both bottom corners, raised it up off her lap, got her arms levered underneath it, and threw it from her boat into his.

The bag landed in the man's boat with a loud plop; Laura,

adrenaline coursing, was surprised at how much force she'd put into it.

So was the kidnapper. His boat actually tipped back a bit, but he righted it quickly and threw an angry glare at Laura.

She shrugged. "Sorry," she said. "I've never done this before."

The man grabbed the bag, opened it, and looked inside. Then he closed it, looked at Laura, and nodded.

"Now there's just one more thing," he said.

"Don't you even think about it," said Laura, not certain at all what he was about to say, but certain that it wouldn't be good.

She looked again at the shore of the island: no sign of Robert, or of the kidnapping accomplice with the flashlight.

"Just one more thing," repeated the man calmly.

"Give me Lord Buxton," said Laura.

"You will get Lord Buxton back. You have my word. But the money is only a down payment."

"I knew it!"

"Relax. We aren't going to ask for the moon, though I wouldn't be surprised if he has some sort of leasehold on it. All we need is for you to do a small task for us. Then your great man will be released."

Laura glared across at the other boat. If she had brought the pepper spray, she would have used it.

"What sort of small task?"

"We want the letters."

"What letters?"

The two boats had drifted apart just a bit. The man hooked the gunwale of Laura's boat with the end of an oar and pulled her boat up against his.

He lowered his voice.

"Bring me the Baker Street letters."

Laura considered that for a moment.

"Can you be a bit more specific?" she said.

"Specifically, bring me a few bits of nonsensical paper and canceled stamps, and I will give you the richest man in the world in return."

Laura did not like this man. She was not fond of sarcasm.

"I didn't say to rephrase," replied Laura. "I said to be specific. Many letters are delivered and sent up and down Baker Street every day. Precisely which ones are you referring to?"

"You should not play games with me," said the man.

"I am damp and cold and beginning to want breakfast. You should not play games with *me*," said Laura. "If you want me to trade letters for lords, you must, unavoidably, tell me which letters you mean."

The man hesitated. Laura was afraid for a moment that he was about to let go of the oar and the whole arrangement.

But then he leaned in.

"All of them," he said. "All the letters delivered to Sherlock Holmes at Baker Street Chambers in the past month. I want every one of them. If I don't get every one of them, complete, then you will not get Lord Buxton back, complete."

The man jerked his head just slightly back toward the shore, where his accomplice was presumably still standing with Buxton. In the dark, it was difficult to tell.

And now, apparently, Laura was taking too long to respond.

"Can you do this?" said the man quite impatiently. "I understood that you have access. I understood that you can do this."

Of course I can, thought Laura, but she wasn't sure she should say it.

"It won't be easy," she said instead. "I will need some time."

The man released her boat.

"You have twenty-four hours," he said.

Then he put the oar against the side of her boat and pushed off.

Laura's boat turned in a half circle; she quickly got it pointed right again, but now his boat was several yards off, and about to vanish in the fog.

Laura looked back toward the shore, where the security team was still in the Range Rover. Then she looked toward the dark little island where she had last seen Robert Buxton.

She began to row toward it.

She knew she wasn't supposed to. But she didn't like it that the demands had changed. She didn't like it that she had been allowed only a distant glimpse of Robert—or the man who presumably was Robert. She didn't like the way this show was being run at all.

Her adrenaline was pumping; she put everything she had into the row, not worrying at all about proper form, drops of water flying down on her on each upswing of the oars.

It felt like forever. But it wasn't. When she felt the bow of her little boat slam into the shore mud, she turned and caught a glimpse of someone running toward the brush on the opposite side of the island.

Laura scrambled out of the boat. Her shoes immediately sank into the soft muck. She abandoned them and began running barefoot on the wet ground.

There was no clear path. She simply had to push on through the branches, dead leaves and twigs crackling uncomfortably under her feet, until she reached the shore mud on the opposite side of the island.

She had made it through. She looked quickly left and right and saw no one.

But then, to her right, in the dark between the island and the opposite Regent's Park shoreline, she heard the sound of an outboard engine.

The kidnappers had another boat.

She heard the motor sputter, then roar; then it whined in acceleration. She couldn't see it; from the sound of it, she presumed it was heading to the far end of the lake. But there was no way to know just where it would put ashore.

Laura stood in the darkness on her side of the shore and could do nothing. The sound of the outboard grew more distant.

Laura shoved her way back through the thicket of trees and trudged toward her own little boat, hoping that even in her haste she had managed to pull it enough onto the shore for it not to have drifted away.

Nothing else had gone right.

Mercifully, it was still there.

She got in and started rowing back toward the shore where she had gotten out of the Range Rover.

This had not gone as planned. But surely, surely, the security team had done what they'd said they would do and would nab everyone before they could leave the park.

It was just barely dawn now; the obscuring dark was beginning to yield to obscuring fog. The park would begin to get populated, especially on the edges, with health-crazed Londoners looking for their thirty minutes of cardiovascular exercise to start the day. Laura continued to row and just hoped the hordes of security operatives presumably watching the perimeter knew what they were doing.

She was getting close to the shore; now she could see Alex and the security chief and all the personnel from the Range Rover standing and waiting for her at the shore.

Somehow, that did not seem like a good sign.

Laura's arms ached as the bow of the boat struck up against the shore.

Alex came down from the road, intending, she presumed, to help her pull the boat up onto dry land, but then he stopped on the edge of the mud, hesitating, looking down at his Italian shoes.

Laura hoisted the boat halfway out of the water herself. Then she got out, and in her bare feet—she had not thought to retrieve her own shoes from the island—tromped up through the several yards of muck.

A passing jogger, and an old man feeding ducks, and a young woman with a baby stroller, all stopped to stare.

On Laura's last step from the muck, the chief of staff gallantly extended his hand to pull her out.

"Thank you," said Laura, grabbing onto his arm. "Did you catch them? Is Robert safe?"

Laura knew from the apprehensive look on his face that she wasn't going to like the answer.

"I'm sorry," he said. "We never saw them."

Laura pulled so hard that the man lost his balance and had to plant his Gucci loafers in the mud to steady himself.

Then she marched on toward Park Road and went right past the Range Rover.

Alex shouted after her: "Where are you going?"

"Home," she shouted back, in a lie. "And you needn't drive me. I'll take a cab. They're more reliable."

19

Reggie had not slept well, and now he was awake at a ridiculously early hour in the morning.

He had been having one of those dreams—or sets of dreams, actually, because it was never just one; it was always themes that merged and morphed—where he literally tried to accomplish in his sleep what he had been unable to complete that day while awake.

When he had been much younger, painting houses to supplement his scholarship at university, there had been times he would wake up at night with his arms waving, trying to trim out the eaves on the building he'd been unable to finish during the day, and at the same time slogging desperately through the set of essay questions he'd been assigned for seventeenth-century European history. And the two would combine—in his dream state, it would be necessary for him to finish layering the blue outdoor enamel on the fascia board in order for Huguenots to escape France after the Edict of Fontainebleau.

Last night had been one of those nights. He had kept trying to put the engagement ring in front of Laura, but the old man from Taiwan, his head dripping blood, had been right there in chambers with them, continually trying to force the letters, or translations, or something written on paper—you could never be sure in a dream—into Reggie's line of sight. And Laura's damned orange cat kept jumping in between.

Reggie didn't like these dreams. They never accomplished anything. Except to focus his mind when he woke up. And it was focused now.

He intended to get to chambers early, look again at the letter Mr. Liu had sent to Sherlock Holmes, satisfy himself that there was nothing of importance there, and then phone Laura, or drive to her house if necessary, and put that ring on her finger. No preliminaries, no more elaborate presentation ritual— just get it done.

He reached Baker Street just before 6:00 A.M. Except for the ever-present vehicular traffic heading toward the interior of the city, the block was actually quiet. No tourists yet in front of the Sherlock Holmes museum, a few doors down. At the corner, the Volunteer Pub would not open for several hours. And even Pret A Manger and the little news agent shop were not quite ready yet. It was that early. Reggie had to skip his morning coffee.

He entered the lobby of Dorset House. It was empty except for Mr. Hendricks, the security guard. Hendricks, white-haired, tall, and thin, was in his mid-seventies, but he had stubbornly kept his job well past the age lesser men would have hung it up. This, Reggie had always assumed, was because Hendricks liked having someplace to go where he could read his papers and drink his tea in peace. No better place for that than the security station at the back wall of the Dorset House lobby.

Hendricks did not look up from the *Daily Sun,* but he did

seem to raise an eyebrow and almost smile slightly when Reggie entered. This was most uncharacteristic; Reggie had no idea what to attribute it to.

Reggie got in the lift alone and took it up to the next floor.

Lois would not be here yet, of course; no one would. He would have it all to himself.

The lift doors opened. Reggie got out on the dark floor and began walking toward his office.

Something crunched under his feet. He stooped down to look.

Mud. Dried mud. And it hadn't even been raining that morning.

The cleaning crew were usually so efficient. He would have a word with them. Someday when there was time.

Reggie continued on toward his office, and then, halfway there, he paused.

Dim light was leaking out from beneath the closed door. That wasn't supposed to be. He always turned the desk lamp off.

Reggie put his hand on the door. The knob turned; it was unlocked. That wasn't supposed to be, either.

He thrust the door open.

There was a crashing sound—something breakable hitting the floor—and the dim light went out.

Reggie flipped the light switch at the side of the door.

The overhead lights came on, and there on the floor, kneeling by Reggie's broken desk lamp, was Laura.

"Oh, thank God," she said. "You gave me such a start."

"Me as well," said Reggie.

"Why didn't you knock?"

Reggie stared back at her.

"It's my office."

"Oh," said Laura. "Yes. Of course. Well. Knocking when a door is closed is still a good habit. Why are you here so early?"

"I couldn't sleep."

"Oh. Why not?"

Reggie shrugged.

"Well, I haven't been getting much sleep, either," said Laura, "so I thought I'd just come in and . . . catch up on a few things."

"In my office?"

It was a perfectly innocent question; Reggie meant it with no suspicion of anything at all, and he sat down comfortably in the client chair in front of the desk.

But Laura, sitting now behind the desk in Reggie's leather barrister's chair, seemed to squirm. She did so in an attractive sort of way. She was wearing gray sweatpants, which Reggie liked because the soft cloth showed the outlines of her legs when she moved, but which, he knew, she regarded as mainly appropriate for jogging and grubby sorts of activities. There was dried mud at the bottom edges.

And she was barefoot.

"Have you been out for a run already? Is this the new style?"

"No," she said. "I mean, yes. Just a short one. And I heard someone say that shoe minimalism is good for the ankles. I gave it a try."

Reggie nodded, but he was still puzzled.

"And then you just popped in to see if anyone was here at six A.M.?"

"I . . . I just wanted to see if your copier is working."

"It is, I presume, but it's next to Lois's desk, not mine."

"Well, I didn't know, never having used it, of course, and neither of you was here, so—"

"What do you need to copy?"

"Oh, no matter. Now that I know where it is and that it's working, everything will be fine. Will we be doing lunch again soon, then?"

"Yes," said Reggie. He put his hand in his coat pocket and checked; the ring was still there.

Laura got up from her chair now and started to move toward the door.

Reggie didn't even move, he was so perplexed. He just stared as she got to the door and opened it.

"Is your cat better?" he asked, at a loss for anything better.

Laura was facing away from him, about to exit, and now she just froze. Her head and neck, in particular, were absolutely still—until they suddenly began to tremble. Reggie thought he knew what this meant, but he had rarely seen it happen with Laura Rankin.

She turned toward him, in tears.

"Robert has been kidnapped," she said with sobbing emphasis.

"What?" Reggie stood up from the chair.

"Kidnapped! Kidnapped!"

Reggie just stared at first. It was taking a moment to sink in, partly because pretty much any sentence that Laura could possibly begin with the name Robert was likely to be annoying to Reggie.

On the other hand—as it did begin to sink in—it occurred to Reggie that "Robert has been kidnapped" might be almost as good as "Robert died in a awful accident when all of his unscrupulously gotten wealth fell on him at Tobacco Wharf." With luck, perhaps that would even turn out to be an accurate, if slightly metaphorical, description of what had taken place.

Robert Buxton kidnapped and never seen in polite society again alive. Such a shame. Could fate be that kind?

But right at the moment, Laura was in tears. She sat down on the edge of Reggie's desk and tried to wipe them away.

"I wasn't supposed to tell you. Or the police, either. They told me not to tell anyone."

"Kidnappers always say that," said Reggie. He sat down next to her on the desk.

"Not the kidnappers. Robert's security team."

"Buxton is kidnapped and his security team contacts you?"

"Yes."

"Why?"

"They said I'm the closest thing Robert has to family."

"Bloody hell," said Reggie. He stood and turned away briefly.

Laura stopped talking and got up from the desk. She knew Reggie was angry now; she wasn't sure over exactly what—there were so many possibilities at the moment.

Now he turned back.

"So it was Buxton's security team got you into this?"

"Yes."

"But you are *not* Buxton's family."

"Well, you know—his parents are gone, and he has no siblings. And from gossip columns, they may have thought—"

"All right," said Reggie, waving that off. He didn't want to hear her say what the gossip columns had been saying about her and Buxton. He already knew; for weeks Buxton had been planting hints in the columns that Laura would marry a mysterious publishing magnate with the initials R.B. As if predicting it in the papers would make it happen. As if he could influence Laura that way.

"All right," said Reggie again, focusing. "I'll call Wembley and see who's handling this for the Yard."

"No," said Laura. "We can't. That 'Don't tell anyone' thing, remember? They were quite adamant about it."

Reggie considered it. It was actually a legal requirement to report a kidnapping. But in practice, no one was ever charged on that. At least not family members, or people acting in place of actual members.

Except that any officer of the court—say a barrister—could very well be disbarred for keeping silent, if it all went wrong and someone had to be blamed.

"All right," agreed Reggie once more. "So, when does Buxton's security team meet with these little entrepreneurs?"

"That's already happened, actually. I've already met with them."

"What? *You* met with the kidnappers?"

"The security team said it was the only way it could be done."

"Bloody gits!" Lines that were not usually visible hardened in Reggie's face. "You should not be involved in this at all. And you sure as hell should not be meeting with them. I want you out of this."

"Well, I'm in it already, and that's all there is to it. I was going to figure this all out and find the bloody things and just get out before you got back," she said, sounding quite frustrated about it.

"What bloody things?"

Laura didn't answer that. Instead, she began to move toward the door, and she said, "I didn't expect you so soon. I didn't want to get you involved in this."

"Are you going to remain involved in it?" asked Reggie.

"Yes."

"Then I am involved in it, as well, aren't I?"

Laura was standing by the door now. She knew that she might still get out of his office alone if she wanted to.

But she didn't want to. She managed a slight smile.

"Yes," said Laura. "I guess you are, then."

20

Tell me all of it," said Reggie. "From the beginning."

Reggie was seated now in his leather barrister's chair. Laura was seated in the client chair. She had gotten the brunch leftovers from the office refrigerator, and she had spread them out on the desk between them.

"I'm not just hungry, I'm famished," she said. She sat back and wiped some stray soufflé from the edges of her mouth. Then, between gulps, she related what had happened after her arrival at Buxton's compound.

She told Reggie how she had delivered the money, but then the kidnappers had kept Buxton anyway, made new demands, and escaped from the park.

"How much more do they want?" he said.

Laura hesitated. "They don't want more money."

"What, then?"

"They want the letters, " said Laura.

"What letters?"

"The letters to Sherlock Holmes."

"Seriously?" said Reggie. He could hardly believe his good fortune—if it were true.

"Of course seriously."

"Well, that's the best news I've had all day. They can bloody well have the letters. But only if they keep Buxton, as well."

Laura glared at Reggie.

"Sorry. Bad joke. It's just that this is like asking if I would be willing to transfer an annoying headache to them. Of course I would. It's just too bad I have to get a nice case of stomach flu back in return."

Laura still glared.

"Sorry," said Reggie again. "So they want the letters, then?"

"Yes. I've no idea why."

Reggie nodded. "Well, let's just go have a look at them."

Reggie got up, and Laura followed him out of the office and down the corridor to the secretary's station.

"I don't suppose they mentioned a specific one?"

"They said everything for the past month."

Reggie grabbed hold of the little cart behind Lois's desk and pulled it out into the corridor.

There were just two letters to Sherlock Holmes on the cart, both of them still unopened.

That didn't seem right. Reggie picked both letters up and quickly opened them.

"Birthday wishes," said Reggie. "Apparently, the Sherlockian community thinks he has one in January, but both of these arrived in just the last couple of days. These can't be what the kidnappers are after."

"I would think not," said Laura. "Since they asked for an entire month. Surely there are more letters?"

Reggie checked quickly around the desk to see if any had simply fallen off the cart.

Nothing.

Then he remembered.

"Bloody hell," said Reggie. "I had Lois send the most recent batch to Nigel. At least a dozen. They were beginning to stack up."

"Well, what more could you hope for?" said Laura, trying to make light of it. "Someone kidnaps Robert to trade for the letters, and we no longer have the letters to get him back."

"I don't get why anyone would want the letters anyway," said Reggie. "I've heard the little museum down the street has coveted them for years, but they can't be behind this; they want the entire franchise, and of course the whole point of that is the publicity of everyone knowing that you receive them. The same would be true for any interested Sherlockian society. You can't acquire something through illegal means if you are then going to immediately proclaim to everyone that you have it."

"Does it really matter *why* the kidnappers want them?" said Laura. "Isn't it enough that we know we need them to save Robert?"

She was standing before Reggie with mud-caked clothes, damp hair, and eyes growing redder and damper by the moment. His guess was that she hadn't slept, and she looked ready to collapse.

"I'll find the letters," he said.

"How?"

"I'll call Nigel. He may have them. He must have them. We'll find the letters and we will get Buxton back. But first I will drive you home and you will swear to me that no matter what his bloody security team does or asks you to do, you will not go near the kidnappers again. You will come to me first."

"Fair enough," said Laura. She offered her hand for Reggie to shake, as though they had just concluded a real estate deal.

And then, for just an instant, her feet just seemed to go out from under her.

Reggie caught her.

"I'm fine," she said.

"Of course you are," said Reggie.

Her neck just below her ears smelled like Chanel, but her clothes smelled like pond muck.

"Nothing that a good night's sleep and a bath won't cure," he said, and she was so exhausted that she didn't even offer a retort.

There was a small couch in the corridor, next to the door to Reggie's chambers office, and he lowered her onto that.

Then he went back into his office and rang Nigel in Los Angeles.

It took six rings before Reggie's younger brother picked up.

"Nice to hear from you Reggie, but I wish you'd learn the time zones. It's well past the dinner hour here, and Mara and I were just about to—well, call it a day."

Reggie ignored that complaint and said, "Robert Buxton has been kidnapped."

There was nothing from Nigel for a moment; apparently, he was pondering it.

Then: "Reggie, wasn't that a bit drastic? I think you already had the inside track with Laura. So to speak."

"Bloody hell, I don't mean kidnapped by me!"

"Oh."

Reggie could hear Nigel saying something to Mara in the same room.

It sounded like "He claims he didn't do it."

"I didn't," said Reggie pointedly into the phone.

"I believe you," said Nigel. "Does Laura?"

"The question hasn't even come up."

"Good," said Nigel. "Who did do it, then?"

"I've no idea," said Reggie. "But what they're after is the letters."

"What letters? "

"*The* letters."

There was a pause from Nigel.

"You mean they want the letters to Sherlock Holmes?"

"Yes. And the most recent batch went out express to you a few days ago. I put the letters on the mailing cart myself. I need you to overnight them back."

There was another pause, a longer one.

"Reggie, I haven't received a batch of letters from your office in more than two weeks."

That news sank in for a moment.

"Bloody hell," said Reggie.

Nigel paused for a moment and then said, "Reggie, are you sure you wouldn't rather just leave this alone? Would it really be a bad thing if no one ever heard from old Bob again?"

"It would be for Laura," said Reggie.

"All right," said Nigel. "I'll catch a red-eye."

Reggie paused and looked past the office entrance to the corridor, where, he presumed, Laura had fallen asleep on the couch—but he couldn't be sure. He lowered his voice.

"Buxton bloody well better still be alive," said Reggie into the phone. "I don't want to spend the rest of my life competing with a ghost."

Reggie hung up the phone. As he did, he noticed that Laura's purse was on his desk.

That could be fortunate. He picked it up. He dug through it and found the little green address book that she used for practically everything. Every entry in it was perfectly legible and complete, with not only the name of the person but also the address and the best hours to call, and in some cases, precautions to take in doing so. Except for one: At the very end, alone on a blank page, was a hastily jotted number with no name, and no other information.

Reggie wrote that number down and carefully put the address book back in Laura's purse. Then he picked up the phone to ring that number.

But now there was a sound from outside Reggie's office, as though someone had bumped into a wall.

Perhaps Lois had arrived early. Perhaps Laura was awake. Reggie went to the door and looked out.

Laura was on the couch, eyes closed. The exterior office was still dark and, to all appearances, empty.

It was still early morning. No solicitor would be visiting at this hour. And the sound couldn't be the cleaning crew; they did their work at night after closing, not in the wee hours before opening. And if it was Lois who had entered—very early for her, as well—she would be heading down the center corridor toward her secretary's desk, and she wasn't.

And now there was another sound from behind the cubicles at the opposite end of the corridor.

Reggie left Laura lying on the couch and began to walk in that direction.

He reached the corridor at the opposite side.

The door to Nigel's office was open. No light was on, but the door was ajar.

Reggie stepped inside. No one.

And then he heard another noise—from the side of the office where he had just been—and he realized his mistake: While he had been coming down the center corridor, some intruder had gone back down the corridor on the north side—in the direction of Reggie's office, and Laura.

Reggie turned from Nigel's office and began running down the corridor.

At the far end, Laura was lying still on the couch. Above her, in dark silhouette, was a tall, heavy-shouldered man, leaning down, his hand showing darkly within inches of her face.

The man turned his head in Reggie's direction, but it was too late for him—Reggie had already left his feet in a flying tackle. He aimed his shoulder for the man's solar plexus and he hit his target square on.

Reggie slammed the man into the wall behind. Reggie's own head hit the wall as well, but it was only a glancing blow; he put his left arm against the man's jaw, shoved hard, and threw him to the ground.

Reggie recovered his own balance, his senses cleared, and he looked down.

Sprawled on the corridor floor, his back against one of the cubicle walls, was a man in a tan sport coat, dark blue jeans, and pointy-toed boots.

The man looked up, his deeply tanned face showing both surprise and anger. He stood. For a moment it was an open question what he would do next.

Reggie's first inclination was to knock him down again, but he held back—Laura was up from the couch now, and she had a hand on Reggie's arm.

"Wait," she said.

And then she stepped between the two men.

"You wait, too," she said to the Texan.

Then she turned back to Reggie. She took a moment to brush her hair out of her eyes, and then said, "He was here earlier. His name is Stillman. I think he's just trying to make an appointment."

"Yes, ma'am," said Stillman. "Thank you."

The man flashed a quick grin at Laura, then immediately let it lapse when he looked at Reggie.

Reggie wasn't buying any of it. "Call back after nine," he said.

"You'll pardon me for insisting," said Stillman. "But I'm looking for a man here who is claiming an association with Sherlock Holmes. I'm guessing that's you?"

"No," said Reggie.

"Sorry for the mistake. His name is Reggie Heath, and I'm told these are his law chambers. Maybe you can point me to him?"

"I am Reggie Heath, but I claim nothing of the kind. And you are on my premises uninvited and before hours, so I suggest you explain quickly."

The man gave Reggie an appraising look, then nodded.

"It's about a letter," he said.

Reggie and Laura exchanged a glance.

"Go on," said Reggie.

"I represent Ms. Hilary Clemens of Shady Oaks, Texas. Do you know the name?"

"I'm sure we've both heard of Texas," said Laura. "I might have even been there once."

"I meant the name Hilary Clemens," said the man.

"No," said Laura.

"No," said Reggie.

"Never heard of Clemens Copper?"

"I believe that was one of the largest mining operations in the States at one time," said Reggie.

"I thought you'd know it," said Stillman. "Though I wasn't sure you'd own up to it so quick. Ms. Clemens was only twenty years old when she inherited the entire fortune. That was eighty-two years ago. Her net worth now is almost incalculable—and she recently decided to change her will."

"And what does that have to do with me? Or the letters?"

"Ms. Clemens never married. She has no children. She had a mind as sharp as a tack when she was younger, and you've never met anyone as careful in her relationships, or as cautious with her fortune. But in the last few years—well, she got kicked by her favorite horse three years ago; that might have had something to do with it—she's become just a little quirky about some things. But not so much as to be indisputably legally incompetent. She can tell you what the opening price of copper was this morning, and she can tell you the name of her favorite cat when she was a young girl. But if you ask her who she spent New Year's Eve with last year, she's as likely to name a character from fiction as anything else."

"I think I see where this is headed," said Laura.

"This nice old lady decided to bequeath her entire fortune to Sherlock Holmes," said Stillman. "And she sent a document here to that effect. I'm here to see that she doesn't get taken advantage of."

"Or to take advantage of her yourself," said Reggie. "But I can't see what you are concerned about in any case. A bequest to a character from fiction can't be enforced."

"Exactly," said the man, glaring hard at Reggie. "Which is why you wrote a letter back to Ms. Clemens, suggesting that she instead bequeath her entire fortune to you. So that, in the same way that courts in the past have delivered money into the hands of a custodian for, say, a cat with an inheritance, you would be put in charge of the money as custodian for the letters that foolish old people write to Sherlock Holmes."

"Nonsense. I wrote no such letter."

"Reggie would never do such a thing," says Laura.

"He already has," said Stillman.

Stillman reached inside his coat pocket; Reggie took a

precautionary step toward him, and the man put up both of his hands, palms out.

"Tell you what," said the man, "Why don't we all just sit down somewhere businesslike, and I'll show you what I'm talking about. The little lady looks like she might want to get off her feet anyway."

Reggie didn't like the Texan's presumption in mentioning that, but before he could respond, Laura did.

"I'm fine," said Laura, "But yes, why don't we all just pretend we're perfectly reasonable people discussing some perfectly reasonable business transaction."

A few moments later, all three sat around a table in the chambers conference room.

Stillman took a letter out from his jacket and unfolded it on the table.

"Last week I paid a visit to Ms. Clemens just to see how she was doing. She was very happy. Excited. She told me she had solved the problem of what to do with all the money and property and invaluable possessions that would be left just lying around after she was gone. She showed me this."

Reggie and Laura both leaned it to read the letter.

It was short and to the point. It presented itself as being from Sherlock Holmes, but it acknowledged that Sherlock Holmes was not a good choice for a bequest. The letter writer suggested that it would be better to leave the entire inheritance to Reggie Heath.

"I did not write this," said Reggie.

"You have motive to do so," replied Stillman. "It resolves to your benefit. And I had a look at some correspondence at your secretary's desk. This looks to me like your hand trying to sign 'Sherlock Holmes.'"

Reggie and Laura both stared hard at the signature.

"Well, I suppose that does rather look like your *H*," said Laura doubtfully.

"No, it isn't. It—well, it does sort of look like it, I'll admit, but it isn't. It can't be. You know whose script this looks like?"

"Whose?"

"Lord Buxton's."

"Oh, please," said Laura.

"Have you ever really looked at his signature? I've seen that ham-handed scrawl on tons of legal documents. I expect half the corporate lawsuits in London—well, maybe not quite that, but tons—involve him in one way or another. Libel, invasion of privacy, plagiarism, hostile takeovers. And he practically punctures the paper every time he puts pen to it, undoubtedly some sort of Freudian compensation. Look there, he actually broke through the paper on the *S*."

Laura was looking perturbed.

"Why on earth would Robert do that?"

"To get me in trouble, of course. Bloody hell, I wouldn't put it past him to have faked his whole bloody—"

"Reggie!"

Reggie stopped himself just in time. He looked at Laura to acknowledge her warning: He had almost said the word *kidnapping*.

Then they both looked at Stillman to see if he had any reaction.

"Uh-huh," said Stillman. "Well, you two can work that out between you. I actually don't give a damn who wrote that initial letter. We're way past that now. Ms. Clemens told me a few days ago that when she received the letter, she immediately executed a new will. I wasn't in town that day to stop her. She lined up witnesses and got the whole thing done up right, bequeathing her entire fortune to Reggie Heath as custodian of the Sherlock Holmes letters, and she fired it off in express mail."

"To this address?" asked Reggie.

"Yes."

"And so you sneaked in before hours to try to find it and take it back?"

"I didn't sneak. I woke the guard at the lobby security station, told him I was here about a letter to Sherlock Holmes, and he just waved me on up. Said it happens all the time."

"And did you find the letter that's supposed to contain this will?" asked Laura.

"No," said Stillman. He looked directly at Reggie. "Where is it?"

For a moment, there was tense silence. Reggie still wasn't sure he believed Stillman's excuse for being on the premises. But quite aside from that, the man's tone was a demand, and Reggie didn't like it.

"Two things," said Reggie now, tightly. "I mean, aside from the fact that you are trespassing uninvited on my premises regardless of what the lobby welcoming committee said, and in a moment I will throw you out."

Reggie was on autopilot now—in his pretrial, last-chance, conference-in-the-corridor mode.

"First," said Reggie, "It occurs to me, just as a theoretical point of law, that perhaps Ms. Clemens is entitled to will all of the copper in the United States to Sherlock Holmes if she chooses to do so. As you acknowledged, people have bequeathed fortunes to their cats, and the courts have enforced that intent, appointing custodians to handle the wealth on the animal's behalf. The lady can do what she chooses, and it's at least even odds that the court will enforce it. Second thing—"

"In other words, you did write the letter asking for the inheritance," said Stillman.

"Of course he didn't," said Laura.

"No," said Reggie. "I did not. But just on matter of principle, the woman has a right. And second thing—if indeed the will you speak of is your only concern—why don't you simply ask Ms. Clemens to change it?"

"I would," said Stillman. "I drove from Austin to Dalhart two days ago to do exactly that. But I couldn't. Because that very same evening after Ms. Clemens had excitedly done her best to dispatch her entire fortune to Sherlock Holmes for the purposes of catching the evildoers that lurk apparently everywhere in your fine city, she suffered a massive stroke. She died."

For a moment there was silence all around.

Then Laura said, "We're sorry for your loss. I mean, not for any money you might have lost, but for her passing."

Reggie glared at Stillman and said, "So you're here looking for a letter that contains a will that would cost the potential inheritors several billions of dollars—which I'm guessing includes you—if you don't find it and destroy it before a court becomes aware of its existence."

Stillman glared back at Reggie and said, "We're done here. If you're telling the truth and you don't have the letter—but you find it—you'll save yourself a world of trouble if you just turn it over to me. The law is far from settled on this. A cat at least has corporeal existence; Sherlock Holmes does not. And whoever is perpetrating this scam is just as likely to be found guilty of fraud as he is to obtain Ms. Clemens's money."

Reggie was about to respond, but Laura put her hand on his arm.

"I'm sure you'll both be just wonderful at trial," she said to

Stillman. "But I don't have time to listen to you and Reggie wrangle legal doctrine all day. We have more important things to discuss. So shoo, please."

"Sure," said Stillman. He stood up from the conference table and turned to exit. But then he paused in the doorway.

Just one more thing," said Stillman. "I'd feel bad later on if something happened and I didn't warn you."

"About what?" said Laura.

"I'm only Ms. Clemens's attorney. I am not, in fact, an heir to her fortune. I'm not a relative. Regardless of what you think, I am not one of those who would stand to lose billions if this bequest were to take effect."

"But you said she never married? She outlived her siblings, and there's no husband, and no surviving children?" said Laura.

"Right. But there's a grand-nephew. Actually, two of them. Before I flew out here, I tried to let them both know that I'm handling this—I reached one of them but not the other, and that second one is a pretty rough guy."

"So you think at least one of them might be here?" asked Reggie.

"No telling," said Stillman. "I don't control him. I can't control him. And I can't say what he will do or what lengths he would go to. But now you're warned."

Now Stillman exited into the corridor and walked back toward the lift, his hard-soled boots clumping on the wood floor. Reggie and Laura followed. Stillman looked suspiciously back over his shoulder at Reggie; Reggie returned a glare, and then at last the lift doors opened, Stillman stepped in, and the doors closed.

"An estate worth billions of pounds," said Laura as soon as the man was gone, "might possibly be sufficient motive for a kidnapping."

"Yes," said Reggie. "But it would be tricky. You can hardly present yourself as claimant at a probate hearing if you're going to be arrested for kidnapping when you show up."

"But that would only be a risk if you could be convicted, wouldn't it?"

Reggie nodded.

"Well, our Stillman wasn't the man in the boat," said Laura. "His voice is wrong. And he wasn't on the island, either. I saw shoe prints in the mud, but they weren't pointy-toed American boots."

"He could have accomplices," said Reggie. "He could be lying about not having an interest in the will. And people do change shoes."

"Yes, and I know not all Americans wear boots, but I doubt that man takes them off even when he goes to bed," said Laura. "Anyway, I don't think it was him. He's far too direct to resort to a kidnapping. But perhaps this grand-nephew person is another matter."

Reggie nodded at that. Then he said something that he'd been dwelling on but trying to hold back.

"If there really was a kidnapping," said Reggie.

"What do you mean? Trust me, I had to row the little boat out to meet them; the kidnappers are real."

"It could all just be a ploy by Buxton to try to drag you back into his sphere of influence. He's got the funds to set it up, and the security team to manage the details, keep you in it, and keep it private."

"That's just foolish. You don't even believe what you just said yourself."

Reggie sighed. "Maybe not. But I don't like having you involved in this.

"Reggie, I can't simply abandon him."

"You can walk away and let the professionals handle this. They can't make you do this."

"No one is making me do anything."

"Then why are you doing it?"

"Because it's the right thing. And because he trusted me to do it. And anyway, I owe him this much."

"I can't see that you owe Robert Buxton a thing."

"Reggie, I owe him for posting your bail in the Black Cab case, if for nothing else."

Reggie didn't like being reminded of that. Buxton had once posted a million pounds to get Reggie out of jail—on Laura's request. Reggie had not been able to prevent it—she had made the request over his objections—but he had known at the time that it would mean trouble someday. And apparently, that day was now.

"He already got his money back on that," said Reggie.

"It's not a matter of the money. It's a matter of his being willing to do a major favor when I asked."

"We both know why he was willing to do that. He didn't mind at all the prospect of my rotting in jail. We both know what he was after."

"Fine, Reggie, you know so much, tell me—exactly what was Lord Buxton after?"

Reggie didn't answer. He couldn't think of a safe way to say it. He and Laura were both standing facing each other, near each other, but squared off in the corridor, and it just didn't seem wise to say it. Probably he'd already said too much.

"Very well, then," said Laura. "I'm going home. Before one of us does some damage."

She turned and pressed the button for the lift.

Reggie couldn't stop her. He knew that. But when she stepped inside the lift, he put his hand between the doors before she could close them.

"When they call again, promise me you won't go to meet them. You'll call me."

"I thought you wanted nothing to do with helping Robert."

"I don't give a damn about Buxton, and he doesn't give a damn about me. But you're in this and I'm in it with you. So promise you won't go to meet them. And you won't rely on the bloody security team. You'll call me."

"I can't see what—"

"Promise."

Laura gave an exasperated sigh. "I promise," she said. "May I go now?"

Reggie brought his hand back and let the lift doors close.

Then, as the lift descended, he went to the exterior window in his chambers office and looked down on Baker Street. He picked up his phone, and as he watched Laura exit the lobby below and flag down a cab, he punched in the number that he had gotten from her address book.

After just two rings, an authoritative male voice answered

"Alex," said the man on the phone

"I take it you are the git in charge of Robert Buxton's security," said Reggie.

"Who are you?" said Alex.

"Reggie Heath."

There was silence for a moment. Then: "Mr. Heath, you should not have this number. You can call Lord Buxton's standard reception line if you want to make an appointment."

"If you make me go through channels, " said Reggie, "I will tell every channel I go through that I know why Lord Buxton hasn't been making any of his appointments."

Silence again, then: "Laura Rankin told you?"

"She had no choice," said Reggie.

"What is it you want?"

"You put her at risk. Don't do it again."

"We took every possible precaution. We had everything under control."

"Apparently, not quite everything. It was Regent's Park, for God's sake—it's surrounded on all sides by a major thoroughfare."

"Obviously. What's your point?"

"And you couldn't keep a good-enough eye on things to stop them from getting away? What sort of control is that?"

"My team had all the exit points covered."

"Again—apparently not. But I'm just letting you know: If you put Laura Rankin at risk again, I will ruin you."

"From what I can see, Laura Rankin pretty much makes up her own mind about things."

"Completely beside the point. If you send her out to meet the bloody kidnappers alone again, and harm comes to her, I will destroy you."

"I'm a professional, Mr. Heath. What are you going to do, sneak up on me in an alley?"

"From what I can tell," said Reggie. "a schoolgirl could manage that."

Then Reggie hung up.

He closed his chambers door, locked it, exited Dorset House, and got in his car.

He hoped Buxton's security team would take his threat personally. But he wasn't about to take that for granted.

He sat in the Jag for several minutes, giving Laura's cab a head start. It wouldn't do to be caught tailing her. And then he started his car and drove toward Laura's home in Chelsea.

21

Robert Buxton was conscious again.

The same stench from before was in his nostrils. He felt like it was permeating his sinuses; he was sure he would never get it out of his head. But this time, it was the voice that woke him. Still the most annoying voice he had ever heard.

"You are still alive, Mr. Buxton. You may wonder, given what you see and smell around you. Imagine, if you dare, what it is like to spend every waking day for years in such a place. But you are still alive, at least. For the moment. If Ms. Laura Rankin brings us the letters on time, perhaps you will stay that way."

"What letters?"

"You bloody well know, Mr. Buxton."

Buxton tried to think. He did not bloody well know.

His vision was clearing more than his head was, or at least that's how it felt, but even so, he got only a general impression of the man's face: very pale, and just barely illuminated by a single electric lantern several feet away.

The letters. Buxton tried to think.

"Hell," he said after a moment. "You mean the letters to Sherlock Holmes?"

The pale-faced man just stared back at him.

"This is about the bequest, isn't it?" said Buxton. "Are you from the States? You don't sound like it. But if this is about that will—hell, that was just a joke. It didn't mean anything. I was just playing a prank on Heath. That's all it was. You sure as hell didn't need to bring me here over that."

The pale man still just stared and said nothing for a moment.

Then he said, "Is Ms. Rankin smarter than you? You may hope so. If she isn't, you'll never get out of here."

"And just where the hell am I?" asked Buxton.

"You are about fifty meters north of the Albert Memorial. Several meters below a park that used to be a private hunting reserve for kings who would shoot deer for sport while the commoners starved. It was a bit of a slog getting you here, and I mean that literally. But if one is looking for symbols of British empire and decadence, and I am, this location will do."

The pale man stood. He picked up the electric lantern and held it out at arm's length to give Buxton a better look at his situation.

"Two hundred years ago, this little ledge was used by the sewer maintenance workers to assemble their equipment. See, right here is a little nook for you to put your lantern—if you had one. Now you can jump down from here if you like—the sewer water here is only about three feet deep at the moment; it'll rise when it rains. But I've put new locks on both the exit grates, so you won't get far, whatever the weather, and I'd advise you to stay put.

"But if you do decide to jump down anyway, do you know what you'd be standing in? I'll bet you don't. Well, maybe you do, in a general sort of way. You can't see it in the dark, but I bet even you can smell it: the queen's shit. And I mean that in a very specific sort of way: the queen's. Though I bet you can't tell from sniffing it the difference between it and anyone else's. Or maybe you can. Do you think? If you had beef bourguignon for supper, would your crap smell different than if you had bangers and beans? Maybe. I haven't done a study.

"But I can tell you that royal shit is what you'd be standing in if you tried to get out, because we are directly under Hyde Park, and just two kilometers to the north of us is Buckingham Palace, which is a main contributor to this tunnel. Everything the royals grunt and strain out of their bums comes through here. Yeah, I know. I do. I know all about it. I spent ten years fixing these sewers back in the day—lively occupation for a young man getting ready to go out and about on the town, don't you think? So I know. Too bad they wouldn't let me make a career of it. But if they had, I would never have found my true calling."

"And what would that be?"

The man with the lantern shook his head and started to turn away.

"Wait," said Buxton. "Don't you have any idea who I am?"

"Of course I do."

"Then think about it. You're mad at the royals, right? I get that. I do. Now, think about the newspapers I own. Think what I could do for your cause if I gave it coverage."

"Your fish wrap is part of the problem. You make the royals a bloody national obsession."

Buxton shrugged. "I can change."

"Doesn't matter. You think I brought you here because of the trash you print? Don't flatter yourself, Lord Buxton. I mean, if you can help it."

"Wait—I'm not even a real lord, you know. That's just for show. Not related to any royals, ever, no matter how far back you go."

The man with the lantern looked back at Buxton, shook his head again, and then turned off the light.

22

It was late in the evening now, and Laura was at home in Chelsea, but she had no thought of sleeping. She made Earl Grey tea with milk and drank it for something to do, and it would be fine if it kept her awake.

All that she was supposed to do—all that she could think of to do—was just to wait.

Wait for the kidnappers to call her. Or wait for Buxton's team to call her, if the kidnappers contacted them first. Or wait for Scotland Yard to arrive with sirens wailing if somehow they had found out, or, worse, if they had found out and already managed to cock it up, wait for a couple of detectives to drive up quietly and walk to her door with bad news.

She wanted to ring Reggie on his mobile and just talk to him; just to hear his voice would help. But she couldn't, and it wasn't because of how they had left things at Baker Street.

It was because she knew exactly where he was, and if she rang him and let him know she knew, he would insist on coming in, and then—well, then things would get just too bloody complicated.

She put her tea down, got up from the chair, and went to

the front window again. She stood behind the opaque drapes and parted the semitransparent curtains only as much as she thought she could without being seen.

Less than twenty yards down the street, just past the second drive, was a Range Rover. She knew—or at least was reasonably certain—that it was the one that belonged to Buxton's security team. It was the largest thing on the street; none of her neighbors had such a vehicle. And although it had arrived more than two hours ago, she had yet to hear a car door slam or see anyone get out.

And another ten yards beyond that, but across the street, and slightly better hidden from her line of sight, but still not completely, was Reggie's XJS.

Laura had heard him drive by more than once since she got home. And then he had pulled up and parked just shortly after dusk. Her orange cat had jumped from the couch onto the windowsill in the way that he did when Reggie came over, and Laura had come to the window in time to see Reggie dim the lights on the Jag.

He had been there for hours; he was probably famished by now. It wouldn't do to ring him anyway; he would be cranky if hungry.

But now, jarringly, her phone rang.

This would be the kidnappers. Laura spilled just a little of her tea into the saucer, but then she took a breath and calmed herself.

She let the phone ring twice more, and then she picked up.

"Yes?" she said.

"Are you alone?"

She knew this voice.

"Reggie, of course I'm alone. Why are you calling me?" asked Laura.

"I just wanted to be sure you're all right."

"Why wouldn't I be all right?"

"Why—well, just think about what's been happening!"

"Reggie, hasn't anyone ever told you that women don't want a man to fix things, they just want a man to listen?"

"Um . . . yes. You told me that. I think. If I heard correctly at the time."

"Well, then?"

"I guess I just see it differently. Personally, I'd think it was great if someone would fix things for me."

"Reggie, it's Robert who was kidnapped, not me. And I already promised that if the wankers call, I won't make a move without telling you, did I not?"

"Well, yes, but . . . even so."

"How about this—you protect me from being tired tomorrow by letting me get a good night's sleep tonight. Would that be fair?'

"Of course."

"All right, then. Good night."

"Good night," said Reggie.

Laura hung up the phone.

His voice sounded so patient when he said good night. He was trying so hard.

Oh well. It couldn't be helped.

Laura managed one gulp of the tea, and then her phone rang again.

This would be the kidnappers. One ring, two rings—she picked up.

"Yes?"

"Have they called?"

Laura knew this voice, as well. It was Alex, Buxton's chief of staff.

"No. And you shouldn't, either. And if you think I haven't seen your great big Range Rover with the tinted windows parked down the street, you are mistaken."

"I'm sorry, Miss Rankin. We have a job to do."

Laura paused. She wanted to tell them just how badly they'd been doing it. But she knew it wouldn't help.

"Your job," she said instead, "at this moment, is to let me sleep. Can you manage that?"

"Yes, ma'am," said Alex.

"Thank you," said Laura, and she hung up.

She checked the time. It was nearly eleven. She knew Reggie knew her routine. Sadly, Robert's team of security spies probably knew it, too. If they all knew what she presumed they knew, then they knew it was just a bit early for her to be going to bed. But given what had been transpiring, they certainly would not think it odd.

So she turned off the porch light. Then she went to the kitchen and turned off that light, as well.

She turned off the light in the front room and went upstairs to the bedroom. She turned that light on; then she turned the light on in the loo. She waited an appropriate amount of time, and then she turned both lights off again in the proper sequence.

There. That should hold them.

Then she walked back downstairs in the dark. She picked up her Earl Grey tea—with luck, she would be allowed now to drink it in peace—and she waited.

23

Reggie waited in his car.

And waited.

He was parked on Laura's street, just three houses down from hers, under a large walnut tree.

Just up the street was an unusually bulky Range Rover with tinted windows and what Reggie guessed had to be armor plate under the bumpers, given how they protruded. It was parked two houses down from Laura's, and across the street from Reggie. It was the surveillance spot Reggie would have chosen himself if he had not been trying to be inconspicuous.

No question. The vehicle had to belong to Buxton's surveillance team. It had the garish personality of their employer.

He had seen Laura turn on the lights in the kitchen. He had seen those lights go off, and then the upstairs lights go on. And then the upstairs lights had gone off, as well.

She had gone to bed. It was just a little early, not quite eleven, but she was no doubt tired.

Reggie was, too. He settled back in his seat to wait. He closed his eyes for a moment, and he faded.

Then suddenly, he was jolted awake. His mobile was ringing.

He checked his watch: It was almost one in the morning.

He picked up the phone. The lights were still out in Laura's house, but it might be her.

It wasn't.

"Mr. Heath?"

A woman's voice, though Reggie didn't recognize it immediately.

"This is Mrs. Winslow," she said. "I'm very sorry to call you at this hour. I hope you weren't sleeping or . . . doing anything important."

"Nothing like that," said Reggie.

"I simply didn't know who else to call. I thought you might want to know. Or maybe you won't. I suppose it doesn't matter now that Mr. Liu is—has passed on, but . . . I just feel like I should tell someone. "

"Yes?"

"I'm just so sorry about it. It turns out that he did not make a mistake after all."

"I'm not sure I follow," said Reggie. Clearly the man had made some sort of mistake, or he would not have died suddenly in a Soho alley thousands of miles from home.

"It's a very well-known rhyme," she said. "And the mistake— what I thought was his mistake—was so obvious. But it wasn't— I mean, it wasn't his mistake at all. It was in the original."

Reggie tried to focus.

"You're saying that, in fact, Mr. Liu translated correctly."

"Yes," she said. "The error—what I thought was an error— was not a discrepancy between his translation and the source material that was sent to him. It was a discrepancy between what was sent to him and what the nursery rhyme is commonly understood to be."

Reggie rubbed his eyes. It felt very late to be talking about this sort of thing.

"You're referring to the 'buckle my shoe' rhyme? The duck?"

"Yes, that one, and some of the others. And I thought he had made the errors. But he had not. All of the errors were in the source material that was sent to him. I don't know how this could have happened, except that a Mr. Sandwhistle, who provided the source material, must have made an accidental change in what he sent on to Mr. Liu. I received a copy of that as well, and ever since you spoke to me earlier, I've been looking for it. I found it. And that's where the errors were—in the source, not in the translation. I've just now called both Mr. Sandwhistle and my client to inform them about their error."

Reggie wondered why the name Sandwhistle seemed familiar. But he couldn't quite place it.

"I'm sure they appreciated that," said Reggie. "At this hour."

"Well, I didn't actually speak to anyone," continued Mrs. Winslow. "I just left messages. They'll have to have both the originals and the translations redone. Or perhaps they won't; not everyone cares about quality the way they used to."

"All right, " said Reggie. "But the point you're making to me is that Mr. Liu actually translated correctly. It was the original that was wrong."

"Yes. And I fired him over it. I'm so very sorry. I feel so bad about it, that he came all this way, and then—what happened to him in that alley."

The woman's remorse over the phone sounded completely sincere. Reggie felt obliged to say something.

"We don't know what happened yet in Soho," he said, "But clearly your misunderstanding with him was not the proximate cause of his death."

It wasn't much consolation, probably. It was the best he could do as a lawyer.

"I know," she said. "I mean, I'm sure that must be true. Still, I wonder if you might want to meet me, and I'll show you what the source material was—and why I thought the translations were wrong."

Reggie was inclined to say no. He was tired. Laura was on his mind; Buxton, bloody hell, was on his mind. And the missing letters. With all of that, he had actually forgotten for the past few hours about Mr. Liu.

"Please," said the woman. "I'd feel better about it. I understand about proximate cause and all that, but I would just like the chance to show you what I found. I know these rhymes so well, and I just didn't see how I could send them on with words that were just the opposite of what they should be. 'Unbuckle my shoe' instead of 'buckle' it. 'Throw down sticks' instead of pick them up. So many errors. And now to see that they weren't Mr. Liu's mistake at all—"

Reggie tried to remember the particular rhyme. 'One, two, buckle my shoe.' He couldn't remember the others.

"Mrs. Winslow," he said. "The rhyming lines with errors—do all of them contain a number?"

There was a pause. "Why, yes," she said after a moment. "The lines in that rhyme certainly do. I'd have to check on the errors in the other rhymes."

Reggie looked across at Laura's house—still dark, of course. He looked in his rearview mirror. The security team was still there in the Range Rover.

"All right," said Reggie. "I can be at your place in ten minutes. But I won't be able to stay long."

"No," said the woman. "That's not where I am. I'm at the Elgar Imports warehouse, where they put all these things together. But it isn't far, just over in the Docklands. Can you meet me there?"

"All right," said Reggie. He took down the address.

Then he got out of his own car and walked directly over to the Range Rover. He approached the driver's side.

The window was tinted too darkly to see in. But Reggie really had no doubt.

He rapped his knuckles on the window.

He waited a few seconds. No response.

He rapped again, harder.

The window rolled down.

"What do you want, Heath?" said the male driver.

Reggie hadn't met the man before, but he recognized the voice—it was the bloke named Alex, the Buxton contact he had spoken with on the phone.

"Just letting you know I'm stepping away for a moment," said Reggie.

"You shouldn't be here at all."

"What I said before still stands," said Reggie. "If you try to use Laura again, I promise you will regret it."

Alex sighed. "You can save your breath, Heath. She's already told us to bugger off. All we're trying to do now is just keep an eye on the place."

Reggie nodded.

The window rolled back up.

Reggie walked back to his car. The kidnappers would surely not show up at Laura's house, not with Buxton's security team parked there so obviously. And he had put the security team on notice. So that should take care of things. At least for the moment.

He wasn't absolutely sure this was the smart thing to do. He was having a hard time being sure of anything. But he started the XJS and drove on.

24

Shortly after one in the morning, Reggie drove down a narrow dead-end alley off West India Dock Road.

To his right was a two-story, nineteenth-century warehouse constructed of aging brick. To his left was a concrete car park for a hotel still under construction.

There were a few energy-efficient yellow lamps positioned every thirty yards or so along the alley, but they did not illuminate much.

Reggie slowed. Even in the dark, the location should be easy to find; vertical aluminum doors had been installed in the entrances to the individual warehouse storage units, and at this hour, all he had to do was find the one that Mrs. Winslow had opened.

But he had reached the end of the alley now, and all of the doors were closed.

He backed up, peering at street numbers that had been hammered into the brick of the warehouse, but it was nearly impossible to make them out.

And then he stopped.

There were no vehicles on the street—except one. It was

covered with a tarp, as if ready for storage. But someone had been in haste; the tarp had not been tied down well, and the rear bumper of a late-model compact car was visible. Reggie got out and lifted the tarp.

A Mini Cooper. Clean, precise, and no-nonsense. If Reggie had to guess, he would have said it was what Mrs. Winslow would drive.

Reggie went to the storage unit door nearest that car. Yes, a small metal sign identified it as Elgar Imports.

The door was closed but not locked; the padlock lay open on the ground a couple of feet from the bottom of the door.

Reggie grabbed the handle and raised the door with a loud metallic clatter.

He looked inside.

Completely dark.

He called out.

No response.

Reggie ran his hand along the side wall until he found a light switch.

And the switch worked, but it was just one sixty-watt bulb hanging from the ceiling at the entrance; it barely illuminated the front of two rows of long storage shelves, each about eight feet high. The corridor between the rows extended some twenty yards to the dark recess of the unit, with a break about halfway.

Something was making a repetitive whirring notice—like a small electric motor, but with interruptions—at the far end.

Reggie walked down the middle corridor toward that sound.

He reached the intersecting corridor, the sound quite close now. He looked around the corner.

And there it was: On the concrete floor of the warehouse, waddling insistently up against the storage shelves but making no progress at all, was a toy duck like the one Mrs. Winslow had shown to Reggie earlier—about the size of a real one, but made of white plastic, with a yellow bill and a red-white-and-blue Union Jack on its back.

"One, two, buckle my shoe," said the duck, the words clearly audible over the whirring of its little electric motor. Its eyes lit up—apparently a feature activated only when the motor was engaged, because the one at Mrs. Winslow's home hadn't done that—shining green in the dark warehouse.

Just a couple of feet from the duck was an opened cardboard shipping box. Directly above the that was an empty shelf where, Reggie guessed, this duck and others like it must have been stored.

A yellow carbon shipping list was tacked to the wood shelving. Reggie could just make out the addresses in the dim light. Three of them.

One of them was the largest souvenir store in Piccadilly. He had never been in, but he had driven by it often—including just the other night, when he'd parked near the Soho alley where they had found Mr. Liu.

Reggie looked in both directions along the storage aisle. Surely she was still here.

"Mrs. Winslow?" he called out loudly, but there was no answer.

"One, two, buckle my shoe," said the duck again. And again. Apparently, the recording was synchronized with the mechanical waddling mechanism. It was getting annoying.

Reggie couldn't help it. He put his right foot against the duck and gave it a little kick, sending it in a plastic clatter to the other end of the aisle.

The acoustics of the place were surprising; the clatter seemed to echo.

"Humpty Dumpty sat on a wall," said the duck now.

Now Reggie was annoyed with himself. Mrs. Winslow had not asked him here to damage the goods. He walked to the dark end of the aisle and bent down to pick the bloody thing up.

And then, where the meager light illuminated the shiny white plastic of the duck, he saw the woman's pale hand.

She lay outstretched on the concrete, on her side, her eyes still open, and the fingers of her hand pointing at the duck as if in accusation.

"Bloody hell."

Reggie knelt by the still body, felt for a pulse at her neck, found none, and this time when he flung the duck away, it was with enough force that it hit the back wall. The toy didn't break, but mercifully, it did shut up.

For a moment, just silence.

And then the hairs on the back of Reggie's neck stood.

He heard someone breathing—at an accelerated, adrenaline-pumping rate in the darkest back corner of the unit.

Reggie didn't turn his head; he tried not to let on that he could hear it, but no one was being fooled now, not Reggie, and not the presence at the back of the room.

Reggie tried to spring to his feet, but at the same moment, the figure in the back made its move. There was only one way out, and that was past Reggie, and someone ran now for all he was worth.

Reggie lunged forward at the torso of the fleeing figure in the dark.

But the man was too quick; Reggie couldn't get his shoulder into the tackle. For a moment, he had a grasp, or thought he did, on both sides of the man's mac. But the man wrenched free; a coat pocket tore away where Reggie had grabbed on. Then an elbow landed hard in Reggie's face, and he fell back.

Reggie was down only for an instant, but it was too long.

The man was fast, and he toppled an entire shelving assembly into the narrow aisle as he fled.

Reggie scrambled past the boxes and debris to the warehouse entrance. But too late. His quarry was gone from sight. Whether the man had hopped the fence to the car park, or gotten all the way out onto the street from the alley, it was impossible to tell. But there was no catching him now.

Reggie went to his car, got his mobile, and rang Wembley at Scotland Yard.

Then he returned to the warehouse unit.

He knelt once more by the body of Mrs. Winslow. But there was nothing to be done.

Then, still at ground level, Reggie saw something on the floor beneath the adjacent storage shelf. Two things, actually— two pieces of paper. In a place where they might have fallen in the struggle between Reggie and the suspect—or even in an earlier confrontation between the suspect and Mrs. Winslow.

Reggie reached under and pulled them out.

One was a single sheet of paper with multiple folds. The sheet was just like the one Mr. Liu had showed Reggie at Baker Street, with rhymes in English and French and Chinese. But there were handwritten changes on this one—in the same lines where Mrs. Winslow had reported errors.

This had to be the original source she had referred to. She had wanted to show it to him. It proved that Mr. Liu's translations had been correct.

For whatever that was worth now. Reggie put the document into his coat pocket.

He looked at the second item: a greeting card with a pastel-colored birthday greeting on the front. Marketed by a company called Fleur de Lis, according to the label on the back, which claimed to be a purveyor to the queen. Nothing remarkable about any of that, but the card was crumpled at one end, as if it had been gripped tightly in someone's hand—Mrs. Winslow's hand, Reggie supposed—and then yanked out by the suspect with force.

Quite some greeting card, thought Reggie, if it was the reason for her murder.

Reggie stood; he didn't open the card, just carefully held it by the edges—it could be evidence—and he went back to the shelves where he had found the duck and the packing boxes.

There were no more ducks. But there were other novelty items on the shelves: plush toys, windup toys, fancy and useless plastic pens and pencils, custom stationery.

And a box that, according to its label, had contained a set of Fleur de Lis birthday greeting cards.

Reggie checked a tag on the box. They cards apparently hadn't come from Mr. Liu; they had been imported from India. But like the toy duck, the cards had been brought in by Elgar Imports.

The box was empty now. But sometimes things fall out. Reggie pushed the box aside, peered into the recess behind it— and yes, one more card.

Reggie reached back and got it just as the entrance to the warehouse was bathed in glaring light, and he heard the sound of vehicles coming to a stop in the alley.

Reggie put the unopened card in his pocket, held on to the crumpled one by its edges, and went to the entrance.

Detective Inspector Wembley had arrived. He had brought just one officer with him.

"I thought you'd bring a full team," said Reggie.

"I did," said Wembley. "Meachem here, right now, is my full team. Go ahead, Meachem, tape it off."

The young officer took a roll of emergency tape and went to do as instructed.

"You brought just one officer," said Reggie. "No one from Forensics. And yet you came to the scene yourself?"

"It's called 'triaging,' Heath. Emergency arrangement of priorities. MI5 and the royal protective services are getting worried about a new anarchist. The fellow has been venting on the Internet, but he's got some other special way of communicating with his fellow gits, and until MI5 figures out how he's communicating and what he's up to, they'll keep tapping my division at the Yard for extra protection on the royals. Half of my detectives have been pulled off their usual cases."

Wembley paused briefly to note whether the new officer was getting by all right with the roll of tape. The lad seemed to be struggling.

Wembley shook his head at that, and then he resumed: "I'd love to tell you that we're doing all humanly possible about your murdered translator in Soho, and that we'll give equally as much attention to the crime scene here. I wish it were so. But the fact is, I just can't afford to put resources right now on anything that isn't a genuine royal emergency."

"We all have our own concerns, I guess," said Reggie. He quickly considered—then as quickly rejected—the notion of mentioning anything to Wembley about Laura or about Buxton's kidnapping. Bumbling Scotland Yard rookies who should have been on traffic patrol were not what Reggie wanted for that.

"So just exactly what brought *you* here, Heath?" asked Wembley.

"Mrs. Winslow asked me to meet her here to look at something regarding Mr. Liu's translation. I came here and found her like this. And then I encountered a fellow lurking in the back."

"Description?"

"I never saw his face at all. I'd say just under six feet, about one hundred and eighty pounds. Strong grip. Callouses. And he smelled like vanilla."

"What?"

"I'm just saying . . . I caught a whiff of something. Vanilla."

"Did you see his attack on her?"

"No," said Reggie. "Of course not. I'd have stopped it."

"So what's your theory? She interrupted a burglary?"

"Possibly. Or she was already here when he arrived, and he wanted something so badly that he'd kill her for it."

Wembley looked around at the shelves of paper and mailing boxes.

"What do we have here that would be worth killing for?"

"I've no idea. For what it's worth, I believe the suspect had this on his person when I struggled with him. I believe Mrs. Winslow had it earlier—and he took it from her."

Reggie handed over the crumpled birthday card.

"He murdered her to steal a greeting card?"

"I'm not saying that. But I think it came out of his pocket when I tried to grab him."

Wembley opened the card.

The card responded with a tinny rendition of "Happy Birthday."

"I hate these things," said Wembley. "If you open it in a public place, everyone knows it's your birthday."

"Humpty Dumpty took a great fall," said the plastic duck.

"What the hell was that?" said Wembley, closing the card. "Happy Birthday" stopped.

"A toy duck," said Reggie. "I believe it was originally in a packing box over here by the workbench. There's still some of this same packing tape on the scissors. I think Mrs. Winslow was unpacking it there, and then she heard something, maybe, so she walked over here to investigate, carrying the box, and then our assailant struck her."

"Then I make it a garden-variety burglary that went wrong," said Wembley. "He wasn't expecting anyone to be here. She got here before hours to meet you. She surprised him; he whacked her to get away, and then he did the same to you when you arrived."

Reggie nodded. "Possibly."

"Hmm." Wembley nodded. Then he motioned for his officer to come over.

"Meachem, get this to Forensics." Carefully holding the mashed card by the edges, Wembley handed it to Meachem.

Meachem promptly opened it up. "Happy Birthday" began again.

"Don't play with it," said Wembley. "Put it in a nice plastic bag to make it look like you know your job, and get it to Forensics for fingerprints. Tell them they can ignore yours."

"Humpty Dumpty sat on a wall," said the toy duck, and it began to whir and move its feet.

"Yes, guv," said Meachem. "Just human nature to open up a card when someone hands it to you, I guess."

"You're not a human; you're a member of the Metropolitan Police," said Wembley. "Try to remember that."

"Yes, guv." Meachem tucked the card inside a Ziploc bag.

The duck continued to whir, waddling up against the shelf where Wembley and Reggie were standing.

"Damn, that thing's annoying," said Wembley. "Can't you make it stop?"

"You press its bill to make it start," said Reggie. "It tends to stop if you throw it against a wall, but maybe there's a better way." Reggie picked up the whirring duck and put it on the workbench. "Ah, here's the switch."

Reggie clicked the switch; the duck stopped moving and went completely silent.

"Good job," said Wembley.

"I've seen a duck like this before," said Reggie.

"Of course you've seen it before. We've all seen toy ducks before. I don't recall them being so bloody noisy when I was three, but we've all seen them."

"I mean, this is the toy that Mr. Liu was translating instructions for. I saw one like it at Mrs. Winslow's house earlier, before she asked me to come to the warehouse."

"And so you're thinking it means something?"

Reggie shrugged.

Wembley motioned for his assistant to return.

"Meachem!"

"Guv?"

"Take this duck to Forensics, too."

Meachem hesitated.

"What's wrong?" asked Wembley.

"I don't have a bag that big," said Meachem.

Wembley sighed. "Just put it in the car and take it along."

"Yes, guv."

Meachem gingerly picked up the duck by its yellow feet and carried it away.

Reggie checked his watch again.

"You got somewhere else to be, Heath?"

"Yes, I have . . . an appointment with Laura," said Reggie in a tone that suggested something more fun than was actually going on at the moment. He didn't want to say that he was just going to drive back to her place, camp out in his car, and keep watch again.

"At this hour? Things heating up, are they, Heath? You're free to go, then. I won't stand in the way."

"Cheers," said Reggie, turning to leave. "You'll let me know when Forensics finds something?"

"If and when," said Wembley.

25

Laura's phone rang.

She almost leaped out of her chair. Her teacup was still in her lap, and what remained in it spilled out onto the floor.

She looked at the clock. Five in the morning.

She had no idea how many times the phone might have rung; she knew she'd been asleep.

She picked up.

"Are you alone?"

This time, it wasn't Reggie.

This time, the voice on the phone was the one she had heard in the boat at Regent's Park. It sounded muffled, possibly an attempt at disguise, possibly a bad connection, but she recognized it.

"Yes," said Laura immediately, and then she was angry with herself. Probably she would have given that answer regardless, but she resolved to try to answer such questions more slowly if they came up again. Probably it was better to lie to kidnappers, or at least consider doing so each time, rather than reflexively tell the truth.

"Are you being watched?"

"No," said Laura after just a moment's thought in light of her new rule.

"You're lying," said the voice.

Damn, thought Laura.

"Or else you're unobservant. The security team is parked two doors down."

"Oh," said Laura. "Thanks. Good to know."

"You will have to evade them. Can you do that?"

"Possibly, " said Laura. "But as you see, I'm not terribly good at this. You can't hold me responsible if someone manages to follow me without my knowing."

"I can and do," said the voice. "You must bring the letters and come alone. If you are followed, Lord Buxton dies."

Laura took a longer moment to answer now.

"I will try not to be followed," she said.

"Do you have the letters?"

Bloody hell. Now what could she say to that?

"Not yet."

There was silence from the other end.

Then the voice said, "If you cannot get the letters for us, then we have no need of Buxton. If we have no need of Buxton, he dies."

"I know where to get them," said Laura quickly. Another lie, pretty much, but this time she had no choice. "It will take some time."

"You have three hours."

"I need more time than that."

"Three hours. We will call with your destination. You will come alone. If no letters, then he dies. If you are followed, then he dies."

Then the voice was gone and the line went dead.

For a moment, Laura didn't move.

The letters had to be somewhere at Baker Street. They simply had to be. She and Reggie must have overlooked something in their search. If not, there was no other hope.

Suddenly, and too late, she wondered whether she had closed the drapes enough that no one on the security team could have seen her pick up the phone.

She looked toward the living room window. It was all right. She had left only the slightest opening. No one from the street had a line of sight in.

It was still dark out. There was no moon. She went upstairs and put on her navy blue jogging suit, the darkest thing she could find. She turned on no lights.

Then she came back downstairs and went into the kitchen.

She put food in Tabasco's dish. Who knew when she'd be back.

She looked out the little kitchen window to be sure she had a concealed path mapped out before stepping outside.

And then she sneaked out the kitchen's side door.

26

Nigel Heath got to Baker Street just after six in the morning.

He came directly from the airport, and the red-eye had lived up to its name. He'd been in the middle of the center aisle on the plane, with a squalling baby on one side and a snoring man on the other, and he had not slept for a moment.

His eyes and body wanted to sleep now, but his mind and internal clock wouldn't let him.

But from what Reggie had told him, there was no time for that anyway.

The Dorset House lobby was almost completely empty as Nigel entered. To the right, the glass doors to the bank's offices were still locked.

But the white-haired lobby guard was present, his chin on his chest, looking down at the *Daily Sun*, either asleep or engrossed. Nigel decided not to disturb him and crossed directly across the guard's path toward the lifts, on the left.

The man's head jerked up.

"Pardon me, sir, but may I ask who it is you wish to visit? That is to say, where are you going?"

Nigel turned and said, "Good morning to you, too, Hendricks."

Hendricks squinted. Nigel took several steps toward him to help out.

"Oh," said the man finally, when Nigel was within about three feet of him. "I'm sorry, Mr. Heath. I didn't recognize you."

"Understandable," said Nigel. "It has been a few months. And I expect I'm looking Americanized, so you're quite right to be suspicious."

"It's not that, sir," said Hendricks. "Although you are a bit sunburned. It's just that I've been told I've been a bit careless of late, and to look out better in the future."

"Who told you that?"

"Your brother."

"Ah. He is a stickler, isn't he?"

Hendricks leaned in, with a conspiratorial whisper. "Just between ourselves? Yes. And more than a little tense lately. He never worried in the past about who made it up to his floor; seemed quite eager for just about anyone, as a matter of fact."

"I think he was hoping for the occasional client," said Nigel. "Ah."

"Now I expect he's begun to find them annoying. Anyway, it's best to keep us informed these days. Especially if it's not daylight when someone arrives."

"Exactly what he said, sir. That's why I challenged you."

"And right to do so," said Nigel. "Cheers."

Nigel took the lift up to Baker Street Chambers.

He got out on the quiet floor and walked toward the opposite wall from the lifts.

The place looked the same, but it did not feel the same.

Months ago, if Reggie had asked him to come out and

investigate anything at all regarding the letters, he would have eagerly jumped at the chance. And, in fact, he had done.

But this time, he had come only because of the danger to Laura. A very different thing.

Maybe it was because of the pressure of studying for the American bar. Or maybe it was something else. Maybe just the jet lag. But he felt different.

He passed Lois's desk. It was much too early for her to be here.

He reached his old office. The door was closed but not locked.

He opened it and looked inside.

It didn't seem to have gotten much use while he was gone. No pens or pencils on the desk. The green felt blotter was still there, with its residual coffee stains from his earlier tenure. There was still a phone. But no yellow Post-it notes or paper clips tucked in the leather corners.

Just one thing of significance was still on the desk—the metal In basket that he had used for the Sherlock Holmes letters.

On the front of it was the hand-printed note that Reggie had attached to it months ago, when the letters first began to be an annoyance—at least in his view: "For Nigel."

Nigel grinned at that.

But the basket itself was empty.

On some reflex, Nigel looked immediately from the empty letter basket to the dark corner at the far right of the room.

The one distinguishing feature of the room—a nineteenth-century four-drawer oak file cabinet more than five feet high—was also still there.

Nigel peered into the dark space behind it, just to be sure: No, there was no one crouching.

Not like the event last summer that had caused him to rush off to Los Angeles.

Nigel laughed at himself over the precaution. Probably someone should just shove the thing flush with both sides of the corner; that way, no one could lurk in the future. But who arranges furniture with the concern that someone might hide behind it?

Nigel knelt down now in front of the cabinet where he had kept letters months ago, when he had occupied the office.

Of course, no one would be putting letters there now—but he had to at least look.

He unlocked the bottom drawer and looked inside. There was one green folder.

And it was empty.

"Damn," muttered Nigel.

And then there was a voice from behind him.

"Mr. Heath. Good to see you. What brings you to London?"

Nigel shut the drawer and whirled around.

He was facing a smallish man in a conservative but expensively tailored gray suit.

It took a moment, but Nigel recognized him.

"Rafferty, is it?" said Nigel.

"Yes. Dorset Leasing."

"What brings *you* to—" began Nigel, but then he stopped, because the desk phone was ringing. He picked up without taking his eyes off Rafferty.

It was Hendricks on the phone.

"Mr. Heath?"

"Yes?"

"You asked me to let you know if anyone went up?"

"Yes."

"Well, then. I thought you'd want to know—a short man in

a gray suit is on his way up. I don't know to which floor. Oh, wait. Yes, I do. Second floor. I know that because of the elevator light. That's where it stopped, you see."

"Yes," said Nigel. "Clever. Thank you for the alert."

"You're welcome, Mr. Heath. I'm keeping my eye out."

"Yes," said Nigel. "Carry on."

Nigel hung up the phone and then said to Rafferty, just a little suspiciously, "I realize that you're responsible for leasing at Dorset House. But how does that bring you into Reggie Heath's chambers at—what is it, quarter after six in the morning?"

Rafferty cleared his throat. He looked about uncomfortably. "May I sit down?"

"For a moment," said Nigel, surprising himself at his own rudeness. "I am rather busy."

"I'll be only a moment, then. This is rather awkward. I had thought to have this conversation with your brother, but he's been difficult to get hold of lately."

Nigel knew it would not do to explain why that was.

"I'm not always a reasonable substitute for my brother," Nigel said instead.

Rafferty seemed to consider that for a moment; then he gave a slight shrug and sat in the chair across the desk from Nigel.

"May I ask—do you plan to remain in London? That is, have you returned to stay?"

Nigel could see no reason for Rafferty to be asking this. But he also couldn't think of any particular reason not to answer.

"No," he said.

Rafferty nodded, clearly disappointed.

"Why do you ask?" said Nigel.

"You know your brother does not like it that letters to Sherlock Holmes are delivered to this chambers."

Alarm bells went off in Nigel's head. Of course he knew this. He also knew he should not acknowledge that Reggie was sending the letters to him in America.

"Doesn't he?" said Nigel.

"No," said Rafferty. "He has said as much, more than once, and just recently."

"Oh," said Nigel.

"Which would not bother me too greatly," said Rafferty. "Under usual circumstances. He is, after all, sending them to you."

Nigel held his breath. Rafferty wasn't supposed to know that at all, but now he continued in a way that Nigel had not expected.

"And we find that perfectly acceptable," said Rafferty.

That was a relief.

" 'We'?" said Nigel.

"I mean," said Rafferty quickly, "that I think two Heaths for the price of one is, in effect, not a bad deal. But there is another problem."

Rafferty paused now. He looked over his shoulder, saw that the office door was still open; he reached back and pushed it shut.

"I'm listening," said Nigel.

Rafferty took a deep breath and said, "An offer has been made on Dorset House."

Nigel took a moment to process that. "You mean someone wants to buy this building?"

"Yes."

"Well, that can't be cheap," said Nigel.

"No," said Rafferty.

"Who is making this offer?"

"I'm not at liberty to reveal that, of course. But it is so great an amount that the leasing board is indeed mulling it over." Rafferty sighed unhappily as he said that, and he slumped in his chair at the prospect. "This is something that we—I—never thought would happen."

There was that "we" again, and it was not clear whether he was still referring to the leasing board. Nigel was about to ask for clarification, but Rafferty continued.

"It is not a done deal in any respect, and I am doing my best to fight it. But I need an assurance."

"What sort of assurance?"

"That if the offer is turned down, and this building remains Dorset House, the letters can still be received here. That the current leasing tenant—that is, your brother—will not reject them. That he will not call the Royal Mail and halt delivery, or offer them to the museum down the street, or any such foolish and irresponsible thing as that."

Rafferty actually seemed to be getting a little heated about the situation.

Nigel tried to take a moment to think it through. He wanted to say this was a bad time for this discussion, but he couldn't possibly let Rafferty know about the kidnapping.

"You say that you have no objection to how things work now—that Reggie sends the letters on to me in the States?"

"No," said Rafferty. "We'll allow that, despite what it says in the lease. We have allowed it, though your brother has never acknowledged that it takes place."

"Then reject the offer."

"You're sure?"

"Yes. The letters will not be turned away from Dorset House. I will see to it."

Rafferty looked skeptical.

"How will you do that?"

"Reggie will change his mind," offered Nigel, and then, as Rafferty did not seem immediately persuaded, he added, "Or I will find a way to change it for him."

Rafferty looked squarely back at Nigel for a moment, and then nodded. "All right, then," he said, and he stood to go. "I'll do what I can with the board.

"But just one thing," said Nigel.

"Yes?"

"Tell me who made the offer for Dorset House."

"You know I can't."

Nigel drummed his fingers on the desk. Probably there was no connection between the offer and the missing letters. Surely no one would buy Dorset House just for that.

But in any case, he could see that Rafferty wouldn't budge.

"All right," said Nigel. "If you can't, you can't. Cheers."

Nigel swiveled in his chair, away from Rafferty and back toward the bottom drawer of the file cabinet.

Rafferty stopped in the doorway.

"I suppose," said Rafferty, "that I ought to just move that cabinet upstairs, given it's not in use. Your brother sends all the letters to you, so he has nothing to store in it."

"Not yours to move, though, is it?" said Nigel, not looking back. "It belongs to Reggie."

Rafferty smiled slightly and shook his head.

"Not exactly," he said. "I provided it to him when he moved in, as the new tenant, but he does not own it."

"Then this is your file cabinet?" said Nigel.

"Well, no, I don't own it either, personally. I have custody, I suppose you might say. For all of them."

Nigel turned toward Rafferty and stared. "I think you should explain."

Rafferty grimaced, as though he had said too much. But then, after studying Nigel for a moment, he nodded. "All right," he said. "The others are upstairs. I may as well show you. Top floor."

Then Rafferty turned and headed for the lift.

27

Nigel caught up with Rafferty at the lift and rode with him to the top floor.

The doors opened onto a bare, shining wood floor. To the right, it stretched some hundred feet, but with no office partitions or tables or chairs or anything else in that space—just empty floor, with windows at the far end that looked out over the street.

Immediately to the left was the only office on the floor; a small one. Nigel started in that direction as they exited the lift.

"No," said Rafferty. "This way."

Nigel followed Rafferty to the corner at the far end.

"I'm sure you've heard the theory," said Rafferty as they walked, "that Sherlock Holmes was, in fact, a real person, that the stories and novels chronicled actual events, and that Sir Arthur Conan Doyle was merely Watson's literary agent in getting them published."

"Of course," said Nigel. "I mean, of course I've heard that."

"And you may also have heard the second theory: that although Sherlock Holmes was fictional, Scotland Yard did what it could to encourage belief in that first theory, so that the criminal element then running rampant in London would have reason to pause and reconsider their activities."

"I may have heard that one," said Nigel.

Rafferty nodded. "It is astonishing what people will believe."

Now they had reached the far corner, and there—surprisingly, not apparent at all when they'd stepped off the lift—was a single unmarked door.

Rafferty unlocked and opened the door. He went inside and pulled the chain on an old metal ceiling lamp at the front of the room.

The lamp illuminated—not quite adequately—a very narrow storage room.

One wall was bare. Against the opposite wall was a row of tall nineteenth-century wooden file cabinets. They looked very much like the one in Nigel's office, but much more imposing, lined up in a formation that extended some twelve feet to the back wall.

Nigel stepped into the room. It was like entering a walk-in safe. The air was still, and the cabinets along the wall seemed to deaden the street noise that was so evident in the main room.

"These go back some years," said Rafferty. "Oldest ones first—starting from the late 1930s—and then decade by decade as you work your way back. The last two cabinets are empty— for future work. The third from the end has this year's archives. It includes whatever was stored recently in your office cabinet. It also includes the files accumulated by the wonderful woman we had working here prior to you—and prior to Mr. Ocher, who was just a temp. I believe you actually met Mr. Ocher?"

"Yes," said Nigel. "Especially if by 'met' you mean I discovered his body with his head bashed in."

"Yes," said Rafferty. "Not everyone works out equally well."

"I had no idea the letters went so far back," said Nigel. He began to walk slowly down the row of golden oak cabinets, perusing the date labels in the little metal frames on each.

"Few people do."

There was a cabinet for a range from 1935 to 1936. Another for 1937 to 1938. In 1939, there was apparently an unusually high volume; it had a cabinet all to itself.

And so it went, year by year or groups of years, until near the far wall.

Nigel stopped at the third-to-last cabinet.

"This one's for this year, then?" said Nigel.

"Yes," said Rafferty. "Including copies of the letters currently in progress. With your brother shipping them across the pond every couple of weeks, I can hardly take the chance that they might disappear in transit. So every week or so, I wait until everyone has left the floor, and then I pop down and make copies on the sly of the ones your brother has put on the cart for the outgoing mail. It's a bother, of course, and I'd love to tell your brother to copy them himself, but if I did, I'd be acknowledging that I know he's breaking the lease by sending the letters to you."

Nigel tried the top drawer of the cabinet as Rafferty spoke. It was locked. Nigel immediately took out his key.

"No," said Rafferty.

"Excuse me?"

"Not allowed. These are archives. No one is allowed to view the archives, except under emergency circumstances."

"But my key will work for these cabinets, will it not?"

"Yes."

"Then surely I am allowed to view the contents?"

"Under emergency circumstance only."

"I see," said Nigel. He paused, looking from Rafferty to the cabinet, and considering what to do.

"If there is an emergency, I have authority to allow you to look at specific archives, under my supervision," said Rafferty.

"I see."

"Is there an emergency? If not, I need to be on my way. I have an appointment in the City."

"No," said Nigel. He stepped back from the cabinet. It simply wouldn't do to let Rafferty in on the kidnapping. Not·unless there was absolutely no other way.

And there was probably another way.

"No emergency," said Nigel.

"Shall we go, then?"

"Of course," said Nigel.

They both walked toward the lift. Nigel hoped this meant Rafferty was leaving the building immediately.

But when they reached the lift, Rafferty just kept walking, on past the lift, to his little office.

Damn.

The lift doors opened, and Nigel got in.

"Cheers," said Rafferty, and he went into his office.

Nigel knew he would have to wait. He remained in the lift, allowed the doors to close, and it descended.

28

Nigel exited the lift on the law chambers floor and went directly down the corridor toward his old office again.

He slowed before he quite got there.

The lights were still off, as he had left them. But the door was open now, and he was sure he had left the door closed.

As he walked to the doorway, he caught a whiff of Chanel.

He looked in.

An attractive—but very untidy—figure of a woman stood at the side of the desk, bending toward the old oak cabinet, so completely focused on it that she did not turn as Nigel stepped in.

"Empty, I'll bet," said Nigel.

The woman turned and straightened.

It was indeed Laura, as Nigel had suspected—but looking so unlike herself that he had not been completely sure.

Her red hair was unwashed and darker than usual and it hung limply; she must have intended to tie it back, but then either forgotten or just not had time. She was wearing what Nigel knew was her version of a tracksuit, but it looked as though she had already run the marathon and then slept in it after.

"You look well," said Nigel.

Laura laughed; then she sighed and sat on the edge of the desk.

"Don't lie," she said. "I know how I look. That nice Mr. Hendricks in the lobby stopped me and insisted on ID and I had to show him a pic in an old version of the *Daily Sun* and strike a pose, just to prove I'm me."

"Reggie's fault," said Nigel. "He told Hendricks to be more cautious."

"Reggie told you about what's going on?" she said.

"Only about the missing letters. And Buxton. And that we need to find one to get the other."

"Well, that's all right, then. We can't have the whole world knowing, but I think it's all right that you do." Laura paused for a moment, then said, "I have a legal question. I mean a law question. Sort of."

"Go ahead."

"If there's a will floating around somewhere that's worth pretty much all the money in the world, and it gives it all to someone other than you, and you're afraid it will turn up and cause you to lose what you think is your rightful inheritance, what would you do?"

Nigel thought about it. Under the circumstances, it didn't seem like an entirely theoretical question.

"I don't know," said Nigel after a moment. "Possibly kidnap Lord Robert Buxton, hold him for ransom, and demand a set of documents that I think will include that will, but without naming the will itself, so that no one will suspect me as the kidnapper?"

"Well, yes, that might be one approach," said Laura. "But suppose you are unsuccessful in locating that nasty will that gives all the money to another person instead of you, the rightful and natural heir? What would you do then?"

Nigel gave that one some thought.

"Probably the traditional thing," said Nigel after a moment. "Cleverly murder the person who is named in the new will, so that with him unavailable to receive the inheritance, it will all revert back to me, the rightful heir."

Laura nodded. "Yes," she said. "That occurred to me, as well."

"Or," said Nigel, "for good measure, I might want to both get the will back and permanently dispose of its intended beneficiary."

There was silence for a moment, then Laura said, "You must help me find those bloody letters."

"Will do," said Nigel. "But seems unfair we should do all the work. I'll call Reggie, wake him up."

"You might let him sleep. I'm sure he's still camped out half a block down from my house, watching to make sure I don't get in trouble, and also watching, I presume, Buxton's security team, which is also camped out half a block from my house, but on the other side. I had to leave my house through the kitchen, hop the fence, and then sneak along behind the neighbors shrubbery to the next street to get away from them all."

"Was that wise?"

"I don't know what's wise lately. I do know Reggie regards my fight as his fight"—she sighed—"which is rather sweet. But I'm not about to risk his life for this. It's enough that I made him feel he must help out. All the help I want now is to find the bloody letters. I can do the rest on my own."

Nigel nodded, though he had no intention of complying with the last part of that request.

"Let's get on that, then," said Nigel.

"I thought the letters might be in this cabinet, where you used to keep them. But as you can see, it's empty."

"Yes," said Nigel, "but there are other cabinets, in an odd little room upstairs."

"Are you saying you know where the letters are?"

"Possibly," said Nigel, "or at least copies of them."

"I'll take what I can get," said Laura. "If the kidnappers want to be picky, they can complain about copies after they show me Robert still alive."

"But getting them is a bit of a process. Rafferty protects them like the crown jewels."

"I don't have much time, Nigel."

Nigel nodded. He picked up the phone and rang Hendricks in the lobby.

"Hendricks. Staying awake, are you?"

"Of course, sir. Why wouldn't I be?"

"No reason at all. In fact, every reason to the contrary. Have you noticed whether Mr. Rafferty has left the building yet?"

"Mr. Rafferty?" said Hendricks uncertainly.

"The smallish chap in a gray suit? Comes in pretty much every day, I think. Did you see him leave in the last minute or two?"

"Ah, sir, yes. He did walk out just now. But I might be able to catch him, if my heart stands for it. Do you want me to chase after?"

"No, not at all. But call and let me know when he returns, will you?"

"Yes, sir. Now, there's also a woman named Lois comes in pretty much every day as well, and claims she works for Reggie."

"Yes, that would be Reggie's secretary."

"She's allowed up, then?"

"Yes," said Nigel.

"And do you want me to notify you when she returns, as well?"

"No, not necessary. And Hendricks?"

"Sir?"

"It's almost seven A.M. What I said earlier about challenging folks arriving after hours?"

"Yes, sir?"

"You can stop doing that now. But do let me know if Rafferty returns, will you?"

"As you wish, sir."

Nigel hung up the phone.

"I'll just sneak upstairs and get the letters while Rafferty is out," he said to Laura, "and then I'll be right back."

"I'll sneak with you," said Laura, starting to get up, though just a bit wearily.

"No, sneaking is properly a one-person operation," said Nigel. "But if I'm not back in ten minutes with a boxful of letters, you can lead the search party."

"Fair enough," said Laura. "Anyway, I'm famished. Do you suppose you left any of those chocolate Smarties in the top drawer?"

"I might have done," said Nigel "They'd be several months old by now."

"Perfectly fine," said Laura.

She opened the top drawer and saw a letter opener, a blank scrap of notepaper, a pencil nub—and one last package of chocolate Smarties.

"Ah," she said. "All the essentials."

Nigel left Laura in the little office and took the lift to the top level.

The floor was dead quiet when Nigel got out, as he had hoped.

There were no overhead lights on. Daylight had begun to seep in through blinds on the street windows, and that was enough to show that the broad expanse of polished wood floor was still empty; there was no one to see Nigel about to break and enter, if indeed he would need to do that.

Nigel looked to his left to verify that Rafferty's little office was still closed and dark.

It was.

Nigel turned to his right and walked quickly to the storage room at the far end.

Locked. As expected.

He'd brought a couple of large paper clips along just in case, but he was hoping not to need them. He tried his first hunch—he took out the same key he had been given for the filing cabinet in his office. He tried it in the door.

It turned.

Nigel opened the door, stepped just inside, and instinctively started to reach for a light switch—and then he changed his mind. This was a very minor transgression he was committing, just barely breaking a rule—or what Rafferty had said was a rule—and it was an unreasonable rule at that. Still, the deep shadows felt better at the moment than a bright light.

He went to the back of the narrow storage room, to the cabinet that should have all the more recent letters.

He opened the top drawer and saw one olive green hanging folder, enclosing perhaps a score of letters and their original envelopes. He checked the folder label—yes, these were the right dates.

He tried to peek inside at one of the letters immediately, but the room was too dark. Now he wished he had turned on the lamp.

No matter. He removed the entire folder and its contents; then he bent down to check the lower drawers in the same cabinet to make sure he wasn't missing something. He wasn't.

They were all empty. He had in his hands a folder of the only set of letters for the past month. He declared a minor victory for himself, and stood.

Or almost did.

Something solid struck him on his right temple.

He slumped involuntarily to his knees.

Now, in the narrow room, there was someone trying to force his way between Nigel and the file cabinet; Nigel instinctively tightened his grip on the folder of letters and got enough strength in his legs to push himself up and back, so that now he was standing again, flat against the wall opposite the cabinets.

His assailant—a couple of inches taller and at least sixty pounds heavier than Nigel—shoved with thick arms, pinning Nigel by his collar against that wall.

"I want the letter," said the man.

The voice was obviously American, so cliché American that it almost sounded fake. Nigel had heard an accent very much like this a couple of years ago when he attended an unfortunate West End production of *The Best Little Whorehouse in Texas.*

"Can you be more specific?" gasped Nigel.

Apparently not. The man just muttered—or growled— something in a low tone in response, and he let loose with one arm to grab for the folder in Nigel's hand.

Nigel knew just one self-defense move, from an extension class during a boring summer years ago; it was only applicable when an overconfident assailant made the mistake of grabbing you by the collar—exactly as the American had just done— and with just one arm.

Nigel rotated his own left arm sharply from the elbow, breaking the grip of the assailant's right hand; at the same instant, he let go of the letter folder and thrust his right hand, fingers extended, into the man's throat.

To Nigel's amazement, it worked. At least for a moment. The man gasped and staggered back. Nigel reached down to the floor, grabbed the folder of letters again, and ran.

Out of the storage room and onto the shining, just slightly slick floor. Nigel ran for the far end, hoping there would be emergency stairs. Surely the place was up to code, but they weren't at this end, so they had to be at the other.

As he passed the lift, Nigel saw from the lights that it was in motion. Someone was on the way up. But Nigel knew from the loud footsteps behind him that he couldn't wait. He ran on to the far end, and there in the corner, just past Rafferty's office— which was open now, Nigel realized; what an idiot he had been not to check more closely—was the door to the stairs, thank God.

Nigel opened that door. He managed to take one step in before getting yanked rudely back and thrown on his arse onto the floor, with such force that he slid up against the wall of Rafferty's office.

The American stomped one heavy foot onto Nigel's right arm, pinning it to the floor, and then he began to reach down for the folder.

That was a mistake. The man had not paid attention at all to what was happening at the lift.

Suddenly, he cursed in pain, and his hand dropped the folder and went to the back of his neck instead. He twisted around, and then received another jolt.

Hendricks, standing just a bit unsteadily at the other side of Nigel's assailant, pressed forward with his Taser, his thin white hair in disarray and his face showing absolutely no fear and only a slight uncertainty in what he was doing.

Nigel, still on the floor, kicked the American's legs out from underneath him, and the man fell.

Nigel scrambled to his feet. He reached to take the Taser from Hendricks, who was having some difficulty bending his knees enough to get down and keep the weapon on the American.

"I can do it, sir!" said Hendricks, not giving up his weapon. With Nigel's assistance, he pressed forward again.

"Enough!" cried the man on the floor. "God Almighty, stop!

29

Laura was making quick work of the stairs, despite her lack of sleep; one always had to stay in shape for the occasional half-naked tabloid photo ambush, and these stairs were nothing compared to her frequent sprints up the Covent Garden tube station.

Moments earlier, Mr. Hendricks had rung her on Nigel's phone. "Nigel asked me to shout out if Mr. Rafferty returns," he'd said, "but not for anyone else."

"Yes. And has Mr. Rafferty returned?"

"No, not that I'm aware."

"Oh."

"But there is an American on his way up. It's just my opinion, of course, but I regard him as much scarier than Mr. Rafferty. Rather large fellow."

"With a Texas accent?"

"I'm not sure I would know, miss."

"Do you remember the American show *Dallas?* On the telly?"

"Ah. Quite well. That's exactly how he sounded to me."

There were other possibilities, of course. But this sounded to Laura like the nasty cousin Stillman had warned them about.

"Hendricks, I'm sorry to ask this, but—are you armed?"

"Certainly. Fifty thousand volts, and I completed a full two-hour training course. Shall I bring it with me?"

"Bring what you can."

Laura hadn't bothered with the lift; she knew Hendricks would need it. Instead, she'd borrowed a letter opener from Lois's desk and headed for the stairs.

Now she had four flights done and just one to go. She heard the stairwell door open from the floor above; someone's voice in a quick curse—quite possibly Nigel's—and then the thumps and groans of a bruising struggle.

Now her adrenaline was up. She powered up the final flight three steps at a time.

She yanked the door open and burst onto the floor, with the letter opener in thrusting position.

"No more!" screamed the American. "No more!"

The man was on the floor, his back against the wall, shouting his desperate pleas.

Nigel was standing over him, but most significantly, Hendricks was standing alongside, his well-trained Taser extended, about to administer the treatment again.

Laura stepped forward, so that now she was standing on one side of the American with her letter opener, and Hendricks was standing on the other side with his Taser. Nigel was in the center.

"Enough," said Nigel to Hendricks. "For the moment."

The green file folder containing the letters was on the floor, just by Nigel's feet. Laura reached down and, saying nothing to anyone, picked it up.

She kept it out of sight behind her back as she turned toward Nigel.

"Here," she said, giving him the letter opener. "Stick him if you need to."

Nigel nodded. Then he looked down at the American's feet, and coat pocket, and he saw that the folder was not there.

He looked down at his own feet, and then behind them. The folder was not there.

He looked to his side. The folder wasn't there, either.

And neither was Laura.

Now Nigel heard the lift doors ping, and he turned and shouted in that direction, "Wait!"

But too late. He saw a fleeting glimpse of the green folder in Laura's freckled hand as the lift doors closed, and then the lift was on its way down.

For a moment, Nigel considered chasing after. But he looked down at Hendricks, bravely but unsteadily holding the Taser in the direction of the brawny American, and he knew he couldn't leave.

Besides, Laura would reach the street well before he could, and from there she would be too fast to catch if she didn't want to be caught.

And clearly she didn't.

Nigel could do nothing but mutter under his breath.

"Bloody hell. Reggie won't like this."

30

Laura exited Dorset House and walked quickly down Baker Street until she found a cab.

As she got in, her mobile rang.

"It's a quarter till," said the voice, still muffled, as before.

The voice did not sound American. But neither had the one on the lake. And given what had just happened, she was no longer ruling the Texas heirs out. The muffling could be an attempt to disguise an accent. And it also occurred to her that one of the two American cousins might have engaged an English accomplice to help negotiate with the locals.

"I know what bloody time it is," said Laura. Immediately after she said that, she worried that perhaps she was supposed to be polite with kidnappers, and not let her annoyance show.

And then she rejected that notion. The kidnappers had an agenda and they would pursue that agenda, regardless of whether she was rude to them.

"Do you have the letters?"

"Yes," said Laura. "As a matter of fact, I do still have the letters. Despite your efforts to the contrary."

There was a long pause.

"Explain what you mean," said the voice.

"Your American accomplice just tried to steal them, did he not?" It was still just a guess. She wasn't at all certain.

Dead silence at the other end for a long moment; then the voice said again, "Do you have the letters?"

"I have them. When do I see Robert?"

"Take a cab to Piccadilly Circus. You have twenty minutes."

"Will he be there? When do I see Lord Buxton?"

"If you do as you're told, you will see him alive at noon. If you do not, you will hear of his death. Catch your cab."

Now the line went dead.

Laura caught a cab.

She reached Piccadilly Circus in eighteen minutes, by her watch.

The voice had not been sufficiently specific beyond that, so she waited by the statue of winged Eros in the center plaza.

It was cold, with the wind channeling down from the four intersecting boulevards. But it was also morning rush hour, and the milling crowd of tourists and commuters was as thick as always.

Laura's mobile rang; she picked up.

"Now what?" she said.

"Go to the British Emporium."

"The British—"

"The bloody big souvenir store at the corner. Go to the first cashier and buy something."

"Buy what?"

"Any bloody thing, but large enough for a shopping bag. Do it now. Be out in seven minutes."

Laura walked quickly across the street to the British Emporium. She guessed she might possibly be out of sight of the kidnappers for a moment, but she couldn't think of how to take advantage of that; there was too little time.

She went directly to the cashier station, and she bought the first thing she could find—a large gray plush toy, some sort of British bear, from a bin right in front of the cashier.

She carried it out of the store in a shopping bag.

Her phone rang.

"Show us the letters."

"What?"

"Hold the letters up high."

Laura stretched her arm out and held the folder of letters up high, so that anyone presumably watching from a nearby building could see it."

"Put them in the shopping bag," said the voice.

Laura did so.

"Now you're done with cabs," said the voice. "You're taking the tube next. Too bad if you regard it as beneath your status."

That was an odd remark, and more than a little annoying. "You overestimate me," she said.

"Shut up. Go across to the underground entrance on Haymarket. Buy an all-day pass for all zones at the automated server."

"I have my own monthly," said Laura.

"Good for you. Buy the pass anyway. Then go through the turnstiles on the left, and take the stairs down to the Northern Line, east platform."

"And then where am I going?" I asked Laura. "I'm an excellent traveler, it would help so much if you would just tell me the destination."

But the line went dead.

With her shopping bag in a tight grip, Laura joined the throng moving across Shaftesbury Avenue, past the statue at the center of the circus again, and then to the Piccadilly tube station on Haymarket.

She entered the tube station. She bought a day pass at one of the automated dispensers, as instructed. That took a couple of minutes, as there was a queue in the crowded station, but she managed to get through the turnstile and join the mad rush down the stairs for the Northern Line.

At the juncture between the passageway for the east platform and the west, a musician had set up against the tiled wall with his violin, its case open for contributions; he was playing fairly well, and Laura had been known on occasion to stop and toss in a few pounds, though it was not commonly considered acceptable in the fast-moving commuter rush to actually stop and listen.

In any case, not today. She pushed on down the stairs, at a pace fast enough, she hoped, to prevent anyone from charging up on her unseen from behind, but taking care not to knock over the elderly woman with the cane in front of her. Two thick-shouldered louts who should have known better came charging up the wrong way on the stairs and bumped her in their progress; but she saw them in time and pulled the shopping bag close in front of her.

Now she was on the platform. On a quiet day, at a quiet station, you could walk from one end to the other of the platform tunnel and actually be alone with your thoughts for a moment or two if you wanted, but not so here—not this station, at this hour. The entire length of the platform was shoulder-to-shoulder with commuters who had not been able to squeeze onto the previous train and were waiting for the next.

The tunnel public-address system crackled something about closures on connecting lines and a couple of stops that were no longer in service.

Now there was a single light and a rumbling and a disturbance in the air of the tunnel; a train was arriving. As it pulled in, Laura could see through the windows of the train that it was absolutely standing room only.

She was on the east platform. But was this the train she was to take? The voice hadn't said. Trains for different ultimate destinations arrived every two minutes or so when things were running properly. Was this the one? Was she exactly on time, or could it have been the one before, or the one after?

"Mind the gap," said the recorded announcement from the train. The doors opened. The standing passengers who wanted to be at Piccadilly Circus pushed outward at the same time that the passengers on the platform who wanted to get away from Piccadilly Circus pushed inward. It was the usual thing, and manageable if you knew where you going and had nothing exposed to the crowd that you had to protect while getting there.

But Laura was at a disadvantage, not knowing where she was going. She was caught firmly in a squeeze, she was being pressed on all sides, and suddenly she realized that this ransom delivery was probably not about getting to the destination at all. That's why it didn't matter which train: The delivery was supposed to take place along the way.

Now she was bumped again from the left side. It was all right, though; she still had the bag gripped in her hands. She could still feel the weight of it—and then she looked down.

Yes, she still had the bag and the damned plush toy. But the folder of letters was gone.

She looked around. In front of her, people were pushing onto the train; in back of her, people were rushing into the tunnel for the stairs directly behind her.

Only one person was moving in neither of those directions; adroitly dodging his way through the throng, toward the exit at the far end.

Laura was about to cry out for help and point toward the thief. But from behind her, somewhere in the crowd, someone else cried out first, "Look! That's Laura Rankin! Right there!"

Many people didn't hear or didn't care, but a few did. A woman with two small children getting off the train saw Laura and stepped right up to her with a camera; a couple of others turned just casually to look, and in an instant the pedestrian traffic congealed, even more than it had been, and she was completely boxed in.

No one was cursing or shouting "Move along"; it was a mostly British queue, after all, and there was a polite custom to be observed.

But that couldn't last forever. And Laura had lost sight of the letter thief. "So sorry," she said, edging back from the train as it now departed the station. She smiled and pushed through the platform crowd. "I'm very sorry. Thank you so very much."

And finally she was able to join the throng moving back up the stairs.

She rushed up the stairs, into the main station, and then out onto Haymarket Avenue.

She looked about, though she already knew: She was far too late.

The sky was filled with the flashing display adverts and the lovely buildings that surrounded Piccadilly Circus. The streets were filled with chattering tourists, giddy teenagers, and intent commuters, and Laura Rankin had failed utterly in the one thing that she absolutely had to do.

For a moment she stood there, blinking in the morning sun, and trying to fight back tears.

She hoped this wasn't becoming a habit.

31

The bank employees in the Dorset House lobby who knew Reggie Heath at all knew enough when they saw his face this morning to stay out of his way.

And, in fact, Reggie had never been as angry with anyone as he was right now with himself.

Instinct had told him early on that something was wrong. Instinct had told him to get out of the car and go to Laura's door and demand again to know that everything was all right.

Instead, he had just waited and watched. Waited and watched, as if everything was normal, just because Laura had turned out the lights in the way she always did. Waited and watched, just because the security team was still in place and everything still seemed all right when he returned from the warehouse.

Waited and watched—until suddenly he was jolted awake in the early.morning by a sound that was familiar but out of place. It came from directly outside the door on his side of the car.

He'd lowered the window and looked down, and there was Laura's cat—her indoor cat—at the break of dawn, meowing at his car door.

He had immediately gotten out of the car, gone to Laura's front step, rung the bell, got no answer, and then let himself in with his key. He ran up the stairs, and found the bed still made and Laura's usual windbreaker missing; ran back down the stairs, and found the tea unfinished on the kitchen sink; opened the kitchen side door—and then Robert Buxton's imbecilic security team had come barreling in through the front door.

That standoff—and the ensuing chaos and cacophony of accusations about who was watching whom and why—had lasted about ten minutes before the two more thuggish of Buxton's team finally backed down. They had personalities uncannily similar to that of their employer, but without even Buxton's modest intelligence.

The team leader—the one named Alex, whom Reggie had spoken to before—finally herded the others back out through the front. Alex said something then, not too loudly, about leaving these things to the professionals, and before Reggie could respond to that, the entire team had gotten back in their Range Rover and roared away, out of Laura's quiet little Chelsea nook and onto King's Road.

Then Reggie's mobile had rung. It was Lois. There'd been a bit of a ruckus. Lois was very sorry about it; it had all happened earlier, before she arrived. Apparently, an American had gotten bruised in a discussion with Nigel. And then Laura had run off without a word, and now she'd come back, but she was not happy.

And now Mr. Rafferty was there, and he had said that perhaps it would be good if Reggie dropped in.

Now Reggie was back at Dorset House. He entered the lobby, noticed that Hendricks was not at his guard station, and then took the lift up to his chambers.

When the lift doors opened, Reggie saw Lois standing at

her desk at the other end of the corridor, keeping lookout. She called out when she saw Reggie, and she hurried toward him.

"They're all in the conference room," said Lois. "They just went in."

"Who did?"

"Nigel. Laura. Mr. Hendricks. Two Americans. And Mr. Rafferty. I think it was Mr. Rafferty called the meeting."

"These are my chambers. Rafferty can't call a meeting in my chambers."

"Well," said Lois. "They all went in the conference room anyway."

"To do what?"

"To conference, I think. All the fighting stopped hours ago."

"Is Laura all right?"

"Yes. A little frazzled, I think."

Reggie started toward the conference room.

"Sir?"

"Yes, Lois?"

"Do you still want me to find that thing that Mr. Liu bought in Piccadilly? I've called all around, and I think I've located one."

"Yes, fine, thank you," said Reggie without much thought, and he went on to the conference room.

Reggie opened the conference room door and looked in.

He saw Nigel and Laura seated together at the middle on one side of the oblong table.

Seated at the head of the table—Reggie's usual position—was Rafferty. Next to him was a worried-looking Hendricks.

At the middle on the other side of the table was Stillman, the lawyer from Texas. Next to him was a slightly larger gentleman, highly tanned and sunburned about the nose and neck, but not so much that two red welts on his neck and a bruise on his throat did not stand out considerably.

Laura looked in Reggie's direction as he opened the door. Reggie had never seen her so bedraggled.

He went immediately to her side and sat down next to her—protectively flanking her, with Nigel on the other side—in anticipated opposition to the two Americans across the table.

Clearly, there was some sort of formal conversation already under way.

"Nice of you to join us, Mr. Heath," said Rafferty, as though Reggie were late for a scheduled meeting.

Now Rafferty turned back to address everyone.

"Mr. Stillman has some items to address that I believe concern all of us," said Rafferty.

"Thank you, Mr. Rafferty," said Stillman, just a little grandly, standing as though he were about to address a court.

Reggie found it annoying.

"Just sit down, won't you?" said Reggie. "We can all hear you with no difficulty."

The man shrugged and sat, then grinned his self-confident grin again.

"You're right," he said. "No need to get formal. I'm sure this won't take long. I just want to wrap up a couple of things before Mr. Darby here has to fly back to Houston. I'm not sure all of you have met him, I know some of you have. Mr. Darby is a great-nephew to Mrs. Clemens, and until very recently, he was one of the two beneficiaries of her will. So. Which do you want to do first? The matter of Mrs. Clemens bequest to Sherlock Holmes? Or Mr. Darby's lawsuit for assault and battery and false imprisonment?"

"You're out of your bloody mind," said Nigel. "It's your client who committed the assault and battery."

"Not true, and if it were true, it would be hard to prove. No one from this office saw fit to call the police. The only reason I can imagine for that is you knew you were in the wrong. So I think the relevant thing will be to look at who has the injuries. Now, Mr. Darby here has severe and obvious bruising about the neck and throat. You, on the other hand, have—well, nothing apparent."

"Doesn't matter," said Nigel. "He started it."

"No, I didn't," retorted Darby.

"Yes, you did," said Nigel.

"No, I didn't," repeated the American, with a straight face.

"There, you see?" said Stillman. "You see how that goes? We have one word against another. The only thing we know for sure, the only thing we have witnesses for, is that Mr. Hendricks here zapped my client twice with a Taser."

Hendricks looked quite miserable, and more than a little confused.

"I guess you must have a license for use of that weapon, Mr. Hendricks, because I know that is necessary, and not easy to obtain, on this side of the pond, and Miss Rankin here—I regret dragging you into this, Miss Rankin, and I hope it doesn't mean you won't have dinner with me before I return to the States—"

Laura rolled her eyes.

"Don't even think about it," said Reggie to the American, quite out loud.

Stillman didn't miss a beat.

"—but business is business, and Miss Rankin did, in fact, threaten my client with that very nasty-looking letter-opening device. So I think we can all see where things stand."

All this while, Rafferty had said nothing, just sat there, fixing his eyes on some imaginary point in the middle of the conference table. But now he looked up.

"What is it you want?" he said.

"Good question. That brings me to the second thing. First, understand that it is American law, specifically the laws of the state of Texas, that will determine the disposition of the will of Mrs. Clemens. That is where the will was made, that is where Mrs. Clemens resided at the time, and it doesn't matter that the document itself arrived here in London.

"That said, it would be a shame for all of us to go to a whole lot of time and trouble over this when we know that the end result will be that her bequest will be invalidated. And so I'm here to—"

"No, it won't," said Nigel, interrupting and glaring across at the two Americans.

"Excuse me?" said Stillman.

"I think I understand the offer you are about to make to us," said Nigel. "And I'm not saying we will turn it down. But just as a point of law—in the United States, as here, an individual can bequeath his or her fortune to whom she pleases, subject to the applicable tax codes of the jurisdiction. The law does not care to whom or what the bequest is made. It is quite commonplace, for example, for people to leave their fortunes to their pets. I'm sure you already know this. A singer here in London just recently left tens of millions to Nicholas the cat, along with a provision that her songs be played for the animal nightly, which one might argue was a high price to pay. The point is, so long as the will was properly made and witnessed and the bequestor was of sound mind when she did it, then it will be enforced, if it can be enforced."

"How could she be of sound mind when she willed her fortune to a character from fiction?" said Stilwell. "That act alone will prove she was not of sound mind when she made the change in her will."

"As matter of fact, no, it does not," said Nigel. "The very

existence of the letters that arrive here daily demonstrates that. There are many people of sound mind who do believe Sherlock Holmes to be real. There is, in fact, a society here in London whose very membership requires that you espouse the belief that Holmes was real, Watson was real, and Doyle was merely Watson's literary agent."

"Sherlock Holmes does not exist," said Stillman heatedly. "You can't bequeath something to someone who does not exist! There's no one to receive it!"

"But that doesn't matter in this instance," said Nigel. "Because Mrs. Clemens revised her bequest to name Reggie Heath on behalf of Sherlock Holmes. The court will do what it can to implement the intent of the benefactor. It can go to Reggie Heath, because her will said it can."

Now the larger American stood.

"Not after we tear the damn thing up, it won't! Give us the will!"

"We don't have it any longer," said Laura, rising out of her chair. "And you bloody well know it, you pompous, self-important cattle wankers—"

"Everyone sit down!" shouted Reggie.

Rafferty looked up briefly, furrowed a brow, and then continued staring at a center point on the table.

"If you sold the will to someone else," said Stillman, "you'd damn well better tell us who—"

"Don't be ridiculous," said Reggie, gesturing the two Americans back into their chairs. "Who else would possibly make use of it but the person it is made out to? Anyway, your objective is simply to make sure that it has no impact on the disposition of the inheritance, that no one can make any sort of claim against the substantial fortune of Mrs. Clemens, correct?"

The Americans sat back down.

"Yes," said Stillman.

"Then perhaps there is a solution. We'll need to talk this over among ourselves," said Reggie.

"All right," said Stillman. "We can cool our heels for a few minutes while you talk it over."

Reggie picked up the conference room intercom and buzzed his secretary.

"Lois, the Americans are going to step out of the conference room for a moment. They can sit in the guest chairs at your desk. They are to go nowhere else, and you won't take your eyes off them for a moment, will you?"

"Not for a fraction," said Lois.

The two Americans exited the room.

Rafferty remained seated at the head of the table, looking expectantly at Nigel, Laura, and Reggie. They looked expectantly back.

"What?" said Rafferty.

"By 'ourselves,'" said Laura, pointing subtly at the brothers on either side of her. "I think Reggie meant just us."

"Oh," said Rafferty, clearly disappointed at that. "Right, then."

Rafferty got up and politely exited the room, taking Hendricks with him.

Reggie looked at Nigel as soon as they had all gone.

"What in hell were you doing?" asked Reggie. " I'm not going to claim that inheritance. I'd be an idiot to try."

"I couldn't help it," said Nigel. "I'm sorry. I just didn't like the man's attitude. And I just finished taking the California Bar exam. The bloody stuff was on my mind."

Laura reached across the table and made sure the intercom was off. Then, she whispered, "The point is, why are the Americans demanding a bloody will that must have been among the bloody letters that I already delivered to them?"

Reggie and Nigel hesitated, looked at each other, and then Reggie said, "I think we have to consider the possibility that you didn't deliver it to them."

"You mean it was just a random snatch-and-run, and someone was just trying to steal my bag?"

"No. He means the kidnapping may never have had anything to do with the bequest at all," said Nigel. "Yes, the Americans want the bequest letter to Sherlock Holmes. But do a kidnapping for it in a foreign country and then show up in person with your American passport in broad daylight in a lawyer's chambers and demand it be returned? Who would be that dim-witted?"

For a moment, they all considered that.

"Well," said Laura, "They *are* Americans."

Reggie shook his head. "Bottom line is that if they had the bequest letter, they wouldn't be here asking for it now. They can't be behind the kidnapping."

Laura didn't like that conclusion. But she knew it had to be true. She slumped back in her chair.

"So I gave away the ransom," she said. "And we don't have Robert back. And we still have no idea who took him."

"First things first," said Reggie. "Let's get the Americans off our backs."

Reggie buzzed Lois.

"Send them all back in," said Reggie.

"Right away," said Lois. "And then do you mind if I'm gone for a few minutes after that? I'll just need to pop down to Harrods for a bit."

"That's fine, Lois," said Reggie, though her timing seemed odd.

A short moment later, the two Americans tromped back in. Then Rafferty entered, shut the door behind him, sat down, and again focused on some invisible point at the center of the table.

"Well?" demanded Darby. Stillman gestured for him to remain calm.

"I believe I have a solution," said Reggie. "Nigel and I will need to draw it up first. If you will return tomorrow morning at ten, we can reach an agreement that will completely invalidate the bequest that Mrs. Clemens made to me, or to Sherlock Holmes, either one."

"I want it resolved now," growled Darby.

Stillman put a hand on Darby's shoulder and kept him down.

"That will work," said Stillman.

Everyone stood.

Stillman turned to Laura before exiting. "Miss Rankin, it seems I'll be staying overnight. So my dinner invitation still stands. I'd sure be pleased if you'd consider—"

"Oh, please," said Laura. "Don't make me call Mr. Hendricks and his Taser again."

32

Reggie, Laura, and Nigel came out from the conference room into the external law chambers office and gathered near the secretary's station.

Lois was still out on her shopping errand.

The Americans were gone from the building, at least for the moment.

Rafferty had returned to his top-floor sanctuary. The man seemed annoyed about something, though Reggie couldn't imagine what.

But in any case, there were more important concerns.

There was a clock on the cubicle wall behind Lois's desk; it was a whimsical clock, with cartoon character cows to show the hours and minutes. But it showed the time very clearly even so.

Laura sat in a chair next to Lois's desk and stared at that clock. She was so tired, she could hardly think. All she knew for sure was that time was running out.

"I gave away the ransom," she said. "And we don't have Robert back. And the kidnappers still haven't called. They said they would by noon."

Now Reggie looked at the clock, too. It was nearly half past ten.

"Why noon?" asked Nigel.

"I don't know why. I suppose that they want to spend the remainder of the afternoon at the pub celebrating. Or whatever kidnappers do after they've won."

"We don't even bloody know what they've won," said Reggie. "They have the letters and they have Buxton. But what bloody use do they get out of either one?"

"Why specifically twelve P.M., as opposed to two, or three, or five?" said Nigel. "Certainly if you're a kidnapper you want as much time as possible before anyone takes any action. You can't say 'We'll get back to you next summer,' but surely you would get as many hours as you could."

"Well, it's not noon yet," said Reggie. "There's still . . . hope."

The moment Reggie said this, the minute hand ticked over, and the clock chimed the half hour.

Laura buried her head in her hands.

Everyone just sat silently now, waiting for the next tick.

Then Nigel got up and began to shuffle the newspapers on Lois's desk. "Something must happen at noon," he said. "Maybe it's public knowledge. Isn't there a society section, or a calendar of events, or something here—"

"Wait," said Reggie. "Stop. Go back one page."

"This one?" Nigel flipped back one page in the *Daily Mirror.*

"There," said Reggie, pointing at a small headline with just two paragraphs.

Nigel read it aloud: "'PEDESTRIAN KILLED AT KING'S CROSS IDENTIFIED. The Metropolitan Police traffic division has released the name of the man killed by a lorry in an accident in front of King's Cross station earlier this month. The victim,

Arthur Sandwhistle, twenty-four, is reported to have dashed out in front—' "

"Sandwhistle," said Reggie. "I've heard that name. The translations that were sent to Mr. Liu came from a man named Sandwhistle. Mrs. Winslow told me that just hours before she was killed."

"Odd that it took the Yard weeks to release the name of a routine traffic victim," said Nigel. "I can only think of one or two reasons for doing that."

"You mean that it probably wasn't routine," said Laura, "and they wanted to keep it from the public."

Reggie nodded. "Mrs. Winslow was murdered last night, at an import warehouse where she'd gone to fetch the original document that Sandwhistle sent to Mr. Liu. I saw the bloody thing. It showed that what Mr. Liu had printed out and sent to us— in his letter to Sherlock Holmes—was all exactly correct; he accurately included all the changes Sandwhistle submitted to him, even though the changes themselves were errors. Anyone raised with those rhymes would have known something was wrong, but Mr. Liu wasn't raised with them. And I think that was the whole point. I think that's exactly why the import company contracted with Mrs. Winslow to have the documents outsourced to someone like Mr. Liu."

"Classic indirection," said Nigel. "Import companies are set up as shells to launder money with that tactic—to provide a legitimate cover and make the funds coming in and out difficult to trace."

"In this case," said Reggie, "information laundering."

"Information for what?" asked Laura.

"We need to see the changes," said Nigel. "Do we still have this document that Liu translated?"

Reggie shook his head. "Not unless we can find the original letter he sent to Baker Street. The Yard took the one from the warehouse, as evidence in the murder investigation. I made sure Wembley has it personally, but it could be days before he gets to it. He's too busy protecting the royals from theoretical anarchist attacks and such—"

Reggie stopped.

Laura, Nigel, and Reggie all said nothing for a moment and just looked at one another.

"Dear God," said Laura.

"Hello, everyone!"

They all turned. Lois had arrived. She had both arms wrapped around a large shopping bag.

"You may wonder where I've been," she chirped, full of shopping energy. "Well, I had to go to three different stores, but I finally found it. At Harrod's, wouldn't you know? And it was their last one."

"Found what?" asked Reggie.

"A toy just like the one that Mr. Liu bought in Piccadilly," said Lois. "You asked me to . . ." But now Lois paused. She was staring at something on the filing shelves just adjacent to her office.

"Oh my," she said. "Oh, Mr. Heath, I'm afraid you're going to be very angry with me. I'm very sorry."

"What? What is it, Lois?"

She put the package down on the desk, then turned to the shelf where the incoming instructions from solicitors were filed.

"I know I told you that only two briefs came in from solicitors last week."

"Yes?" said Reggie. He followed her line of sight.

There were three briefs on the shelf.

"I don't know how this could have happened," said Lois as

she picked up the thickest of the three rolled-up documents. "I stopped accepting new ones last week, as you instructed; I don't remember receiving this one at all—but obviously I must have. It fell behind the others, I guess, and I just didn't notice. I'm so sorry. I hope the deadline for it hasn't passed."

"I've never known you to forget a brief, Lois," said Reggie.

Reggie took the rolled-up brief from her. He untied and unrolled the several sheets it contained. The he turned to Laura and Nigel.

"The letters," said Reggie.

"How—"

"I've no idea," said Reggie, separating one sheet from the others. "But these are the letters that arrived last week. The schoolgirl crush in Iowa. The bequest from Texas."

Now Reggie unrolled the single largest sheet.

"And this is the sheet of nursery rhymes that we received from Mr. Liu."

"And those rhymes go with this thing?" said Nigel. He reached into the package that Lois had plunked on her desk, and he held up a large white plastic toy.

"Yes, that's the bloody duck," said Reggie.

"This is what Mr. Liu bought at the British Emporium," said Lois. "Or one just like it."

"I'm sure he thought it would help him prove to Mrs. Winslow that his translation and printout were correct," said Reggie. "But I think it would have shown just the opposite. We'll know as soon as we press the beak."

"Press the beak?" said Laura.

"I think the duck will say one thing," said Reggie, "and Mr. Liu's printout will show something else."

"Okay, press it," said Nigel. "I'll compare it to the document from Mr. Liu."

Laura pressed the beak.

"One, two, buckle my shoe," said the duck.

"Bu that's not what Mr. Liu's document says," said Nigel. "It's 'One, two, unbuckle my shoe.'"

"Well that's just wrong," said Laura. "It's not how the rhyme goes."

"Exactly," said Nigel. "All right, press it again."

Laura pressed the beak again.

"Three, four, shut the door," said the duck.

"That one's correct," said Nigel. "The document is the same as what the duck says. Press it again."

"Five, six, pick up sticks," said the duck.

"The document is wrong again," said Nigel. "It says 'throw down sticks.'"

"The opposite of what it is supposed to say," said Reggie. "Mrs. Winslow said there are errors like that throughout."

"Then it's a bloody code," said Nigel. "And the cipher is based on the errors. During Word War Two, the allies did something very similar with crossword puzzles published in *The Sunday Times*. They put in deliberate errors in the answers, and each incorrect answer conveyed information about the coming invasion in Normandy. This is like that, and there's a reason why we're seeing exact opposites in rhymes that have numbers in them. If the line is the opposite of what it is supposed to be, then the numbers in that line get included in your password, or phone number, or whatever the hell the thing is that is being conveyed. Someone was supposed to go to the souvenir store, buy one of these ducks, and look at the errors in the printout to see the numbers that matter. And if you have any doubt about what the line is supposed to be, all you have to do is press the duck's beak to confirm."

"Someone did buy one," said Reggie. "Mr. Liu bought one, and then he was killed for it."

"We don't have time for all this beak pressing," said Laura. "Let me see the document. I know my rhymes: 'Baa Baa Black Sheep'—says it doesn't have any wool, but that's completely wrong. It has three bags full, so we include the number three. Is that how this works?"

"Exactly," said Nigel.

"All right, then," said Laura after a short moment. "I've circled them all. These are the numbers we get from the lines with obvious errors."

She handed the sheet back to Nigel.

"Seven digits," said Nigel. "Could be a phone number."

Laura, with the plastic duck still in her lap, looked from Nigel to Reggie.

"Well," she said. "What do we do? Do we call it?"

"Let's," said Nigel. He took out his mobile and started to punch in the numbers.

"No, wait," said Reggie.

Nigel stopped, three digits short.

"What?" said Nigel.

"What?" said Laura. "We're finally getting somewhere. And we don't have much time."

"If we ring that number and it is the kidnappers, they'll know that we know that what they wanted all along was just this one document."

"You mean that they'll know we know they wanted a translation sheet for a talking duck?" said Nigel. "That's bloody all we know."

"At this point," said Laura. "Maybe it would be good if they think we do know something. Certainly it will make me feel better."

Reggie considered that.

"All right, then," said Reggie.

Nigel began to punch the numbers in again.

"No, wait," said Reggie.

Nigel stopped, two digits short this time.

"What?" said Nigel

"There was something that happened at the warehouse. Something we were doing—me, Wembley, or his assistant—kept setting the duck off."

"Yes?" said Laura.

"Probably doesn't matter," said Reggie. But then he stood and took the duck out of Laura's lap. He set it on the desk and stared at it.

"Now?" said Nigel.

"No, wait," said Reggie. Nigel, Laura, and Lois all gave Reggie puzzled looks.

"Sorry," said Reggie. "Just bear with me."

Reggie picked up the duck and walked some ten paces down the corridor, to the far corner. He set the duck down, then returned to the desk with everyone else.

"All right," said Reggie. "Now."

Nigel began to punch in numbers again.

"Wait," said Laura.

"Now what?" said Nigel, stopping just short of the final digit.

"When a kidnapper answers—if a kidnapper answers—I do the talking," said Laura. "Agreed?"

Reggie and Nigel both nodded.

"Of course," said Reggie.

"All right, then," said Laura. "Now."

Nigel picked up the phone again and quickly punched in six digits.

Then he paused before the final digit and looked at both Reggie and Laura.

They both nodded.

Nigel punched in the last digit.

Two seconds of silence crawled by. Reggie looked in the direction of the duck.

"It's ringing, " said Nigel. "Once. Twice. Third ring. Now the line's dead."

"Try it again," said Reggie.

Nigel punched in the numbers, and they all waited through the sequence of rings again. Reggie still looked in the duck's direction.

Again, nothing.

Reggie let out a huge sigh of relief.

"What did you think it was going to do," asked Nigel. "Explode?"

Reggie's look back at Nigel and Laura said yes.

"Why would anyone put a bomb in a plastic duck?" asked Lois. "It would be so silly. Might as well put one in your knickers."

Nigel went and got the duck and brought it back to the desk.

"Huh," said Nigel. "I didn't notice these green eyes before. Did you?"

"No," said Laura. "I don't think they were lit before."

"Then the coded number did have an effect," said Reggie.

"Booted it up, like a computer," said Nigel.

"Or armed it," said Reggie.

Nigel placed the toy duck on Lois's desk, as if preparing it for surgery. He took a letter opener from the desk drawer, located a plastic panel on the bottom of the duck, and pried it open.

"It was too light to have an explosive in it," said Nigel. "I mean, not yet at least." He lifted the duck up and peered into the shadowy plastic cavern inside.

"There's enough room for it, though. And it does already have something that normal ducks—I mean, normal plastic ducks—do not have."

Nigel pried farther inside the duck with the letter opener. A thin brown electrical component board, no more than an inch square, dropped out onto the desk.

"I'm no expert on this, but it looks to me like there are two receivers on this chip," said Nigel. "One of them gets the coded signal that we just dialed from a mobile phone. The coded signal prepares something on this chip to happen, in advance. When the time comes, something else has to communicate with the other receiver to make the thing happen in real time."

As Nigel pushed the component back into the duck, Lois tried to peer into it from the other side of the desk.

"Where's the part that makes the duck talk?" she asked.

"There's a little speaker board attached," said Nigel. "That part, I'm sure of. It's just like what you see in those greeting cards that sing happy birthday to you."

As Nigel closed the duck back up, Reggie reached into the inside pocket of his mac and pulled out the greeting card that he'd taken from the warehouse.

"One of these kinds of cards?" said Reggie. "There was a box of these at the warehouse, brought in by Elgar Imports, just like the duck."

Reggie put the card on the desk for everyone to see. It was unopened; it still had a seal on the edges.

"One more test," said Reggie.

"So you think this one will do more than play 'Happy Birthday'?" asked Laura.

"Let's find out," said Reggie, and he prepared to open the card.

"No, wait," said Nigel.

Nigel picked up the duck and carried it over to the same far wall where Reggie had taken it moments before. Then he returned to the desk.

"Better safe than sorry," said Nigel.

Reggie nodded. Then he broke the seal and opened the card.

"Happy Birthday" played from the card.

"Humpty Dumpty took a great fall," said the duck, and it began to waddle toward them.

Reggie closed the card.

"Happy Birthday" stopped. And so did the duck.

Nigel exhaled. "All right, then. Seems to me we armed it by phone with a secret code. And then we activated it by opening a birthday card. I suppose there might be several innocent scenarios where you want that kind of sequence. Right now, I can't think of a single one, but then, I'm no expert."

"Scotland Yard is," said Reggie. "And they already have one of these bloody things. Wembley had his assistant take it from the warehouse for analysis."

"Then they should already know if—"

"They were treating it as just an ordinary crime scene. They probably haven't even gotten to this thing yet."

Nigel stood and put the computer chips in his pocket. "Someone should go to the Yard and give them a nudge."

"Perhaps it would help if we knew whose birthday it is," said Laura. She took the greeting card from Reggie and opened it.

"Happy Birthday" played again as Laura read the printed inscription on the inside of the card. This time, they let the song run all the way through to the end: "Happy birthday dear Lady Ashton-Tate," sang the card. "Happy birthday to you."

"Oh dear God," said Laura. "The Lady Ashton-Tate birthday party. That little bash is today."

"Oh yes," said Lois. "I have it right here in my newspaper:

'Lady Ashton-Tate Birthday Bash to Support Red Squirrels.' The procession starts from her home in Hampstead and goes to Serpentine Lake at Hyde Park, where one of the lesser dukes joins her with his own procession, everyone sings 'Happy Birthday,' and then they all go on a jog around the park to celebrate the lady's efforts on behalf of the endangered red squirrel. It's supposed to happen at noon."

All eyes turned to the clock.

It was quarter of eleven.

Laura hid her head in her hands and said, "Tea at noon, detonation code courtesy of Laura Rankin."

"It's not even eleven yet," said Reggie, trying to sound upbeat. "We've got a solid hour and fifteen minutes before the lady opens her birthday card."

Nigel nodded. "No worries."

Reggie picked up a phone. "I'll call Wembley. He'll get right on the bomb thing, cancel the event, and then I think it's time we let him know about Buxton. I mean, assuming he is still— well, point is, whether or not they've done anything to him—"

"Reggie," said Laura, as plaintive as he had ever heard her. "Please, just call."

Reggie rang the detective inspector.

As they all waited for someone to pick up, Nigel said, "How are they getting the bomb into the event? Security will be everywhere."

"Some, but not so much as you'd think," said Laura. "Most of the focus will be on the Prince of Wales's dinner with foreign dignitaries across town. Our event is just the duke, Lady Ashton-Tate, and assorted celebrities in trainers."

"Yes, but how do they do it? Is someone going to walk in carrying a plastic duck under his arm? And why a duck in the first place? Why not a red squirrel or something?"

"Ducks float?" said Laura.

"Well, yes, but you'd still have to get it onto the lake some-how. Surely it will be cordoned off. So how do they get it in?"

"I've got someone," said Reggie. "No, damn it, bloody hell—just another recording."

"We can't wait," said Laura. "I'll go to Ashton-Tate's estate and see if I can stop the procession from departing. Apparently I wasn't on the invite list, but I know some of these people."

Reggie nodded. "I'll go direct to Hyde Park. If you can't stop the procession from embarking, maybe I can find some-one to turn it back when it arrives. Lois can keep trying Wem-bley's number from here while Nigel goes to the Yard."

Now there was the tiny, innocent sound of Lois's clock chim-ing. They all looked at the clock, and then at one another.

"Good news," said Nigel. "We've still got a full hour."

Laura picked up the plastic duck.

"You're taking it with you?" asked Nigel.

"I work better with a prop."

"What will you tell the procession?"

" 'Beware the damn duck,' I suppose."

33

Reggie drove from Baker Street onto Park Road, intending to turn south onto Gloucester Place, toward Hyde Park. But he paused at the intersection. Just one block north, at Regent's Park, was the duck pond where Laura had met with the kidnappers.

Something about that first meeting still bothered him. It still didn't feel right. And although there was very little time, the road along Regent's Park would be a very short detour.

Reggie took the turn. He drove slowly along the road that paralleled the duck pond. He stared across at the little island where Laura had had her encounter.

There was not much to the strip of land; it really had no more right to be called an island than the pond had to be called the boating lake. The perimeter was lined with trees and shrubs, though, and there was indeed enough cover for someone to hide—temporarily—from the sight of people on the shore.

Buxton's chief of staff had said they had all vantage points covered. And as incompetent as they were, it should have been true. For the entire circumference of the park, there was no structure or foliage that anyone could have hidden behind to get across the Outer Circle road. For the kidnappers to have escaped the boundaries of Regent's Park as they did, Buxton's security team had to have been either blind or fools beyond belief.

Unless one of them was lying: a distinct possibility, which Reggie had not yet ruled out.

But another possibility had occurred to him. If there were sufficient time, there was no question he should check it out.

There was not sufficient time. He knew it.

But he pulled over anyway. He got out of the Jag and walked to the boathouse where Laura had embarked before to meet the kidnappers.

The boathouse was open. There was no queue, which was lucky.

"Can I rent a boat with a motor?" said Reggie to the attendant, though he was pretty sure he knew the answer.

"No, sorry," she said. "You can only rent a rowboat. Or a pedaler."

"Oh," said Reggie. "Didn't know. Someone told me they'd seen an outboard on the pond before."

"The only outboard with access belongs to the Royal Parks Service," said the young woman. "I'm afraid it's not for let. Only park rangers and water district workers can use it."

"Fair enough," said Reggie. And now he had to decide. This would take more time than he had hoped.

"I'll take one that rows, then," he said.

Reggie paid for his boat and waited impatiently, staring out at the little island and checking his watch, as the attendant unlocked the boat from the rope.

Then Reggie got in and rowed as hard as he could.

This was a probably a wild-goose chase. So to speak. But he kept rowing.

Finally he bumped the bow of the boat up against the island mud. He got out into four inches of water and muck and hauled the boat onto the shore after him.

He dropped the boat, straightened up, and looked about.

It had not rained since Laura was there before. Reggie looked down at the mud, silty where she had dragged the boat up, but firmer approaching the shrub line on the shore—and there they were: Laura's footprints, where she had pursued the kidnappers into the trees. He even found one of her shoes.

Reggie followed that path. He pushed through a narrow gap in the bushes and entered a small clearing, roughly forty feet in circumference. It was flanked by trees on all sides, with shrubs and water reeds that would have provided sufficient concealment from anyone watching from the shore.

Reggie began to walk along the circumference of that area. In just a few moments, he reached the point where Laura had pursued someone across the island to the other side. Yes, there were her footprints again—and someone else's, as she had said.

Reggie looked at the prints and could make nothing of them. He had not made a science of this. They were shoe prints. A man's. No, two different men, given the different sizes. Any more information than that would require Wembley's forensics team, and there was no time for that.

But an identity from the prints wasn't what he was looking for.

Reggie stooped down and began to walk slowly along where the foot-high grass and weeds grew up against and between the shrubs.

He broke off a thin branch from a tree and began to prod the ground.

Mud. Mud. More mud.

And then something solid.

Reggie bent down for a closer look. He pushed aside the grass, which parted easily, as if someone had done this before and then pushed it back. He got down on his hands and knees and brushed aside some loose dirt.

And there it was: a rectangular brass plate, roughly twenty inches by thirty, set in a concrete casement. The letters forged in the top of the plate read ROYAL PARKS WATER AND SEWER.

All of it was concealed from the casual observer—or even the halfway interested one—by the dirt and leaves and high grass that had been pushed over it.

And it was the only way Reggie could think of for anyone to have gotten off the island and out of Regent's Park unseen.

Forget the motorboat. That boat, in Reggie's opinion, had been a ruse. It might even have been empty.

What mattered was this sewer cover. Quite possibly the thing had been in place for the past forty or fifty years, untouched. And Reggie knew that if that were the case, he wouldn't be able to dislodge it now, for the first time in ages, without tools. Years of dirt and rust would have locked it in place.

He almost hoped that would be the case.

He got down on the muddy ground, put two fingers though a narrow horizontal opening at the top of the plate, and tried to lift it.

The plate moved. Not much—it had to weigh more than sixty pounds—but it did move.

So someone else had been here, and recently.

Reggie adjusted his position for a better grip and managed to slide the front of the plate forward onto the lip of the concrete.

Now he was able to get one hand on each side. He lifted

again, got the entire plate clear of the concrete casement, and shoved it aside, into the damp grass.

"Bloody hell," muttered Reggie.

He was looking down at the top of a series of iron bars, set in the concrete to serve as steps, leading straight down into a pitch-dark chamber.

He wished he had not been successful in prying the thing loose.

But he had done. He checked his watch. Forty-five minutes remained. And he still couldn't be really certain he was on the right track.

But he had come this far. There was no choice but to follow through. And if his hunch was right, he would get to the location at Hyde Park almost as quickly this way as he would driving in heavy traffic.

He took off his mac, tossed it across a tree branch, and began his descent.

Eight feet, straight down—and then he stepped into a chamber some ten feet in diameter, constructed of very old tan and red brick.

It could have been from the nineteenth century, or maybe the eighteenth—he wasn't sure. But the brick was old, and smooth, from years of water running over the fine edges of the brick, and slime accumulating on its surface.

There were two tunnels, both seven or eight feet high. One went north, the other south. It was an easy choice. The one headed south would lead to Hyde Park.

Unless he had the whole thing totally wrong.

Reggie stooped down at first to make sure he had cleared the tunnel ceiling, then began to slog.

The muck oozed over the tops of his shoes, soaked his socks, and got down in between his toes, and the scent of the place began to assault his senses.

So far, it was just the odor of old water, mud, and slime.

He hoped it would not turn into something worse. But he was almost sure it would.

34

In the refurbished commissary on the fourth floor of Scotland Yard, Nigel sat across a square glass café table from Sergeant Meachem and wondered whether the Yard was having trouble attracting qualified recruits.

Sergeant Meachem was simply dense. There was no other way to describe him.

Well, physically, Nigel would have said Meachem was tall, narrow-shouldered, and the typical age for someone fresh out of the Metropolitan Police training school, in his mid- or late twenties.

Mentally—which was all that mattered—the man was dense.

Nigel had been tracking Meachem down through the corridors at Scotland Yard for the past half hour. Detective Inspector Wembley, according to the desk sergeant, was already out with most of his team on the detail that was protecting the prince's international dinner at Clarence House. Meachem was the contact everyone in the building kept referring Nigel to in Wembley's stead, but Meachem always seemed one step beyond wherever the last person said he was supposed to be.

Nigel followed doggedly, and now he had finally cornered the man, just steps away from the commissary coffee urn.

"I don't think you fully understand what I'm telling you," said Nigel. He held the little computer chip up within inches of Meachem's face, so close that Meachem should have felt obliged to push it away. "I think this is a detonator," said Nigel for at least the third time.

Meachem was apparently not easily provoked. He stirred his coffee before responding.

"And you found it inside a plastic duck," said Meachem, as if that settled the matter.

"Yes," said Nigel. "A plastic duck like the one my brother said you brought from a crime scene at a Docklands warehouse to the analysis lab here at the Yard. Detective Inspector Wembley told you to do that, did he not?"

Nigel was overstepping his bounds in the way he said this, and he knew it, but observing the proprieties was getting him nowhere.

Meachem looked away for a moment, nodded, and then looked directly back at Nigel, his eyes narrowing and lines suddenly appearing in his smooth forehead.

"Yes," said Meachem. "Your brother was at that crime scene. And he intruded himself at an earlier one, as well. Some other people here at the Yard apparently feel that he is entitled to special privileges. Perhaps because of that thing with the Black Cab case a while back. But I, for one, do not see it."

"The duck," said Nigel, holding up the microchip. "Can we get back to this and the duck?"

Meachem's forehead got even more severe.

"I did deliver the plastic duck to the lab, as Detective Inspector Wembley requested that I do, and not because you or your brother have any say in the matter. When the lab has finished its work, they will notify me. But they have not yet done so."

Meachem stood now, and he forced a slight smile, in a falsely apologetic, public-relations sort of way.

"Now I'm afraid I must attend to my other duties. Thank you for your interest. Scotland Yard is always open to input from the public and we thank you for your comments. Please pay for your own coffee on the way out, and bear in mind that you have only a visitor's pass and you are not entitled to the police officer's discount."

Meachem turned on his heel and walked toward the exit from the commissary, heading to the interior corridors of the building.

Nigel was furious at the intransigence, but he restrained himself. With the large plastic visitor's pass hanging from his neck, he stopped at the cashier and paid for his coffee, and considered what to do.

First, he decided, get rid of the visitor's pass. He tucked it inside his shirt as soon as he got into the corridor. Better to be showing no ID, and let someone wonder and ask, than to be advertising that he had no official capacity.

Second: bypass Meachem and go directly to the lab.

Nigel took the stairs down to the second floor. He walked comfortably down the corridor as though he belonged, and he reached the glass door to the lab without being challenged.

But now there was a problem: The entrance to the analysis lab was always locked; it required an identity card key for entry, and Nigel, of course, did not have one.

Nigel stepped back from the door; the only thing to do would be to lurk inconspicuously at the corridor drinking fountain, wait for someone else to enter the lab, and tailgate in— with luck.

Then he paused. Peering through the glass entrance, he had a clear view of the center portion of the lab, all the way back to the far exit. At the moment, no lab workers were visible. But he did not have a clear view of the evidence lockers on the left side of the room, and now, from that side, Meachem had stepped into the line of sight. He had something in his arms.

This was odd. Scotland Yard had its procedures, many of them. Sergeant Meachem had access to the lab, but once evidence was delivered there, he had no business touching it in any way without a lab operative present.

Nigel saw Meachem glance up, as if that very thought had just occurred to him, as well.

Nigel shrank back against the wall, barely out of Meachem's line of sight, waited a moment, and then peeked past the door again to watch.

Apparently satisfied that he was alone, Meachem was now placing the object he had taken from the evidence lockers onto a long steel lab table.

Nigel could see the object clearly now, the white-and-yellow plastic reflecting on the shining metal: It was the duck.

Now Meachem took a large plastic evidence bag from a drawer beneath the table; he put the duck inside, closed the bag, and with one more cautious glance around, he headed for the exit at the far end. Nigel saw the automatically locking door close behind him.

Nigel took a breath. So Meachem was not dense. He was something worse.

Meachem had to be heading for the car park. He wouldn't likely take a chance on going out the front door. He had only a slight head start, and he didn't know that he had been seen, so at least that much was in Nigel's favor.

Nigel turned and ran back down the corridor. He took the

stairs, allowing his visitor's badge to flap back and forth in front of him as he ran.

He reached the ground floor. He looked out through the front window toward the exit gate for the car park. The gate was still closed; no one had just gone through. That meant there was still time.

Nigel ran through the main exit.

A public-minded officer on his way in started to ask if something was wrong as Nigel passed by, but there was no time to explain.

"Been lovely," Nigel shouted back, not pausing. "Don't want to miss tea."

At the front entrance on Broadway, the contemporary cube sign announcing New Scotland Yard was slowly turning. Directly beneath it was the gate for the car park, always kept closed until a car approached with a valid pass.

Nigel ran to the gate; just as he reached it, it began to open, in response to someone punching in from the car park.

Nigel stood in the middle of the exit as the gate arms raised; he pivoted and looked back in the direction of the car park. An older-model Saab was coming directly toward him.

And behind the wheel was Meachem.

Nigel couldn't think of anything else to do. He stood his ground, his feet planted in front of the gate, and thrust his arms forward, palms facing out, as if they would constitute an effective barrier, and shouted, "Stop!"

And then he hoped for the best.

35

Laura's cab was arriving in Hampstead. The driver turned left from Kentish Town into a long road that ran along Primrose Hill. They began to pass large private estates, positioned with spectacular views of Hampstead Heath and the London skyline.

If housing was a reliable indicator of social class, this ride told Laura that she had not yet arrived.

Yes, she had achieved some success on the London stage and in her first movie role. But the small mews home she had managed to afford in Chelsea was nothing compared to what she was passing now in Hampstead, and her position in the London theater community was nothing compared to that of Lady Ashton-Tate.

They had never met personally. But Laura had seen the occasional rumors in print that she, Laura, had been getting the sort of lead ingenue roles that Lady Ashton-Tate was no longer young enough to take.

Laura hoped this would not pose a problem today. She knew that her own eligibility for such roles would soon begin to fade. Perhaps Lady Ashton-Tate was equally philosophical.

Laura checked her watch, anxiously. "How much longer?" she asked the driver.

"We're there now," he said, and Laura looked out the window and saw that, yes, they were. The cab turned into a long driveway that led to an expansive home with green lawns and a white-columned porch in the front.

Lady Ashton-Tate's procession had already assembled. There were four limos in all, and the first was already pulling out of the drive.

"Let me out here," said Laura. She paid the driver, did not wait for change, and ran quickly to the nearest limo, the next to last in line.

Laura rapped on the driver's window. "Stop the car, please."

The car did not quite stop, but it did slow. The passenger window rolled down. It was the lady herself.

"I didn't know you did causes," said Lady Ashton-Tate, sounding only slightly catty as Laura walked briskly alongside to keep up. "Lovely day for a jog, don't you think? I'm sure it will be in the fifties, at least. And I would have been happy to invite you. After all, it isn't really about my birthday at all."

"Oh, I know. And I would have been delighted to attend even so. But this is very important. Please stop the car. Now."

"Oh, I'm very sorry. But as you can see, my car is quite full, and we're running late," said Lady Ashton-Tate. "However, there is another right behind me. There may be a space, and if there is, I'm sure you'll be welcome to it."

This didn't sound promising. Laura considered the possibility that Lady Ashton-Tate had indeed been reading the tabloids.

And before Laura could say anything more, the window rolled up and the limo picked up speed as it moved through the gate.

That had not gone well.

Laura ran up to the next car in line—the last in the procession—and pounded on the passenger window.

The window rolled down.

"Laura—how nice to see you!"

Laura recognized the young woman inside, a makeup artist. Not someone in direct competition, and younger than Laura. With luck, that would make her feel empowered and benevolent.

"You, too, Bernice."

"Why are you jogging alongside our limo?" asked Bernice. "I know you're a bit of a runner, but we're supposed to ride to the park, and then—"

"May I get in?"

"Of course!"

The limo came to a stop, the passenger door opened, and Laura slid in.

Then they continued on.

"I saw you talking to Lady Ashton-Tate just now," said the makeup artist. "I'm so glad you chose to join us instead. After the basic birthday toast, we're all going to jog about the park a bit to celebrate red squirrels, and if we see any of the big brutish American gray ones that are taking over just everywhere, I think we're allowed to kick them."

"Do we have a way of communicating with the lead car?" asked Laura.

"I think so," said the makeup artist. "Say, why do you have a plastic duck in your lap?"

"It's a long story," said Laura. She pressed the intercom to speak with the driver. "Can we speak with the lead car?"

The driver held up a mobile phone.

"I have this, ma'am."

"Call them, please, and tell them to stop the procession."

"I'm sorry. Say again?"

"Tell them to stop the procession."

The driver glanced back at Laura. She gave a look in return that made it clear she wasn't joking.

Now the driver made a call on the mobile and exchanged a few words with someone at the other end. Then he turned back to Laura.

"Sorry, I'm afraid we can't stop. But not to worry, we'll be at our destination in just a bit, if you forgot to powder up."

"Just let me speak with the lead car," said Laura brusquely. "Right now."

The driver hesitated just briefly; then he passed the phone to Laura through the partition.

"You must stop the procession," said Laura immediately into the phone. "You must cancel the event and disperse any crowd that has gathered."

It took a moment, and then an official-sounding male voice finally responded.

"Who is this, please?"

"Laura Rankin."

"And which party are you with?"

"It doesn't matter," said Laura. "You must stop the procession. There is a bomb."

"Making a bomb threat is a very serious offense, miss," said the man.

"I am not making a threat. I am telling you what is about to happen." She hesitated for just a moment. "Probably. I think. Let me speak to the person in charge."

"That would be me, miss. Sergeant Tooley, Scotland Yard."

THE BAKER STREET TRANSLATION

"You are in charge of this specific detail, Sergeant. But Detective Inspector Wembley is in charge of the current royal events. Call the Yard, tell him what I told you, and tell him who said it. And tell him Nigel Heath should be there at the Yard at this very moment. He has all the details. He will confirm what I'm telling you."

"One moment," said the sergeant.

There was a pause of almost three minutes. Laura looked through the window. The procession was moving slowly, but it was already in sight of the Lancaster Gate at Hyde Park. Laura guessed they had less than five minutes.

But now, mercifully, there was someone new at the other end of the line.

"Detective Inspector Wembley is on site at Clarence House for the prince's dinner," said Sergeant Tooley. "But I have Sergeant Meachem on the line at Scotland Yard. Would you like to talk with him?"

"Yes, let's."

Laura waited for Meachem to come on the line. Looking through the window, she could see the glistening frost on the trees on the perimeter of Hyde Park. A beautiful winter morning; no snow, just crisp, perfect for a jog. And they were getting close. They were almost there.

"Miss Rankin, this is Sergeant Meachem. How may I help you?"

"Sergeant, you must stop the procession. You must cancel the event and disperse any crowd that has gathered. There is a bomb, and it is set to go off the moment the birthday festivities begin."

"Making a bomb threat is a very serious—"

"Sergeant, I am not making a threat, I am telling you what I know!"

"I see. Can you help us out just a bit more, then? We have security completely surrounding the park. So just how is this bomb being delivered?"

"It's in a duck. Like the one I have here in my lap. I could show it to you, but that will be too late."

"If you have a plastic duck in your lap that you believe contains a bomb, Miss Rankin, may I suggest that you discard it?"

"The bomb is not in my duck, Sergeant; it's in another duck, just like the one I have, at the event."

"I see. And why would anyone choose to put a bomb in a duck?"

"I don't know, Sergeant. Because it would go unnoticed among all the real ducks in the park? Because it floats?"

"Well, there's where your theory goes wrong, miss. The event is not on the lake. It's in the meadow. So how would that work, exactly?"

"Sergeant Meachem, the lake and the meadow are right next to each other, are they not?"

"Don't know, miss. I'll have to check on that."

"Sergeant, please page Nigel Heath. He should be in your building at this very moment. He will confirm what I am telling you."

There was a short pause, and then: "Oh, yes," said Sergeant Meachem. "Nigel Heath is in the building. We have him in custody at this very moment."

"In custody—"

"Thank you for your interest in Scotland Yard, Miss Rankin. We do appreciate and encourage comments from the general public. And have a nice day."

And now the line went dead.

The limo driver took the phone back and switched off the intercom.

And then he turned his attention—as did Laura—back to the road.

The procession was coming to a stop.

They were in Hyde Park.

36

Reggie had no good idea of the time, and it was beginning to worry him. It might have been ten minutes since his initial descent; it might have been twenty. If it was thirty, then he had made a bad choice, and all hell would soon be breaking out above him, with him slogging like an oblivious fool below. The thought of this was making his chest tighten, much more so than just the claustrophobia induced by the tunnel.

It was the type of tunnel euphemistically referred to as "mixed-use." Reggie knew that now from the stench. It was a storm drain for water, yes, but it was also a sewer.

There was not enough light to see his watch; he should have bought one of those with the damn fluorescent dials.

He had continued straight on from the first chamber and had not yet encountered another that was equally wide. Three times he had reached junction points, at which a small overhead cover allowed the most minimal light, and he could see tunnels leading off to either side. But two of those tunnels had been covered by grates, and the third was so much smaller than the one he was in that he had decided—or at least hoped—that it could not possibly be a valid choice, that it was just some sort of ancillary dead end for maintenance.

Aside from those brief illuminations at the intersections, he'd been working forward in pitch-black darkness. To maintain his balance, he kept one hand in contact with the smooth brick wall, which was slimy from what Reggie presumed was the congealed accumulation of hundreds of years of damp and evaporated filth.

Now he heard something. A rumbling overhead. He wiped his hand on his coat and then touched the sweating brick wall again. It was faint, but it was there. Just the slightest vibration made it down this far, but it was detectable.

There was no mistaking it. It could only be one thing—the tube. A subway train was passing overhead.

It had to be the Northern Line, heading into Baker Street station—no other line could possibly be within the distance Reggie had trudged.

So that meant he had come at least a half mile due south from where he had entered at Regent's Park. It meant he was heading in the right general direction—toward Hyde Park.

Surely, then, even if the suspicion that had formed in his mind was incorrect—that the sewer system was being used by the bomber to get past security and into Hyde Park—at least it would still get Reggie there.

He slogged on.

And with luck, there would be steps leading to a grate that would not be locked, and he would be able to climb out to dry ground, and would not end up slogging all the way down to the outfall at the Thames, and be trapped and drowned when the afternoon tide came in.

What bloody time was it? Would he be too late?

Had Laura been able to stop the procession?

Or had she been caught up in it—trapped in the motorcade? That possibility hadn't even occurred to him before.

He never should have let her go on that errand. He had completely and utterly failed.

He slogged on.

If he had done what he properly should have done when the translator first came to him, perhaps things wouldn't have come to this. The translator might not have been murdered. The bomb plot might have been foiled. Laura would not be in danger.

And if he had done what he properly should have done when Laura first came to him with her Buxton problem, things might not have come to this. Buxton might still be alive— which he probably no longer was. The bomb plot might have been foiled.

And Laura would not be in danger.

He tried to slog on. The nasty slurry on the floor was getting more watery, but it was getting deeper as well, almost to his knees now. He began to slosh forward faster, not bothering to steady himself against the wall any longer, but with arms outstretched ahead of him in the dark.

Surely he was running out of time. Had Nigel reached Wembley at Scotland Yard? Had Laura managed to stop the procession, and were they all back at Hampstead having tea? God, he hoped so, because if it was up to Reggie this time, all was lost.

And then, suddenly, though it must have been there all along, he saw it.

Light. It almost made him laugh to think of it that way, but there it was—light. Light at the end of the tunnel.

Or at least somewhere in the tunnel.

He rushed forward, almost giddy. There was some sort of chamber ahead, like the one where he had begun, but better lit.

Within fifty yards of that opening, Reggie slipped. He fell forward.

He managed to get one arm down in time to catch himself; that arm was now up to the elbow in the watery filth; he thrust his other arm into it as well and pushed back off the floor before his face become completely immersed. He staggered back up to his feet.

Only a few more yards. He was almost there. He could see a gleaming yellow lamp swaying slightly back and forth, pointing in his direction. It was blinding, it was so bright. Reggie pushed forward.

And then, at the very edge of the raised chamber, he fell again.

But this time, he didn't get his arms down. This time, he went face-first into the vile river.

And then—his head submerged, his arms slipping on the smooth tunnel floor as he tried to push himself up—Reggie felt someone grab the back of his collar and pull.

"Bloody tourist!" said a man's voice.

Reggie got both hands on the raised chamber floor now, pushed, and with that and the assist on his collar, he managed to stand.

Reggie shook the filth from his hands and stepped forward onto the semidry floor. Then he tried to wipe the sewer water from his eyes and focus. He gestured for his rescuer to lower the industrial-strength electric lantern that was shining in his face.

The man lowered the light slightly, and now Reggie got a look. He saw a man in knee-high rubber waders and a pale green uniform, with the logo of the Royal Parks Service on the shoulder. The man didn't introduce himself, but the name Aspic was sewn in red onto his shirt pocket.

"You're going to need more shots than you can even count. More gamma globulin than the Health Service even keeps in stock," said Aspic. "You've no idea. Why anyone thinks it a lark to come take a stroll in a sewer is beyond me. It's not a recreation area. But you'll wish you hadn't. Bloody sewer tourer."

"I'm no—what did you call me?"

Reggie took a moment to assess his benefactor. Aspic was about Reggie's height, of thick build, probably mid-fifties. White skin, pale even by London standards. A working-class accent much like Reggie's own before Reggie had gone to university, but with a bit of an affectation.

He wore a uniform that Reggie had seen frequently on Royal Parks workers; it wasn't a new uniform, and it fit as though he had been using it for a very long time. He carried the lantern as though he had done so for years.

"Sewer tourer," said Aspic. "You're not the first I've found. There've been others. You think just because it's not easy to get into the sewer, and unpleasant once you do, that it makes you an explorer. It doesn't. And you can call it an underground river, you can claim you're exploring the hidden Westbourne River, or Tyburn, or whatever you want—but you're not. You're just a slogger about in turds and pee. You're a sewer tourer."

"Believe me," said Reggie. "I would not be here if I didn't have to be."

The uniformed man regarded Reggie suspiciously.

"Look at me," said Reggie. "Would I wear a suit like this into a sewer voluntarily? Would I have worn these shoes?"

The man nodded.

"All right," he said. "I see your point. A chalk-stripe suit. That does make you a bit of a toff. I'll give you that."

"Thank you," said Reggie.

"What are you doing here, then?"

"I must get to Hyde Park immediately," said Reggie.

Aspic considered that. "When people say 'take the underground,'" he said, "they usually mean the tube—not the sewer."

"In minutes," said Reggie, "I believe there will be an explosion at an assembly in Hyde Park that will kill dozens of people. If my guess is correct, it will come from down here. If my guess is wrong, it will come from somewhere above. Either way, I must get there immediately."

The park worker's face was hard to read as Reggie said this; Reggie couldn't see him clearly. But the man's posture stiffened.

"Sounds unlikely to me," he said to Reggie. "Just who are you?"

"Reggie Heath, QC, Baker Street Chambers," said Reggie, hoping it would sound impressive enough to enlist cooperation.

Aspic aimed the lantern at Reggie again and studied his face.

"All right," said Aspic after a moment. "I'll take you there."

He took the lantern off Reggie for a moment and scanned it quickly around the little chamber they were standing in. There were three tunnels, not counting the one Reggie had come from. The one in the center looked much like a continuation of the one he had been in. The ones on each side were slightly narrower, but still high enough that Reggie would have to stoop only slightly, and they were much drier.

"You can follow me," said the man, illuminating the tunnel

on his left. "I'll warrant you would have gone the wrong way if I hadn't come along. No one would have seen you again until they found you drowned and floating like a chalk-striped turd in the Thames."

37

At Scotland Yard, Nigel was in the interrogation room re-served for only the most frightening terrorist suspects.

There were not just one, but two uniformed bobbies stand-ing guard outside the locked door.

There were not just one, but two separate wall-length one-way windows, from which representatives from various agencies, if any of them were available, which they were not, could look in on the proceedings.

And Nigel had not just one, but three interrogators—a plainclothes detective named Pierce, in his late fifties, a woman from the forensics lab, fortyish, named O'Shea, and Sergeant Meachem himself.

Amazingly, when Nigel had blocked Sergeant Meachem's car at the gate and accused the officer of concealing a bomb detonator in a plastic duck, no one had taken his word for it.

Possibly, Nigel acknowledged to himself, this was the fore-seeable result—but he just hadn't been able to think of what else to do.

The duck itself was now resting in the center of the table.

"Now then," said Pierce. "Let me be sure I understand. You

are saying that Sergeant Meachem here was attempting to drive past the Scotland Yard security gate with a bombing device in the boot of his car, concealed in the body cavity of a plastic duck. This duck we have here on the table in front of us."

"Yes, but not the explosive itself," said Nigel. "Just a detonator."

"Yes, as I said," said detective Pierce, just a tad annoyed. "A bombing device."

"Correct," said Nigel as agreeably as he could.

"You may not be aware," continued Pierce, "that Sergeant Meachem graduated third in his class last year in 'Detection and Handling of Explosive Devices.'"

"I was not aware," said Nigel. He checked his watch. Time was running out, but it was a close call as to whether saying so would move things along or slow them down.

"If he had not," continued Pierce, "I would never have saw fit to recommend my wife's nephew for such a position in assisting Inspector Wembley."

"Understandable," said Nigel.

"Well, then," said Pierce, and he sat back with his hands folded, as if he had settled the matter. Then he leaned forward and added, "You do understand that interfering with a Metropolitan police officer in the performance of his duties is a felony?"

"Sergeant Meachem wasn't performing his duties," said Nigel. "He was smuggling evidence in a murder investigation— including a detonation device intended for use at an event that takes place, as I've been trying to tell you, within the hour. Time is running out."

"Well now, if there is a detonation device, as you claim, and if it is right here in this duck, as you claim, then there's not so much urgency now, is there?" said Meachem. "We already have it in our possession."

"There are other ducks like this one," said Nigel. "I don't know how many, but I believe each of these toys brought into the country and assembled by Elgar Imports is a potential bomb—containing a microchip for detonation and lacking only the explosive and the action of a person who knows the code to set it off."

"Total rubbish," said Meachem.

Now O'Shea, the forensics examiner, leaned forward and put her hands on the duck.

"Let's just have a look for this microchip, then, shall we?" she said.

"Fine by me," said Meachem. "Let's."

Nigel breathed a sigh of relief. Now they would get somewhere.

The woman carefully touched the toy all around the edges.

"So. We appear to have a plastic toy duck. Or possibly goose. Roughly fifty centimeters long and twenty wide. White plastic body. Yellow plastic beak." She picked it up and set it down. "Weighing approximately twenty ounces."

"Check the compartment underneath," said Nigel.

She gave Nigel a look that told him to stop giving instructions. She proceeded to check the battery compartment.

"We have a battery compartment," she said, "approximately four centimeters by six, containing"—she peered inside—"two double A batteries."

"The other compartment," said Nigel. "Right next to it. There. There's no tab on it, but you can pry it loose."

Nigel received another one of those looks, but the forensic examiner proceeded to pry open the second compartment.

"A second compartment," she said. "Approximately two centimeters by three. Containing"—she peered inside—"nothing."

"Are you sure?" said Nigel to O'Shea.

She held the duck up, underside out, for Nigel and all to see. Empty.

Meachem and his uncle by marriage both gave Nigel a smug look.

"A felony," said Meachem, with great satisfaction. "Interfering with a police officer in the performance of his duty is a felony."

For a moment, Nigel could say nothing.

He looked up at the clock. Ten minutes remained before the birthday celebration was scheduled to commence at Hyde Park.

Nigel glared across at Meachem.

"He could have put it in his coat. Or his pants pocket. He had just enough time."

"This is completely unnecessary and more than a little insulting," said Meachem.

Nigel looked for help to the forensics examiner.

"Coat, please," she said to Meachem.

Meachem sighed, as if greatly put out. Then he stood and removed his coat. He handed it to O'Shea.

She checked the pockets. All empty.

She pointed at Meachem's pants.

Meachem, without further prompting, began to undo his belt buckle.

"No, no, please," said O'Shea. "Just pockets inside out. Please."

Meachem did as he was told, showing the cheap white inside linings of his pockets.

All empty.

"A felony," said Meachem's uncle by marriage.

Five minutes remained.

This was getting extremely problematic. Meachem had to have the chip on him; Nigel had kept him in sight except for the briefest moment, and there'd been no place where he could have discarded it in the car park without it immediately being found in a search, and they had, in fact, done a search. The Yard was nothing if not thorough.

It would be found. It would have to be. But it would be too late.

Then, suddenly, Nigel realized the obvious.

"May I make a call?"

"You are allowed two calls from the public phone before we take you to your holding cell," said Meachem with something of a smirk.

"Won't be necessary," said Nigel. "Just one call—right now—from my mobile."

Meachem looked suspiciously at Nigel.

"If it will wrap this up, go right ahead," said Pierce.

Nigel took out his mobile and quickly punched in the coded number that they had identified at Baker Street.

From the look on Meachem's face, Nigel could see that the sergeant realized now what was up and was about to object—but too late.

"Humpty Dumpty sat on a wall," said a plastic duck's voice.

But it wasn't coming from the duck.

Pierce looked at Meachem.

"Did you say something?"

Panic began to register on Meachem's face.

"Pardon me," said Meachem, and he shifted uncomfortably in his seat.

Nigel dialed the number again.

"Humpty Dumpty sat on a wall."

Now everyone in the room looked in the general direction of Meachem's stomach.

Nigel dialed again.

Meachem leaped up and bolted for the door.

38

Reggie stooped down to clear the six-foot ceiling and followed the Royal Parks Service worker into the tunnel.

Aspic moved quickly, as if on a mission. He shone the lantern ahead of them as he went, but never with a pause to actually look about, just charging straight ahead, and Reggie, not being so familiar with the tunnel, had to scramble to keep up.

After some five minutes, Reggie's shoulders and the back of his neck were beginning to cramp up. He tried to stretch them out, and he stumbled in the process; when he stood back up, he forgot the ceiling height for a moment and slammed the top of his head into the hard brick above.

Now he was so far behind that the light vanished for a moment. But then the worker came back.

"Get up! Come on! We're almost there! Fifty yards will do it."

Reggie didn't see how that could be; he could see nothing on ahead of the lantern's beam. But he pushed on.

And then Aspic and his lantern halted at what looked like a dead end.

But it wasn't. Reggie caught up and saw Aspic unlatch a solid-steel gate that had been blocking that end of the tunnel.

"It diverts the flow," said Aspic as he pushed on the rusty iron latch. "Not many know about this one. There are tunnels under London that no one but me has seen in a hundred years. This one's a shortcut. You're just lucky it was me that found you, lad."

He pushed open the gate, and suddenly there was a rush of fresh air.

It brought with it a whiff of vanilla. Reggie tried to remember where he had encountered something similar recently.

He stepped through the opening. He and the Royal Parks worker were in yet another small chamber of intersecting tunnels.

The worker seemed to be having trouble getting the lantern focused on their next turn.

"Ah, here it is," he said, motioning Reggie forward. "You first; I'll just fix the light, and I'll be right behind you."

Reggie wasn't sure he liked that plan of action, but he took a step forward in the dark.

And then suddenly he remembered where he had noticed that scent of vanilla before, but it was too late—he had stepped forward onto nothing.

His left leg went down first; he grabbed with both arms for the floor of the tunnel; but his right knee and leg collapsed into the hole now, as well; the surface of the floor was just too slick, and he could not hold on.

Reggie dropped into the hole and down.

He slid. It wasn't a free fall; he realized after perhaps a second that he was on a slope.

And then it was over. He landed.

It was a hard surface; brick, like the floor of what he'd already been on, but with no mud or muck to cushion the blow. He landed on his ass more than his legs, and the impact sent a momentary shiver up his spine.

He got his hands on the floor and gathered his legs beneath him. Perhaps nothing broken. He tried to stand.

Yes, thank God. He could. He began to straighten up.

"Careful," said a voice. "Don't step forward. There's a damn bloody ledge. I almost went over it myself."

Reggie knew that voice. It was too dark to see him, but he knew the voice: It was Buxton's.

"Where are we?" asked Reggie.

"Heath? That's you?"

"Bloody hell, yes."

There was a long pause, during which, Reggie presumed, Buxton was trying to figure out just why Reggie was there.

"We'd given you up for dead," said Reggie. "Or at least I had. And please don't say it was nice of me to drop in."

"Wouldn't dream of it," said Buxton. "But I can't say I'm not glad for the company."

Reggie could hear water flowing somewhere; he hoped it was water, but it might not be, given the acrid stench in this chamber.

And he thought he could hear something else, above the ceiling and perhaps a bit to the south. The muted sound of traffic.

But now there was a clang of metal from somewhere in the chamber.

"He's going to appear over there," said Buxton, pointing at some area in the darkness across from them.

And then Aspic did indeed appear. He was still in waders and his green uniform. He now had a large leather rucksack slung over one shoulder.

Aspic held his electric lantern aloft, and for the first time Reggie got a look at the chamber they were in. It was broader and higher than the others he had been through—eight feet high, and there was a distance of at least ten feet from the ledge where Reggie and Buxton stood to the one where Aspic stood now. Behind Aspic was a set of steps, straight up, which Reggie guessed had to lead to the surface—or at least to another chamber higher up.

"Impressive, isn't it?" said Aspic. "The effort they put into the brickwork a hundred years ago. Built to last. Build to withstand the occasional flood of London rainwater and the continual flood of detritus from the city's inhabitants. Maybe not built to withstand six pounds of C4 explosive, though. We shall see. Or you will, at least. I intend to be aboveground."

Aspic put down the rucksack.

"This chamber and the large tunnels you see over there are what we call 'mixed use,'" he continued. "Some of that use is for water, storm water, water that goes into the lakes and out of them. The other use, your nose can tell you. There are connecting tunnels for each use."

Aspic took an object out of the rucksack as he spoke.

"One of those water tunnels is right up there," he continued, pointing at the ceiling above the steps. "It carries water into the eastern end of Serpentine Lake, which is directly above where you are now standing. It's the lowest point in Hyde Park, the quickest point of access for someone who knows the tunnels, like me. And it's also the place where royals are most fond of having their little public picnics."

Aspic unwrapped the object, and Reggie recognized it immediately: a white-and-yellow plastic duck.

Aspic picked up the toy and opened the bottom panel with a screwdriver.

Then he reached into his rucksack and brought out several small slabs of gray-white material that looked rather like Play-Doh. He began to pack them into the duck's compartment.

"Why are you doing this?" asked Reggie.

Aspic now screwed the bottom panel back into place.

"Eighteen years," said Aspic, kneeling by the toy duck and inspecting his work. "Eighteen years, starting from when I was just a lad. But I did my job for eighteen years—keeping these tunnels clean, slogging through the stench when it backed up. You can never get the smell out, you know; you put on slickers before you climb down the steps, you put on a mask for the fumes, when it gets really bad, but it still gets into your skin somehow, and when you go back up to life aboveground, you can never really get it out. You try to cover it up with vanilla, but you know it's still there."

"Eighteen years?" said Buxton. "Then you're just two years from your pension. Why mess it up now?"

Aspic stopped what he was doing and shot back a glare. He put the duck down and stood.

"Eighteen years," he said, "of cleaning up royal shit, and then the Royal Parks Service let's me go."

"Oops," said Buxton under his breath.

"Me and my partner were working the Thames outfall during a storm, trying to clear out the debris before the tide came in. We were almost done. It was his turn to go under and mine to stay above and stand guard at the manhole cover. We were outside a pub. I was thirsty. I put cones all around the cover and made sure it was unlocked, and then I popped inside for a brew. Not strictly according to regulation procedures, but we'd both done it. We'd both done that, many times before."

Now Aspic knelt down to do something with the duck again. He didn't look up as he spoke.

"Couple hours later, I wonder why my partner hasn't come in to join me. I'm ready to buy him a pint, and I come out— and a bloody lorry has ignored the cones, knocked them all over, and parked there anyway. It's parked on the manhole cover. Not just over it, but it's rear wheel actually on it, holding it down with all the weight of the vehicle. I run back in the pub, I find the owner of that bloody delivery truck, and I drag him out by his ear to move the thing. But it's too late. The tide was in. Someone had locked the escape gate on the other tunnel—we didn't know—and my mate couldn't get out through the tunnel where we'd come in. The Thames came in, and he drowned."

Now Aspic stood again, the duck in his hands.

"The Royal Parks Service fired me. I disputed the firing in court. I won a settlement. I never went back to work for them—no way I would—but I kept my uniform and I kept my memory of all the stink hidden beneath the royal palace."

Aspic set the duck on a shelf behind him now and started digging into his pack for something else. Reggie saw him take out two paper items and place them in a small canvas bag.

"That was twenty years ago," Aspic continued. "I swore I would make the royals pay for what happened to me. I didn't go to university like you, Heath. And I sure as hell wasn't born into money, as you were, Lord Buxton. But I learned. I started my own import business. I learned how to make connections on the Internet. Set up my antiroyals Web site. Got a young police officer to join as a way of expressing his family rebellion. Added a lazy techno-geek who thinks that if he can be an anarchist with money, that will get him girls. Hired a limo chauffeur who's driven just one too many celebrity toffs. I networked. Made friends, influenced people, you know? Set up a perfect system for keeping everything under the radar, and it was all running smoothly—until I get a subcontractor who thinks every little thing has to be perfect, and a freelancer who comes all the way from China on a point of honor. What are you going to do with people like that? Anyway, those were just bumps in the road. Now I'm ready."

"You know, I sympathize with your cause entirely," said Buxton. "And I've been thinking for some time now that its time to run an exposé on the Queen Mum."

Aspic just shook his head and continued what he was doing.

Reggie glanced over at Buxton and said, "Might be best not to mention the queen at all."

"Well, why don't you say something, then? You're the bloody barrister. Argue us out of this."

Reggie nodded, thought about it for a moment, and then turned to Aspic.

"You know, these things never really accomplish what you hope. Maybe there's a better way. My guess is, your little bomb will just end up missing the royals entirely and you'll blow up the serving staff instead."

"You think so?" said Aspic. "I'll let you assist, then."

Now Aspic threw the small canvas bag across from his ledge to theirs.

It landed at Reggie's feet. He picked it up.

Inside were two birthday greeting cards—just like the one Reggie had tested back at chambers.

"Share, boys," said Aspic. "You each get one."

Buxton hesitated, then took one card from the bag. Reggie kept the other.

"Now then," said Aspic. "Just how much do you love the royals? Are you ready to die for one? Unknown, out of sight, below ground, not being certain at all whether your act will even accomplish anything?"

"You mean that in just a rhetorical way," said Buxton. "Right?"

"You each have a card exactly like the cards the birthday guests will have when they assemble upstairs by the lake. As soon as someone opens one of the cards—any of them, one of yours or one of theirs—all the C4 explosive that I just now placed in this duck will explode."

"I'm not sure what you mean," said Buxton.

"I think your friend gets it. He and his people have been working on it long enough. Mr. Heath, explain it to Lord Buxton, will you?"

Reggie looked at Buxton and said quietly, "The bomb is in the duck. The wireless detonator is in the card. He's inviting us to set it off now, before the royal party arrives, thereby possibly saving their lives."

"If we do that, we die," said Buxton.

"Exactly," said Aspic, calling across the ledge. "You die now, or the royals die later. You choose."

Buxton thought about it, made up his mind, and then acted quickly. He threw his card down.

"God save the queen," said Buxton. "But it's not my job."

Reggie was still holding on to his own card. He glared across at Aspic.

And then Aspic's mobile phone rang. The sound of it made all three men jump.

Aspic turned it on speaker.

"They will arrive in five minutes," said a conspirator's voice over the phone.

"Very good," said Aspic, and he turned toward the steps.

Then his phone crackled again.

"One thing," said the voice, still on the speaker.

"Yes?"

"There is an addition to the procession. This Laura Rankin person. The actress. Do we consider her a bonus?"

Aspic paused to consider it, and at the same moment, there was a scream—from Buxton.

"No! Don't!"

But Buxton wasn't screaming at Aspic. Or at the man on the phone. He was screaming at Reggie.

But Reggie paid no attention. He opened his card.

Buxton cringed against the slick wall.

"Humpty Dumpty sat on a wall," said the duck.

Aspic, still holding the duck, but completely nonplussed, looked back over his shoulder at Reggie.

Reggie looked in surprise at the card in his hand.

Then he looked defiantly back at Aspic—and he closed and opened the card again.

"Humpty Dumpty sat on a wall," said the duck again. And that was all.

"Ah," said Aspic, smiling, and holding both the duck and his mobile phone. "There, you see. I haven't yet punched the arming code into my phone. Silly me. But no matter. I'll do that after I get upstairs. And far away."

He paused, with his foot on the first step, and said, "I was wrong about one of you, perhaps." Then he shrugged. "No matter. I was merely curious."

Aspic set the lantern down where it would give him just enough light, and he started up the slimy, smooth brick steps.

And then he slipped.

Aspic still had both arms around the duck and one hand on his mobile; unwilling to let anything go, he could not grab on, and he slipped from the steps back down to his ledge. The phone clattered from his hand, and the lantern went skidding across the ledge into the water.

The entire cavern went dark. There could never be a better chance.

Reggie leaped in the dark as far as he could from his ledge toward Aspic's; he landed with his arms on the slick ledge floor and his legs dangling in the water below.

And then, with one foot, he found an indent in the tunnel wall, the rare space of a missing brick. He had leverage now, and he pulled himself onto Aspic's ledge.

Aspic was scrambling on his hands and knees, searching for the phone. Reggie scrambled after him, and then felt a collision as Buxton managed to come across, as well.

In the pitch-black, Reggie lunged for where he thought Aspic was, and missed him. But his hands landed on something else—smooth and plastic. He had the duck.

Now, on the steps leading out, the pinpoint lights of Aspic's mobile phone came on. Buxton was on the steps as well, behind Aspic. But Aspic had the phone—and he was punching in the numbers. One, two . . . all seven.

"He's armed it!" shouted Reggie. "Don't let them open their cards!"

Aspic was on the steps now, climbing out. And Buxton was right behind him.

And Reggie was on the floor with the damn duck.

39

Laura rode in the last limo as Lady Ashton-Tate's procession passed through Lancaster Gate into Hyde Park.

In the meadow at the east end of Serpentine Lake, every-thing was already in place for the lady's Birthday Bash and Charity Celebrity Jogathon. As they approached, Laura could see through the limo window that the duke's contingent had already arrived and assembled at his bandstand, and most of the celebrators were already seated at picnic tables covered in white linen alongside the lake.

The first Ashton-Tate limo arrived now at the destination, parking on West Carriage Drive, adjacent to the meadow. The other limos fell in behind.

Lady Asthon-Tate was the guest of honor and so had some dispensation to arrive fashionably late—later than intended, due to Laura, admittedly—but you can only keep a duke wait-ing for just so long, and his introductory speech was already in full stride.

"What more can one say about Lady Ashton-Tate? What can one say about the woman who coined the famous phrase

'The invading American gray squirrels are like our American cousins from years ago—oversized, oversexed, and over here'?"

Lady Ashton-Tate disembarked from her limo now and began walking—smiling and nodding along the way to well-wishers—toward the table at the front, nearest the bandstand, and nearest the water and tall reeds of the lake.

And now the duke himself, having seen that Lady Ashton-Tate was finally present, picked up an unopened Fleur de Lis birthday card and held it aloft. And so did every one of the celebrators at the picnic tables.

Laura jumped out of the car and began running toward the bandstand.

She knew she would not get there. She knew the Scotland Yard security detail would stop her before she quite got there, that she would attempt to warn them, to explain—and that by the time she could persuade them, it would already be too late. Time was already up.

"And now," said the duke—the crowd all hushed—"let us all open our cards and render a rousing Happy Birthday song to our red squirrel guest of honor, Lady Ashton-Tate!"

With the uniformed bobbies moving to intercept her now, Laura began waving her arms wildly, as if to frighten a murder of crows. She could think of nothing else to do.

The thought crossed her mind that when the bomb went off, this would be the last anyone would ever know of her—a wild woman running across the lawn at Hyde Park, waving her arms for no apparent reason.

Oh well. Perhaps they'd eventually suss it out.

"Don't do it!' screamed Laura, just as two bobbies caught her in front of the bandstand. "It's a bomb!"

All the guests opened their cards.

"Happy birthday to you" rang out in tinny unison from thirty-six individual detonating devices.

And then—nothing.

Laura stopped.

"Oh," she said.

She disentangled herself from the bobbies. She looked about. "Already opened them, did we? Very sorry. My mistake. Sorry."

From the crowd, there was a puzzled silence for just a moment—and then the beginnings of murmurs and titters.

Lady Ashton-Tate came right over to help. "Laura, dear," she whispered in Laura's ear, not unkindly, "the plan is that we will do our jog first, and then drink the champagne after. This is exactly why it's best not to mix up the order of things."

"Yes, I know, you do have a point, but you see . . ." Laura paused and looked toward the lake, just some twenty yards away.

White ducks were floating everywhere.

In for a penny, in for a pound, thought Laura. All the real ducks should be able to fly away. Anything left behind would be the bomb.

Laura charged toward the lake.

"Fly! Fly!" she shouted, waving her arms once more.

There was a sudden rush of wings, a clamor of cackles and quacks, and the lake erupted in a glorious spectacle of beating wings.

And then—nothing.

More murmurs.

Well, thought Laura. At least this is better than if I had helped end the world as we know it.

But now—with all eyes on Laura, who was standing by the

reeds at the edge of the lake—something stirred in those reeds. Something in the muddy ground moved.

A heavy iron plate pushed up from the mud, like a hatch opening on a submarine.

A man in a Royal Parks uniform climbed out.

The crowd stared. How clever; whatever it was, it must be part of the celebration.

Fully out of the access tunnel now, Aspic—the man in the uniform—stood and blinked once or twice to focus his eyes.

And then he began to run as fast as he could for Carriage Park Road.

And now a second man came out of the tunnel. The crowd gasped.

No uniform on this man. And though he was a little worse for wear, his expensive dark suit and his girth were well known and easily recognized: It was Lord Robert Buxton.

Buxton didn't even bother to look around. He got his feet on solid ground, staggered just for a moment, and then ran full speed after Aspic.

Someone in the crowd began to applaud the spectacle, and it rippled through from one table to the next. Buxton had always claimed to everyone that he was fit. No one had ever believed him—until now.

"Bravo!" The duke applauded.

The ground sloped upward between the lake and the road, and it slowed Aspic's progress; Buxton gained ground.

And then Aspic slipped.

In an instant, Buxton was on top of him, hammering the man's back and shoulders and head with his fists, and shouting.

"A bloody sewer? You hold me in a bloody sewer? As if you have no clue who I am?"

More murmurs from the crowd. Perhaps this wasn't part of

the planned festivities. The duke began to look concerned, and three members of the Scotland Yard Royal Protection Detail now ran over—and not a moment too soon for Aspic.

Laura remained standing by the lake. This was all well and good, so far as it went. She began to consider the possibility that they might all live through the day.

But where was Reggie?

She walked over to the sewer-maintenance opening, got down on her hands and knees, and peered in. It was very dark, but she saw movement.

"Can you use a hand?" she called out, not entirely sure who it was she saw below.

"I bloody well can" was the response. And it was Reggie's voice.

In another moment, he had climbed far enough on the ladder to be visible to Laura, though not yet to any of the crowd.

"Take this," he said.

With one hand, he pushed the plastic duck up toward Laura. She took it, set it on the grass behind her, and then reached back in to pull Reggie out onto solid ground.

They were both just sitting there on the ground now. Most of the crowd was still focused on the tangle of Buxton and Aspic, and for a moment, for Reggie and Laura, it was almost as though they'd just come out on a sunny day to lounge a bit on the lawn and have a picnic.

Laura pointed at the duck.

"Is it—"

"Completely disarmed," said Reggie. "I don't think it will even quack. Broke my thumbnail unscrewing the damn thing."

Now Reggie stood, and he helped Laura off the ground.

She started to brush the water and mud and slop off the sides of his pants with her hands.

Then she stopped. She felt something hard in a pocket. Hard and perfectly square.

"What's that?" she said.

"You know me," said Reggie. "I'm just happy to see—"

Laura reached into his front pocket.

"Laura, everyone could be watching—"

She grabbed the jewelry box and pulled it out.

Then she leaned in to Reggie and whispered something in his ear.

40

On Monday morning, just a few minutes before ten, Reggie and Nigel sat in the conference room in Baker Street Chambers. Several copies of a newly prepared legal agreement were spread out on the table before them.

"Do you think the Americans will go for it?" asked Nigel

"I think they'll be thrilled."

"Any second thoughts yourself?" asked Nigel. "I mean, granted, it would be a long shot, but if you prevailed, it would be an incredible amount of money—life-changing."

"I like my life in the direction it is changing already," said Reggie. "I would just like this thing to go away."

Nigel nodded. "Me, too. Let's get it done. It's time for me to head back. Mara said my bar results have come in, and she wants me home to celebrate."

"She's already opened them?"

"No," said Nigel, smiling. "She just assumes I passed. She's like that. Just always thinks I'll get it right. Doesn't know me that well yet, does she?"

"Here they come," said Reggie, pointing at the conference room door.

The two Americans had arrived; Stillman, the lawyer, entered first, looking confident; Darby, the potential billion-dollar heir of the Clemens fortune, entered second, looking angry.

Then Rafferty entered, looking unfathomable.

They all took their seats. Now Reggie stood, and Nigel pushed copies of the legal document across to everyone at the table.

"This document, " said Reggie, "states that, on behalf of myself, and on behalf of Sherlock Holmes, whether he is fictional or otherwise, and on behalf of whatever connection I may have to Sherlock Holmes, whether he is fictional or otherwise, and any connection I may have to the letters written to him, whether they were intended for a fictional character or otherwise, I give up any and all claims on the estate of Mrs. Clemens. I will sign this document as tenant of 221B Baker Street and on behalf of Baker Street Chambers and all employees thereof. And Mr. Rafferty will sign on behalf of Dorset Leasing and all occupants of Dorset House."

Rafferty jerked his head up on that last part. He looked across at Reggie, but Reggie was focused on just the two Americans.

Darby looked at Stillman, who was mulling it over.

"I believe our proposal is considerably better from your perspective than simply the return of the document you were looking for," said Reggie.

"I should say so," said Rafferty, so softly that the conversation continued as if he had not.

Stillman nodded. "That will work."

"And in return," said Reggie. "You will agree to renounce any and all civil or criminal claims against Baker Street Chambers and all employees, and Dorset House and all employees, and specifically including Mr. Hendricks and my brother and

Miss Rankin, regarding any and all incidents that have taken place since your arrival in London."

"Now wait a minute—" said Darby, starting to rise out of his chair. But Stillman immediately pushed him back down.

"Agreed," said the lawyer. "Let's get it signed."

There were sighs of relief all around the table. Almost everyone began to stand.

"No," said Rafferty. He had not stirred. "It is not agreed."

Everyone else now froze in place. And then Rafferty brought out a document of his own.

"Regarding the events that took place upstairs," said Rafferty, "any possible civil suit would cut both ways. It would be presented to an English jury, and although English juries are the most fair-minded and least provincial in the world, I would not take it as a given, Mr. Darby, that they would accept your word over Nigel's. And as to injuries—well, Mr. Hendricks, who bravely hurried upstairs despite his advanced age, has yet to see his physician. I, for one, am worried about his heart."

Reggie raised an eyebrow at that but said nothing. Laura had told him once that she frequently encountered Mr. Hendricks in her runs around the lake, Hendricks jogging and muttering along in the opposite direction.

Rafferty continued. "And most important, I am not absolutely convinced that Mrs. Clemens did not, in fact, intend to bequeath her fortune to Sherlock Holmes in a way that will be upheld. As you know, the document has been recovered. I have it here with me. And I call your attention to the last line."

Rafferty now pushed forward onto the table the will that had gone missing—that had been rolled up by Buxton along with other letters and tucked away into the shelves behind Lois's desk.

Everyone leaned forward to read the last line.

Nigel read it aloud: "'I therefore bequeath my entire fortune and all my possessions to Reggie Heath, as custodian and recipient of the letters to Sherlock Holmes.'"

The American lawyer glared and said, "What's your point?" just as though he didn't know what the point was.

"My point," said Rafferty, "as I'm sure everyone at this table knows, is that the bequest is not merely to Reggie Heath. It is also to the custodian and recipient of the letters to Sherlock Holmes."

"No," said Stillman heatedly, "it is to both, but only as long as they are one and the same. And Heath has already said he will sign it over."

Rafferty looked across at Reggie and then Nigel. "Mr. Heath? And Mr. Heath? What are your opinions?"

Reggie shrugged. "Arguable."

Nigel nodded. "Arguable."

"We had a deal," growled Stillman.

"And I believe we still do," said Rafferty. "But there is just a minor modification."

"Let's hear it," said Stillman.

"An offer has been made for the purchase of Dorset House. Dorset National Building Society does not wish to sell, but great pressure has been brought on them to do so.

"The current offer can be thwarted, if it can be shown that another bidder would be capable of making a competing offer. If another bidder—one with very substantial funds, such as the heirs to the Clemens Copper fortune—were to express an interest, I believe the current hostile offer would be withdrawn, and Dorset House would remain as the recipient and custodian of the letters to Sherlock Holmes."

"You're asking us to buy Dorset House?" said Stillman.

"Absolutely not," said Rafferty. "I'm assuming you have no interest whatsoever in the building. Is that correct?"

Stillman looked at Darby, who nodded.

"It is correct," said Stillman.

"Then all I will need from you," said Rafferty, "is your commitment that, should the time come, with the vast funds that you will receive from the Clemens inheritance, you will be prepared to threaten such an offer. I believe that threat will be sufficient to discourage any other unwelcome bidders."

Stillman looked over at Darby again, and then at everyone else at the table. Darby nodded.

"Then we have a deal," said the American lawyer. "We're willing to trade one fiction for another."

41

THE NEXT DAY

It was Tuesday, and Reggie wanted to get back to some routine work, but he could not do so quite yet.

First he had a letter to write. And before he could do that, he had to deal with Detective Inspector Wembley, who was sitting across from him in Reggie's office.

"I thought you might want to know," said the inspector, "that we won't be asking the Crown Prosecution Service to press charges against you."

It took a moment for Reggie to let that sink in. It had not been the first thing on his mind.

"Good to know," said Reggie. "Charges regarding what, specifically?"

"You are an officer of the court, and you are expected to inform us when a crime has been committed. You did not tell us that Buxton had been kidnapped."

"Oh," said Reggie. "That."

"It's a statutory duty, in fact, as I'm sure you know," said

Wembley. "Miss Rankin should have informed us, as well. And so should have Lord Buxton's security team. Technically, you could all be charged."

"But you're cutting us all a break, then?"

"Yes," said Wembley. "Under the circumstances."

"It seems to me," said Reggie, "that Lord Buxton should be charged with breaking and entering at Baker Street Chambers."

"Well now, he didn't actually break in, though, did he? I believe he entered openly and was allowed up by the building's security guard, even though it was before hours."

"He tampered with my mail," said Reggie.

"Technically speaking, it was mail addressed to Sherlock Holmes. Do you really want to make a public issue of that?"

Reggie thought about that for a moment, and then said no.

"In any case," said Wembley, "it wouldn't do for the Crown Prosecution Service to charge him with something like that at the moment, given the other action that's being planned for him."

"Yes?" said Reggie hopefully. "And what is that?"

Wembley told him.

"Bloody hell," said Reggie. "I slogged through a sewer, you know."

Wembley shrugged. "Next time, try to do it in full view of the duke and his company. Anyway, rumor has it that you're going to get what you really wanted. Don't muck it up."

Wembley stood now, but then he looked down at the desk, at the letter that Reggie had begun to write out in longhand.

"Who's that to?" he said.

"Mr. Liu has a granddaughter," said Reggie. "And Mrs. Winslow asked me to send something to her. I'm just trying to figure out what to say about two people who were both trying to do the right thing, and then both died because of someone who wasn't."

"Virtue is its own reward?" said Wembley.

"Most of the time," said Reggie, "I guess it pretty much has to be."

42

TWO MONTHS LATER

On a morning in early spring, Reggie Heath woke alone in his penthouse at Butler's Wharf.

He was running late. Fortunately, everything was already prepared. He even managed a cup of coffee before he got into his tux.

Now he stood at the west window and looked out over the Thames. He could see St. Paul's Cathedral easily from here. And he could also see the garish new sign that Robert Buxton had put up over his headquarters.

Reggie struggled with his tie as he looked out. That was unusual; he never had trouble with his tie.

The phone rang, and he picked up.

It was Laura. She said hello, and then she sighed. As though she were waiting for him to say something, Reggie thought. But then she spoke first.

"Don't be bitter," she said.

"I'm not."

"At least you were invited to the ceremony. That's something, isn't it?"

"Yes. It's something."

"You're not jealous?"

"I think the word you mean is *envious*."

"You're not envious, then?"

"Of course not. Neither one. It doesn't mean a thing to me. After all, who cares that it was me who defused the bomb?"

"Well. All right. I was just worried how you'd feel about it. Are you going to be on time?"

"Of course. Just tell me one thing."

"Anything."

"What sort of knot does one use when attending a knighting ceremony? I mean, I'm sure half of London will choke anyway when we all have to start saying '*Sir* Robert Buxton.' Is there a special kind of knot I can use to get started on that early?"

Laura laughed. "Just pick me up on time. And don't sweat in your new tux. You're going to need it again."

MYSTERIES FROM
MICHAEL ROBERTSON

"For Anglophiles, crime-o-philes,
and all fans of wonderful writing."
—*Booklist* (starred review)

After two brother lawyers who now live on London's Baker Street start receiving letters to Sherlock Holmes, they find themselves in the midst of an investigation that would stump even Holmes himself.

The Brothers of Baker Street | *The Baker Street Translation*
Moriarty Returns a Letter

CPSIA information can be obtained
at www.ICGtesting.com
Printed in the USA
LVHW04s1907041018
592417LV00002B/280/P

9 781250 043917